LAWRENCE BIRD

THE SPECIAL RELATIONSHIP

A TRUMP BEFORE HIS TIME?

CONTENTS

Introduction 7

CHAPTER 1: All change at the top 15

CHAPTER 2: Travis starts work 29

CHAPTER 3: USA rules 41

CHAPTER 4: Reds under the bed 50

CHAPTER 5: The Americans arrive 79

CHAPTER 6: Resistance 90

CHAPTER 7: Protests 106

CHAPTER 8: Getting serious 116

CHAPTER 9: Taking charge 127

CHAPTER 10: Time to negotiate 146

CHAPTER 11: Missing 162

CHAPTER 12: The deal 173

CHAPTER 13: A visit from the police 195

CHAPTER 14: A presidential holiday 204

CHAPTER 15: Unwelcome visitors 212

CHAPTER 16: Talks about talks 225

CHAPTER 17: Time for negotiations 232

CHAPTER 18: A deal at last 248

CHAPTER 19: All roads lead to London 260

CHAPTER 20: Repairing public relations 277

CHAPTER 21: Back in the limelight 286

APPENDIX: Fact or fiction? 304

Acknowledgements

The author is grateful to the following friends and family members who read several drafts and made many helpful comments:

John Bird
Helen Brown
Paul Brown
Bob Cadden
Louise Courtney
Frances Davis
Richard Masters

INTRODUCTION

O ver the years we have become accustomed to seeing soldiers patrol the streets of distant countries, sometimes there by invitation, but more likely because politicians have perceived that country to be a threat, or they simply do not like the way those regimes operate. Understandably the indigenous population can resent any military presence and frequently rebel against it, even to the point when they are labelled subversives or terrorists within their own country.

Since the days of William the Conqueror, Britain has not had to suffer this indignity, although there have been several attempts. There have been many scenarios based on what might have happened had Adolf Hitler been successful and how the British would have dealt with it. However, after WWII another foreign power could have seized the opportunity because Britain's forces were much depleted, with thousands of military personnel elsewhere in the world and many still in the Far East awaiting transport to return home. The threat to Britain could have come from the east or the west, because it was clear America was paranoid that the USSR wanted to take over the world, while of course the USSR had a diametrically opposite view of America. It is likely that the USA were concerned that the newly elected Labour government, with its socialist agenda, had set in motion a plan that was totally alien to America, with the British seemingly a little too aligned with the USSR. Did the Americans apply any pressure on the newly elected Atlee government? We shall never know, but the British people, being mostly behind their prime minister, would surely have resented such interference.

Of course, we know Harry Truman, Roosevelt's successor, didn't push it that far, but would a more gung-ho right-wing president have seen things differently? If that seems improbable, imagine if someone had written a story predicting the 2016 US election campaign and Donald Trump's four-year presidency, followed by his involvement in the events of 6th January 2021. It may have been regarded as entertaining, but pure fiction! But had Roosevelt and Truman not been at the helm in 1944 and beyond, could events in the UK have taken a different course?

Thus, two possible events inspired this story: first, the imagined impact of foreign soldiers patrolling one's own streets, and second, the possibility of a Trump-like character becoming president of the United States in 1944. Whatever your views of Trump and his politics, and he has many supporters, he is nevertheless a larger than life personality who enjoys being the centre of attention, as if he had been cast in a film about a fictitious US president.

In rewinding history back to 1944 and the immediate post-war years I have involved many real people in the story and hopefully not defamed them as a result. However, I named the president David Travis simply because at the time of writing Donald Trump is still very much alive and may not find the likeness totally agreeable! Where possible I've attempted to intertwine actual events with my fictional version and for those whose knowledge of 1940s history is a little hazy I've added a short appendix where real facts are identified as such.

LEB

Cast of Characters

Real people who existed in 1944 and beyond

Franklin D Roosevelt	Outgoing USA President
Thomas E Dewey	US Republican candidate
J Edgar Hoover	Head of FBI
John Foster Dulles	USA Politician
Alan Dulles	USA Politician
General George C Marshall	USA Army & Secretary of State under Truman
Averell Harriman	USA Politician & Ambassador to Moscow
John G Winaut	US Ambassador to UK
Joe Stalin	USSR President
Vyacheslav Molotov	USSR Foreign Secretary
King George VI	British King 1936-52, succeeding Edward VIII
Winston Churchill	British Prime Minister (Conservative)
Anthony Eden	British Foreign Secretary (Conservative)
Clement Atlee	British Prime Minister (Labour)
Ernest Bevin	British Foreign Secretary (Labour)
Herbert Morrison	British Minister (Labour)
Sir Stafford Cripps	President of the Board of Trade. Knighted in 1931
Hugh Dalton	Chancellor of the Exchequer 1945-7
John Maynard Keynes	British Economist
J Robert Oppenheimer	USA Scientist
Richard Dimbleby	BBC Radio Journalist
General Charles de Gaulle	Acting leader of French Government in waiting
Wernher von Braun	German Rocket scientist

Admiral William Leahy	US Navy
Sir Walter Citrine	TUC General Secretary (Retired)
Thomas E Dewey	US Republican candidate
Harry S Truman	Incoming USA President
Dwight D Eisenhower	5-star General & 34th US President

Fictitious people

Lord Rufus Drakeford	Barrister & spokesman for BFG
Lady Christine Drakeford	Wife of Rufus
George Drakeford	Brother of Rufus
Jeanette Drakeford	Sister of Rufus
David Travis	Incoming USA President
Joe Delaney	USA Vice President
Donald Travis	Son of David Travis
Tara Travis	Wife of David Travis
Tamara Travis	Daughter of David Travis
Joe Thompson	USA Financial expert
General William Sykes	USA Army
James Palmer	USA Civil Servant
Robert McIntyre	British Civil Servant
Martin Tyler	British Civil Servant
Colonel Graham Downton	British Army (Retired)
Bill Johnson	BFG Team member (Former British Intelligence)
Major Charles Brown	BFG Team member - British Army (Retired)
Charlotte Joubert	BFG Team member (Former British Intelligence)
Susan Watson	BFG Team member – Office Manager
Andy Price	BFG Team member (motorcyclist)

Terry Bell	BFG Team member (Telephone engineer)
Jeff Davies	BFG Team member
Anthony Jones	BFG Team member (Photographer)
Ben Godfrey	BFG Team member (motorcyclist)
Harry Mitchell	BFG Team member
Joe Cole	Daily Mirror Reporter
Bill Binder	Daily Mail Reporter
Major Sir Rupert Stevenson	BFG Team member
Michael Millerchip	Professor - Communication intermediary
General Howard Thomas	US Army Officer
Major Bill Sutherland	US Army Officer
Les Harvey	US Army Officer
Jim Dale	US Army Officer
Brad Lomas	Anglo-American Unification Campaign
Victor	Anglo-American Unification Campaign
Joan	Anglo-American Unification Campaign
Clive James	Detective Superintendent
Bob Lindsey	Detective Chief Inspector
Sergeant Dixon	Police Officer
Thomas Baldwin	Police Officer (Detective)
PC Stephens	Village PC
General Gus O'Donnell	US Army Officer
Chief Constable Perkins	Scotland Yard Police Chief
Paul Green	US Army GI
Ian Ryan	US Army GI
Bill Healey	Manager Blair House
Jim Watt	White House Tour Guide
Jack Lambert	Labour MP
Ted Campbell	Labour MP
Harold B Crosby	US Senator
Geoffrey Anderson	Civil Servant (Board of Trade)

Kevin Bowman	RAF Squadron Leader
Charles B Hampton	Staff member – US Embassy
Mary Martin	Assistant to TUC General Secretary
Fred Kinsella	Yorkshire Miner
Bill Jackson	Farmer
Lizzie Jackson	Farmer's Wife
George Morgan	Sergeant – British Army – awaiting demob.
Tommy	British Army – awaiting demob.
Dick	British Army – awaiting demob.
Mike	British Army – awaiting demob.
Rev. Phillip Caruthers	Village Vicar
Alan Oliver	US Army Captain
Robin Brady	US Army Lieutenant
James Cleaver	US Army Lieutenant
Jo Brindley	British Civil Servant (Stenographer)
Paul Robinson	White House Head Chef
Clifford C Smith III	New York Judge
Charles Kleinsmith	Business Associate of David Travis
Arnie Hunter	Business Associate of David Travis

THE GEOGRAPHY

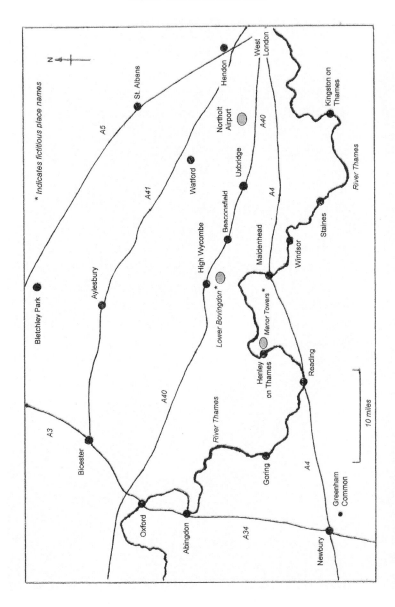

* Indicates fictitious place names

CHAPTER 1

ALL CHANGE AT THE TOP

R ufus Drakeford was a Peer of the Realm, a title he inherited on the sudden death of his father in 1942. His father had been a prominent lawyer and Rufus, in his early forties, was himself a successful barrister, specialising in international law. He was deemed unsuitable for National Service as a result of a climbing accident when he was 18, resulting in a broken femur and complications leaving him with a slight limp. He was a little above average in height, dark haired, clean shaven and his legal training made him a confident, eloquent speaker. He had enjoyed being one of the youngest peers permitted to sit in the House of Lords and although regarded as one of the 'traditional ruling class' he had never been comfortable with the political aims of the Conservative Party and openly described himself as being in the centre-ground and sat as a cross-bencher. It was now September 1944 and although the UK had been ruled by a wartime coalition government, he could see an early return to the normal party system quite soon as it was only a matter of time before the inevitable victory over Adolf Hitler. Nevertheless, he had many concerns as to how Britain might return to normal life, especially if it involved the politics and high unemployment of the thirties.

He lived in Lower Bovingdon, a quiet village on the outskirts of High Wycombe; rural, yet close to the A40 for the drive into London. Rufus ran a large black 1939 SS-Jaguar, a fast, good looking car, although he much preferred driving his wife's Morris 8 Series 'E' around the local country lanes. The village was small, yet large enough to have a village pub, a post office and general store. He and his wife Christine lived in a large traditional-style house, with oak beams and an open fire. They had a long back garden sloping down to a stream with willow trees overhanging. Christine worked part-time as a researcher for the Liberal Party; more a labour of love as the pay hardly covered her travel expenses. They had met twenty years before when Rufus was assisting a Liberal MP in a legal case and they married soon after. The couple had two teenage children who were at boarding school, and Rufus had a younger brother, George, also a lawyer who lived on the other side of the village. They had a younger sister Jeanette who had recently qualified as a doctor and worked in Salisbury hospital, having been inspired by the notion of a National Health Service, as set out in the Beveridge Report, published in 1942 and adopted by the Labour Party as an essential plank in any future peace-time government. The Drakefords' mother had died in 1940, so on the death of their father they had decided to sell the London family home and divide the assets between the three of them. The peerage was automatically inherited by Rufus as the eldest son, a legal process over which he had no control.

He surveyed his copy of *The Times* spread over his breakfast table. Prominent on page one was a report on the

USA presidential campaign, with the forthcoming election to be held in November 1944. The headline read:

"New Challenger for Ailing Roosevelt."

The article explained the Republicans' original choice, Thomas E Dewey, had been taken ill unexpectedly and admitted to hospital for an emergency operation. With the election only two months away, the Republican Party had to make an urgent decision, with Dewey unavailable for campaigning and requiring a period of convalescence for an indefinite period, effectively excluding him from the presidential election. The short and easy answer was to adopt his running-mate, David J Travis, as their candidate. Travis's reputation had grown rapidly as he emphasised his priority to establish the USA as the most powerful nation in the world. He was a New York property developer, with strong right-wing views and considerable financial backing. He was aged 63, a well-built man, and claimed to be six feet three inches tall, although this was often disputed. He was always popular with the ladies and now married to Tara, his third wife, and had two grown up children from his first marriage. The newspapers loved him as he was always good for a spontaneous quotation and he often appeared on the rapidly developing media of television. There was concern when Travis had been Dewey's unexpected choice as a potential Vice President since he had no political experience, but he enjoyed a popular relationship with the public. To endorse their decision, his performance since his appointment as Dewey's number two had been well received by the public;

consequently the GOP's elder statesmen realised they were onto something. The Republicans saw their opportunity, since until then they had rated their chances as no better than 50-50, such was FDR's reputation. However, with the President's ailing health obvious for all to see, a complete change from the usual career politician presented an unexpected opportunity. After twelve years of Democratic rule, they thought perhaps it was time for a new approach.

The Times article reported that public opinion had begun to swing, particularly as world events were reaching a critical point. The Republicans saw their opportunity to seize power and bring in a candidate who could lead America in the battle for Europe and in the war against Japan.

Lord Drakeford turned to his wife and said, "I fear the worst; this is not good news for Britain. We've always had a high regard for Roosevelt and he's been a big friend of Churchill, but this guy's going to do us no favours – he wants to rule the world and we'll be out in the cold. Now with the Germans retreating, the Allies have a foothold in France and are making good progress, while Russia is closing in from the East, so it's only a matter of time before Hitler concedes. Stalin will have his own ideas about how Europe is carved up and I fear Travis will have other priorities."

"But he's not been elected yet, aren't you being pessimistic? We can still hope," she replied.

"We shall have to watch closely, I'm afraid he might just make it."

* * *

Lord Drakeford had taken a keen interest in international politics since the early 1930s and was better equipped than most politicians to predict the outcome of the many scenarios that had been speculated upon when the war was finally over. He was well aware that the USA's intentions would have a major impact on world politics, hence his close attention to the forthcoming presidential election. He read all the newspapers and listened to the radio reports as the election in the USA proceeded with its usual razzmatazz. Travis had selected Joe Delaney as his running mate, a popular New York Senator and seen as a calm, experienced politician. Despite having three previous victories, Roosevelt, with his ailing health, was no match for his noisy opponent and Travis became more confident as the campaign approached the final days.

The election took place on 7th November 1944 and as the results began to filter in, everyone was glued to their radios. Inevitably, FDR's supporters were crestfallen as the truth began to dawn and Travis was duly elected, with 60% of the Electoral College votes and 52% of the popular vote. The Republicans were overjoyed, seeing as they'd been in opposition for twelve years. What's more, they had won a slim majority in the House of Representatives and now had 52 Senators to the Democrats' 48, the implications being that they could force through almost any law they chose. Travis spoke to the media as soon as the result was declared, and his speech was relayed by radio across the USA and beyond.

"For too long we've endured this Democratic rule where we've tried to please everyone, including some of our enemies. We're currently fighting a war on two fronts and many people have questioned whether we should even be involved in the European war. We need to take a tougher line and when this war is won, as it surely will be, we should make sure we're justly compensated by Germany and all the other countries that have benefited from our military aid and the loss of so many American lives.

"I think the war in Europe is close to victory, Hitler cannot recover and it's only a matter of time before the Russians move into Berlin and string him up. I'm more concerned about the war with Japan; we must win there, they can't be allowed to rule the Far East the way they have done. During my time in this office, it's my intention to make America beyond doubt the world's most powerful nation."

That was the speech many Americans had hoped for. Travis stood proudly up there on the podium, his wife Tara by his side with the new Vice President Joe Delaney next to him, while his son Donald and daughter Tamara stood in the background. There were rapturous cheers from the hall, packed full of celebrating Republicans, decked out in various designs of American flags, worn as rosettes, hats and even clothing. It took several minutes after he had finished speaking before he and his family left the podium and disappeared through a passageway behind the stage.

In a radio interview that followed he was asked whether he intended to follow FDR's ambition to see the formation of a United Nations. He replied, "I don't see it as a priority. With the proposed format I'm unhappy with us only getting one vote, considering our size and population. I want to see the USA having a significant role if this goes ahead, that's what I campaigned on."

He then moved on to a celebratory party which continued into the early hours. Next morning, as reality kicked in, it was time to get down to work, with another press conference followed by meetings with Republican Party officials and key personnel. After so long in opposition there was no shortage of candidates eager to be part of Travis's team. He also needed to make arrangements for trusted aides and family members to take over the day-to-day running of his New York-based business empire. It was clear that Donald and Tamara would be in charge, there was no dispute about that, although their father would have a big influence on future direction.

Back in the UK there was much speculation about what was likely to happen when Travis officially moved into the Oval Office and the Drakeford household was full of scenarios as to what he might do. Rufus turned to his wife and commented wistfully as he closed his copy of *The Times*:

"As we feared, he's won the election and everything we said appears to be a possibility. Based on his comments so far, he's looking for a head-on collision with Stalin. Unless he has some secret weapon, he could be heading for a nasty surprise.

"I think we should keep a record as events unfold, we could be moving into a new era. It's always interesting to look back and re-visit one's thoughts which may have become cloudy with the passage of time," suggested Rufus. He had always kept a pocket diary, but this was mainly for appointments. Now he took a hard-backed exercise book, the sort of thing handed out in the more affluent schools, so that he could record events as they happened.

"A lot depends on what happens when things return to normal in the UK," he continued. "Everyone's assuming that Churchill will be re-elected as Prime Minister and that will suit Travis and his new regime. I'm not so sure how they will react if Atlee wins; somehow I can't see much common ground there."

"We'll need a strong government to resist whatever he has in store for us. Let's just wait and see," replied Christine, ever the more optimistic.

* * *

Fortunately, the American presidential system has a period between the election and the inauguration to allow a smooth transition for the incoming president to make suitable arrangements and be brought up to speed while the previous incumbent is still in office. Travis had not visited Washington DC that often, but now he was shortly going to move into the East Wing of the White House. He made the journey to Washington by air, something he would be doing on a regular basis over the next few years, and on this occasion it was by his own private plane, a rare sign of affluence in 1944. As a temporary measure, he stayed in nearby accommodation, Blair House, normally reserved for visiting heads of state and diplomats. He was accompanied by his personal bodyguard on the flight from New York and Travis insisted he stay close by. Normally this service is provided by the US state and Travis was keen that whatever protection came with the presidential office, he wanted his man to be retained and have a significant role.

Next morning at nine o'clock, a large black limousine picked him up and took him the short distance to the White House. Travis had gained a reputation for hiring and firing, and the staff awaited with some trepidation as he arrived for the first of several briefings. As he entered, everyone lined up and greeted him respectfully, unsure of their futures. He brought with him his son, Donald, J Edgar Hoover, head of the FBI, and brothers John Foster Dulles and Allen Dulles, both lawyers and Republicans. Allen Dulles had recently returned from Switzerland where he had spent much of the war years as head of the OSS operation based in Berne. He was named as Travis's future Chief of Staff. Travis strode in confidently, wearing an immaculate dark blue double-breasted suit and a red tie. He had a healthy head of hair, although many people thought this could be a wig on the assumption that man of his age would be unlikely to have retained all of his natural hair with its original colour.

Travis was shown into the Oval Office, looking around at a place he would soon be occupying on a daily basis. FDR greeted him warmly from his wheelchair and explained, "I've arranged for you to meet the key people you'll be working with in this interim period. They're waiting for you in the cabinet room, there's more seating available in there. You're in good hands, so I'll leave you at this point. This meeting is to bring you up to speed with the many things that are going on, things that the public are unaware of. I'm sure you will have a few surprises. Good luck."

Travis and his associates were led a short distance along the corridor to the meeting room where six men and one woman were already seated. They stood up as he entered and there were firm handshakes all round. Representing the military personnel were General William Sykes and General George C Marshall, who was one of Roosevelt's closest advisors and shortly to become Travis's Secretary of State. The meeting was initially chaired by General Sykes and they began by discussing a few generalities, but as the meeting progressed Travis became more impatient. He was not accustomed to having to wait his turn and began to assert his authority. It was clear he wanted to move on to the more pressing matters of the day, particularly the military situation.

Travis took over the meeting. "Let's move on to the important things. America is fighting wars in both Europe and in Japan in the Far East. How close are we to winning both these and bringing our soldiers back home?"

General Sykes was slightly offended by Travis's impatience, but replied: "In Europe, Allied forces are progressing well in the west and beginning to move into Germany itself. The USSR is now into eastern Germany and will probably reach Berlin first. The Nazi forces are putting up stiff resistance, but it's only a matter of time."

"What about the V2 rockets? Could they swing it for Germany?" asked Travis.

"They're quite formidable, especially for Londoners where most of these are targeted. Technically the V2 is unique, it's quite brilliant and no one has anything like it at the moment. However, they're not going to win the war for Hitler. These rockets have been very expensive to develop and to build in any meaningful quantities, and they use expensive rocket fuel. And despite the publicity, the number of casualties in London is relatively low compared to the bombing raids we're carrying out on German cities and factories. In London the deaths are mostly in the hundreds, but in Berlin, Dresden and Hamburg it's more like several thousands. We are targeting mainly military and industrial sites, but we're also hitting town centres. Hitler can't last much longer."

General Marshall then spoke. "Japan is rather different. We're beginning to gain the upper hand, but we really need the help of the USSR to attack them from the north. For some time, FDR has been trying to do a deal with Stalin, hoping that our support for the war in Europe would enable the USSR to attack Japan from mainland Asia. It makes sense to continue with those negotiations."

"Will Stalin be willing to cooperate?" asked Travis. "What will he want in return?"

"That could be the problem," replied Marshall. "He'll probably want to take over China, having wrestled it from the Japanese. And he'll want to keep all the European territories he will be occupying when Hitler surrenders." He then paused for a few seconds before continuing. "However, we literally have a secret weapon that could make all the difference."

Travis's team went completely silent, stunned by Marshall's announcement. No one moved and everyone looked at Marshall.

He continued: "Since 1942 we've been working on an atomic bomb at a secret location at Los Alamos in New Mexico. This is known as the Manhattan Project and is led by Robert Oppenheimer, a brilliant scientist."

"I've heard of him," countered Travis. "Isn't he also supposed to be a communist?"

"Yes, we know he has communist sympathies and has friends who are known to be politically active, as is his wife, but he's under constant surveillance by the FBI, so we don't think he's a risk. After all, he was born in the USA and has German-Jewish parentage. He built a reputation as a Professor of Physics at the University of California and is a world authority on quantum theory, whatever that is. But that is the basis of nuclear physics and his talent is considered essential for this project."

"So how destructive is this bomb?" asked Travis.

"It's equivalent to twenty thousand tons of TNT. That could flatten a medium sized town and cause damage for anything up to ten miles beyond. Very soon we hope to test it in the desert. It may be that when the full extent of the weapon's potential is known, our enemies may be prepared to come to the conference table."

Travis's eyes lit up when he realised what he had inherited. His immediate comment was, "Why bother with a test in our own back yard, let's try it out on Berlin?"

His generals were taken aback by his reaction. General Sykes said, "We honestly don't know when the first test will be ready. By then it's a fair bet that soldiers of USA, Britain and the USSR will be closing in on Berlin and they would be caught up in the damage and its after-effects, along with millions of German citizens. Even if we were to give a warning, Hitler might ignore it as he would assume it was a bluff. Then again, he might invite us to use the bomb so he can go out in a blaze of glory, effectively triggering his own suicide. It can't be long before even Hitler realises it's all over and whatever happens he's not going to let himself be taken prisoner. Of course, some people have suggested that he could be arranging his escape to a sympathetic country, possibly South America, but we've no evidence so far."

"I agree," said General Marshall. "If we use the bomb on Germany we could turn all our allies against us. We can win this war without resorting to such drastic action. But Japan is different, we don't have any forces on the Japanese mainland, so to use the bomb on Japan would mean that casualties would be limited to the Japanese population. That is, assuming we still have to use it."

Travis thought for a while. Even he realised there was no way he could convince the vastly experienced personnel around the table that using the bomb on Germany was a good idea. He replied, "OK, I take your point. I guess a lot depends on how Stalin reacts when he sees what our bomb could do."

Sykes came back quickly. "I should point out that the Manhattan Project is top secret. We suspect he has spies who may have fed back some information to him, but its existence is not something you should mention in any negotiations. FDR had built up a reasonable relationship with Stalin and it's in our interest not to antagonise him."

"Stalin, I can't stand the man," retorted Travis. "He's the last person I would want any favours from."

"You'll probably get to meet him in person sooner than you might expect," countered Sykes, "We're in the process of setting up a meeting with yourself, Stalin and Churchill. We had hoped for somewhere neutral, but it's most likely to be in the Ukraine because Stalin is reluctant to fly. The meeting is essentially about how we carve up Europe when the war has ended, but it's also an opportunity to see how Stalin feels about Japan. As we mentioned, FDR had a brief discussion as to how they might help, but nothing was agreed."

"We'll need to get a team together," said Marshall. "The outcome could have a major influence on worldwide history."

With that the meeting broke up, everyone somewhat wiser than when they had started. Travis now had a better idea of who in the White House staff he should keep and who he should discard in order to change America's role in this post-war world.

CHAPTER 2

TRAVIS STARTS WORK

Quite soon the date for Travis's inauguration arrived, 20th January 1945. Everyone was well wrapped up against the cold Washington winter and thousands thronged along Pennsylvania Avenue. He began his speech by repeating much of what he had said at his victory speech in November. He resolved to take a tougher line in Europe, declaring:

"Many people have said that the Treaty of Versailles was too severe and this brought about an adverse reaction from the German people in the 1920s and 30s. Personally, I don't think the Treaty was tough enough. If we had taken a stronger line, Hitler would never have gotten into power, the advances into Alsace Lorraine, Austria, Czechoslovakia and Poland would have been prevented, and World War Two would never have happened. However, the field was wide open for someone like Adolf Hitler because he wanted to free up Germany and even expand it. Once in power a lot of people admired him because he restored a united spirit among the German people, bringing about full employment, killed off opposition from the trade unions and the communist party, and restored a sense of national pride. He could have tolerated the Jews and had no need to take over those other countries or wage war against the USSR. Other countries might not have liked it, but they would not have fought Germany and he could have stayed in power for as long as he wanted. Instead, he's become the most hated man in the world and when this war is won I want to see Adolf Hitler on the end of a rope. For those reasons I will not hesitate to insist on appropriate reparations from Germany."

This was met with polite applause.

Travis was paranoid about the influence of the Soviet Union and made no secret of his mission to suppress communism, a very popular position to take in the USA. He continued, "As long as we've been fighting Germany, Joseph Stalin has been our friend. However, we have to be very careful to guard against his expansionist ambitions. He's already brought virtually all of his neighbouring countries into his Soviet empire and I'm certain that the likes of Finland and Poland could go the same way. I suspect that even the inclusion of Germany is not out of the question if he is allowed to get away with it."

He then moved on to the war with Japan. "I have every confidence that we will be victorious in our battle with Japan. If we have to, I know we have the capability to blow them out of the water."

He now had the knowledge of the Atomic Bomb, which he almost blurted out, with his aides cringing as he spoke, since its existence was still a closely guarded secret.

He finished his speech with some predictable promises. "My priority is to end these wars as soon as possible so as to bring all our brave guys back home. I intend to get people back to normal peacetime activities, with full employment and good healthcare. I want to see America as the best in the world, in every way possible."

He waved to the cheering crowds and, taking his wife's arm, quickly moved into the warmth of the Capitol Building.

He was barely sworn in at his inauguration ceremony when his newly appointed Secretary of State made it clear that Travis should be briefed before attending the Yalta conference, scheduled to begin on 4th February. Next day, they sat down with their top military men to explain what was planned.

Dulles began, "As the replacement for FDR you'll be meeting Stalin and Churchill. You'll recall that the three of them met in Tehran in 1943 and FDR was very keen to be pushing his idea of a United Nations, with Stalin not so keen. Everyone will have their senior politicians and military people with them. You will have myself, along with General George C Marshall, Admiral William Leahy and others we're still to decide. The American delegation will be staying in the Livadia Palace. The Ukraine is not the easiest place to get to, but Stalin claims that his doctors have advised him that he shouldn't travel too far, although it's been said that the real reason is a fear of flying.

"The situation is that the war is still raging in Europe as forces are closing in on Germany, with the Allied forces on the western border, while the Soviets are only forty miles from Berlin in the east. From our point of view the conference has two purposes: the first is the obvious one of what happens to Europe when Germany surrenders; the second is to what extent will Stalin help us defeat Japan. There is also the ongoing issue about FDR's pet project, the formation of the United Nations."

"Will Averell Harriman be there?" asked Travis. "After all, he was our Ambassador in Moscow."

"Yes," explained Dulles. "As you know, President Roosevelt sent Harriman to London in early 1941 to take charge of the Lend-Lease lifeline that provided Britain with the resources to continue fighting in the most desperate months of the war. He quickly became known as the most powerful American in Britain. Then later he became the USA Ambassador in Moscow. Meanwhile John G Winaut has been the US Ambassador in London, since 1941 in fact. It's now your decision whether to replace him."

"I'll have to think about that," replied Travis.

Things were moving fast. In just over a week President Travis and his team were boarding the plane for the long and tiring journey to the Ukraine. It was a proud moment for Travis to be replacing FDR in this meeting on equal terms with Stalin and Churchill, he felt he had truly arrived on the world stage. His back-up team included Averell Harriman, while Churchill brought his Foreign Secretary Anthony Eden, and Stalin brought along Vyacheslav Molotov, Eden's opposite number. All three leaders were supported by teams of interpreters and lawyers, ready to draft agreements as the discussions proceeded.

As they arrived it was clearly still winter, but the scenery of the Crimean peninsula was impressive. Yalta had been an elegant seaside resort, but there was clear evidence that the Germans had left in a hurry just a few months earlier as the roads were strewn with rusting tanks and other debris. The plan was that each delegation be accommodated in separate palaces. These had been left in a sorry state by the retreating Germans, but the Russians had worked feverishly over recent weeks to restore them, with teams of craftsmen and masses of fixtures and fittings brought from Moscow. The USSR delegation stayed in Yusupov Palace in Koreiz, the Americans nearby in Livadia, while the British were thirty minutes away in Vorontsov Palace. To make the guests feel as welcome as possible, almost all the staff in the palaces had been brought down from Moscow.

The conference started on Sunday 4th February 1945, with most of the meetings taking place in Livadia. That location had been chosen because when the conference was planned it would have been best for the wheelchair-bound FDR; few outside America had foreseen him being replaced by Travis. Everyone was aware that the French had not been invited, primarily because Stalin, it was said unofficially, found General Charles de Gaulle impossible to deal with.

Having met in Tehran fifteen months earlier, each delegation was aware of the aims and concerns of the others, but the introduction of Travis led to some uncertainty because FDR had been less concerned with Europe, with his long-term ambition being to form the United Nations.

When they had first met there was an element of hatred and mistrust between Stalin and Churchill, but gradually relations thawed and they developed a respect for each other. Initially Travis took a dislike to Stalin, leaving Churchill as the compromiser to enable some progress to be made. Travis's team soon realised that their President was no negotiator, having rarely been challenged in his years at the helm of his own business empire. They were particularly concerned that his tough line with Stalin would have a negative effect, particularly as they were seeking the USSR's help in the war against Japan. At the time they had to assume that Japan could only be defeated by conventional military means since they couldn't be sure the atomic bomb would actually work effectively, or even be ready in time. Moreover, there was still the political decision as to whether they should actually use it. At the time, the development of the bomb was still a secret, although Stalin couldn't let on that he was well aware of its existence through his own espionage channels.

FDR had been less concerned with Europe, whereas Churchill was prepared to confront Stalin over the future of the many countries bordering the USSR. He was particularly concerned with Poland, since this had become a corridor between Russia and Germany in two world wars and by that time at the conference the Soviet troops had retaken Poland and were advancing towards Berlin. They agreed on holding elections in Poland as soon as practicable, but could not agree on who would be allowed to stand for election and whether neutral observers would be allowed. Stalin refused to include the Polish government in exile, based in London, and insisted that his Soviet-sponsored provisional communist government be able to stand for election. Stalin had clearly seen his opportunity to bring Poland under his Soviet umbrella and was not going to give it away.

Meanwhile, Churchill's team was working on a plan for dividing Germany and who should be responsible for controlling those regions. They were very aware that the

Versailles Agreement after the 1914-18 War had been too severe, leading to the emergence of Adolf Hitler and his kind to fight against the reparations. By contrast, Stalin wanted no compromise and was all for severe reparations to punish the Germans. A map was eventually produced in which the east and west borders of Poland were moved to the west, so some Polish territories were taken over by the USSR and Poland gained part of eastern Germany. Occupation of Germany itself was to be shared between Britain, USA and USSR, with France later being given part of the areas originally allocated to Britain and the USA. Berlin, as the capital, was divided on similar lines.

Some progress was made on FDR's ambition to form the United Nations. All had agreed it was a good idea, but the main area of dispute was the number of votes any one country was allowed to have, with the USA delegation insisting they have more than one vote.

The defeat of Japan was also in the best interests of the USSR and so a grudging agreement was reached where Soviet forces would take on Japan in the north. Stalin agreed to help in exchange for Soviet expansion to include territories to the north of Japan, including Manchuria. China had not been consulted on this, since they were currently under Japanese control and would be liberated by the fall of Japan.

The conference ended with a 'Declaration of Liberated Europe' and the leaders returned to their respective countries. On returning home each delegation had to face a press barrage and they did their best to show they had got something out of the time spent at Yalta. Probably Stalin could justifiably feel most satisfied as he had conceded the least. Lord Drakeford was particularly interested in the outcome, and over a period of days gathered newspapers from many different countries, including a translation of the leading article of the USSR state newspaper. It was clear that Stalin had been very pleased with his week's work, even allowing for the fact that the reporter had been told what to write. Nevertheless, Drakeford was able to add to his library of press cuttings which he glued into his diary, convinced this was going to help him understand future events.

As if thinking aloud, he said to Christine, "It's so frustrating having to spend days trying to piece together all the reports. Perhaps one day we'll have international communications, maybe even by television, where we can receive news almost as it happens?"

"I think you've been reading too many of those science fiction books," she replied. "I'm sure it will come, but in our lifetime?"

"Yes, I suppose I'm getting carried away. Looking at the outcome from Yalta it could have been worse, Stalin wanted it all; it's a good job Churchill was prepared to stand up to him. Clearly Travis wasn't that concerned about Europe, providing Britain remained independent and he still sees us as his best friend. I suspect we'll never know what was really said behind closed doors. These kind of events don't happen very often, I would like to have been there."

"Maybe one day," she replied.

* * *

It was only a matter of weeks after Yalta, on 12 April, that Roosevelt died of a cerebral haemorrhage at his home in

Warm Springs, Georgia, aged 63. It was a sad moment for all those that had known him, and newspapers on both sides of the Atlantic featured prominent front page articles. President Travis was quoted as saying, perhaps somewhat grudgingly, "I hadn't met FDR until recently, but I found him very honest and straightforward." By contrast, George McDonald, a Democrat Senator had rather more to say about his former President: "FDR was an amazing President. He was elected as a Senator in 1910 and even though he contracted polio in 1921 he went on to became President in 1932. The USA was suffering from the great depression when he was elected and he turned things around, famed for his 'New Deal' and his 'fireside chats'. He made thirty radio broadcasts and was the first politician to appear on TV. He was credited with the decision to build the Pentagon as the USA defence HQ. I doubt if any President in the future could achieve so much."

Drakeford read many tributes in all the newspapers. Most were complimentary, although the more right-wing were reluctant to acknowledge that FDR's policies had proved successful – the USA recovery was more down to astute American businessmen.

Events were unfolding rapidly in Europe. The war in Europe ended on 8th May 1945 with an unconditional German surrender. Hitler was nowhere to be seen and reports were filtering through that he had committed suicide along with many of his henchmen in the Berlin Fuhrer Bunker. This was now the time when the provisional outcome agreed at Yalta would now become a reality, and the three leaders agreed to meet at Potsdam, near Berlin, on July 17th.

Meanwhile Britain had the small matter of a general election to resolve with a date fixed of 5th July. There was an assortment of parties contesting this election with wartime Prime Minister Winston Churchill leading the Conservatives, while Clement Atlee, his coalition Deputy Prime Minister, in opposition as the leader of the Labour Party. Churchill had been quite scathing of Clement Atlee, describing him as "a sheep in sheep's clothing" and "a modest man who has a good deal to be modest about". It was generally reported that the Conservatives conducted a poor general election strategy, misjudging the mood of the British people. In his first election broadcast on 4th June, Churchill denounced his former coalition partners, declaring that Labour 'would have to fall back on some form of a Gestapo' to impose socialism on Britain. Attlee responded the next night by thanking the prime minister for demonstrating to the people the difference between "Churchill the great wartime leader" and "Churchill the peacetime politician" and argued the case for public control of industry.

People can have long memories when it affects them personally and Churchill's record had been marked by his opposition to the Suffragettes movement, his attitude to striking dockworkers and the fact that he had initially opposed the abdication of King Edward VIII, some people wanting him to head up a new 'King's Party'. He quickly declined this possibility and changed his mind about the abdication as the outcome became inevitable.

It was said at the time that many British soldiers were scattered around the world, some in prisoner-of-war camps in the Far East, therefore unable to vote, but would have voted for Churchill. In fact, thousands of military personnel did vote, but many were influenced by a statement made by Churchill in the latter stages of the war, when he had promised all military personnel financial compensation for their efforts. However, they were disappointed when they found this amounted to just 6d (six pence) per day and this became known by many servicemen as "Churchill's tanner".

There was some delay in announcing the outcome because it took some time to bring the votes cast by servicemen back to Britain. Eventually the result was finally announced 26th July and it proved to be a win for Labour with an overall majority of 145 seats. A significant majority of voters did not want a return to the hard times and unemployment of the 1930s, preferring Atlee to the wartime leader Churchill, based on his peacetime record.

The delay in confirming the election result could not prevent world affairs from moving on. The Potsdam conference went ahead as scheduled, with Churchill representing Britain, supported by his Foreign Secretary Anthony Eden. However, once the British General Election result had been declared the conference was suspended for two days on 26th July to enable Churchill and Eden to be replaced by Clement Atlee and Ernest Bevin. The other delegations were taken aback by this change, especially as they thought Churchill was invincible as a politician. Nevertheless, the conference resumed, concluding on 2nd August with what became known as the Potsdam Declaration.

* * *

Back in London Atlee had appointed his first cabinet and this included several ministers who had served in the wartime coalition government. These included Herbert Morrison who had served as Home Secretary and Ernest Bevin, Minister of Labour. As is customary, suitable candidates are contacted and invited to meet the Prime Minister at 10 Downing Street. Lord Drakeford was in his office at his chambers in London and asked to come to Downing Street. He readily agreed, having never previously set foot in there, feeling rather curious as to why he had been invited. On arrival he was ushered into the Prime Minister's office and met by Clement Atlee in person. After a few brief pleasantries, Atlee said, "I know you are not a member of the Labour Party, or indeed I suspect any Party; however, I would like you to take up a position in the House of Lords as our spokesman on legal affairs. I knew your father very well and you may not be aware, but as a fellow barrister I've followed you career thus far. I think you would do rather well and we need people with a good professional background in the Lords."

Taken completely by surprise, Drakeford answered, "Yes of course, thank you very much." He couldn't think of anything else to say, so unexpected was this offer. He shook hands with Mr Atlee and left the room, the meeting having taken little more than a few minutes.

When the new cabinet appointments were announced in the press, his name appeared in the under-card since few people had heard of him and he suspected few people even noticed.

CHAPTER 3

USA RULES

B ack in the USA, Travis was now pressing to sort out the so-called Lend-Lease Agreement which was originally intended to provide equipment and resources to Britain during the war on the basis it would eventually be returned. Later it was agreed that Britain would be allowed to keep what it still had for £1.075bn, equivalent to 10% of the original value. However, at the end of the war the US decided to terminate the Lend-Lease Agreement and Britain was invited to a meeting with representatives of the suppliers of the equipment, USA and to a lesser extent Canada, where Britain was represented by the famous economist John Maynard Keynes. The outcome, announced on 21st July 1945, was that the Lend-Lease Agreement would be replaced by an Anglo-American Loan for $3.75bn (marginally less than £1bn at prevailing exchange rates), at 2% interest, to be paid annually.

Meanwhile it was decision time on the war with Japan. After some delays the bomb was tested on 16th July 1945 at 'Jornado del Muerto', about two hundred and ten miles south of Los Alamos, New Mexico. Known as Operation Trinity, the predicted devastation of the bomb was confirmed. Observers were taken aback by the blinding flash as the bomb was detonated, followed by a delay of more than twenty seconds before the noise of the explosion reached them at the base camp some five miles away, a clear demonstration of the speed of light being almost instantaneous, compared to the speed of sound.

Back in Washington it was now time to decide whether to use the bomb on Japan. The experts calculated that it could shorten the war, based on the assumption that a conventional war would last another two years and cost many more lives, particularly American lives. By now the news of the atom bomb test was leaking through, a deliberate tactic as they felt sure the Japanese would show indifference if confronted with news directly. Stalin had his sources and knew far more about the bomb than the Americans had realised, while through code interceptions it was known that he had links with the Japanese. The Americans hoped that the threat of such a powerful weapon would bring the Japanese to the conference table, but such was their pride and stubbornness that nothing transpired, possibly calling America's bluff. Having reached that point in the war of nerves, the USA could not back down and had little option to continue with their intention to confront Japan. Travis needed little persuasion that the nuclear weapon was the only way. He was becoming impatient and convinced that it was his duty to save American lives; the only decision that remained was the target.

Travis convened a meeting of his top military personnel and his political inner circle. After a short introduction he made his thoughts clear. "I think we have no option but to use the bomb and I think we have to hit them where it hurts, so that means Tokyo, the capital." There was a silence and collective intake of breath, while some just rolled their eyes or looked anywhere but at Travis.

"I'm not so sure," countered General Marshall. "There could be massive casualties, more than we need in order to make the point. I think we should go for a small to medium sized town, where the destruction and casualties will be limited, but still enough to show the full potential of the weapon."

"I agree," responded General Sykes. "What's more, Tokyo will be heavily defended, they will be expecting raids on Tokyo. It will be embarrassing if the plane carrying the weapon is shot down before it reaches its target. Remember also we have limited supplies of nuclear material, so I think we should choose somewhere well away from the capital." There were several nods of agreement.

Maps were produced and the meeting then discussed the options. Eventually they concluded that Hiroshima was the preferred target, with the island of Nagasaki as a backup if the Japanese refused to surrender. Everyone, including Travis, agreed with the decision and orders were immediately passed to the military personnel who had been on standby, having planned for this possibility for some time. Everyone waited with trepidation as the mission set off.

The weapon, equivalent to twenty thousand tons of TNT, was used on Hiroshima on 6th August 1945 with devastating results. Much to everyone's surprise there was no response from the Japanese, so three days later another bomb was dropped on the island of Nagasaki.

Travis was following events closely and was surprised that the Japanese were holding out after the USA had clearly demonstrated their superiority. He called another meeting of his cabinet and military experts on 12th August. "I believe we have no alternative but to escalate the A-bomb campaign," he declared.

"Let's give it a while longer," replied Sykes. "Their campaign is on hold, maybe it's time for a diplomatic intervention. Surely a week or so is not going to make much difference."

"I disagree," Travis declared. "We have to get tough; the Japanese mentality is such that surrender is not an option. I believe we have to use a third bomb. I will authorise an attack on Tokyo on the 15th of August, that's the only thing they will understand. They will have no choice once they've lost their emperor."

There was much consternation amongst the military and scientific personnel as they had not planned for three bombs, having worked on the basis that one bomb would be sufficient to bring the Japanese to the table, possibly two if the first did not produce the required reaction. A third bomb was hastily prepared and flown to the air force base at Pearl Harbor. The plane was made ready and the bomb loaded, as in the two previous missions. Just as the crew was preparing to board, the simple message came through:

"Japanese have surrendered. Cancel attack on Tokyo."

The station commander ran across the runway, clutching the message on a flimsy piece of paper, shouting at the crew as they walked towards their aircraft. The crew stopped in their tracks and threw their flying helmets in the air, cheering as they did so.

It was later reported that Emperor Hirohito had declared, "The situation has developed not necessarily to our advantage," clearly a classic understatement. The abrupt end to the war against Japan was met with intense relief by all concerned and, more importantly, rendered Russian involvement unnecessary.

Back in the United States there was much celebration because at last both wars were over and American personnel would be returning home. However, not everyone was rejoicing, particularly those who had had direct involvement with the atomic bomb and had witnessed the devastation. Most prominent among these was Robert Oppenheimer, head of the Manhattan Project, and as a brilliant physicist he had done more than any single person to bring it about, almost certainly within the timescale necessary to bring the war to a conclusion. After much thought he requested a meeting with the President.

He met the President in the Oval Office. Oppenheimer began, "I have barely slept since the bombs were used on Japan. The thought of all those people, either killed, or suffering a slow painful death as a result of the after-effects, has haunted me. Surely the bomb on Hiroshima would have been sufficient; did you have to bomb Nagasaki as well?"

"It was a military decision," replied Travis. "I'm sorry you feel this way. Frankly you should have thought of the consequences before you got involved."

"Perhaps I should. For that reason I'm resigning my position as head of the Laboratory at Los Alamos."

With that he left. The President shouted to his aides, "Don't let that man near my office again."

Clearly no one had grasped Oppenheimer's dilemma. Until then he had seen the project through the eyes of a scientist. Having successfully demonstrated the power of the bomb he had hoped that its very existence would deter them from using it, particularly against the Japanese as they were an obvious target. He had hoped they might offer some compromise short of an unconditional surrender, but he had seriously underestimated the Japanese mentality. After his resignation few had sympathy for his position as his communist views made him a security risk, despite him having been born in America. Scientists have traditionally mingled with international colleagues, learning from one another, and his opponents were convinced he could be sharing his knowledge with the USSR.

* * *

It was now September 1945 and shortly after Oppenheimer's visit General Marshall made an appointment to see President Travis. He had heard that the President was not in the best of spirits and he wore a serious expression as he entered the Oval Office. Travis gestured for him to take a seat.

Marshall began, "As you know we've been keeping a close watch on the situation in Germany since the surrender. We know that hundreds of engineers and scientists, many who had been working at Peenemunde on the 'V' project, fled as soon as they could see what was going to happen. Hitler did not want them to be captured and had set out to have them gassed. The majority of them were more scared of being captured by the Russians and they easily evaded Hitler's SS who themselves were more concerned about their own futures. The scientists fled to Southern Germany and arrived in May at Oberammergau where 450 of them willingly surrendered to the Allied forces. These numbers have grown since then and many have applied to come to the USA."

"Could be a unique opportunity," responded Travis. "We could benefit from their experience, and we can afford to be choosy. Maybe Britain will want to take some as well?"

"Exactly," replied Marshall. "We've developed a secret system to identify the people we want. Top of that list is a guy called Wernher von Braun."

"I've head of him," interrupted Travis. "Wasn't he the guy leading the V2 project?"

"Yes, he was the leading German rocket expert. He'd been involved in experiments with rockets since his teenage years. His ambition was to build a rocket to get to the moon! As it happened, the war came along and he was forced to join the Nazi Party if he wanted to stay in a job."

"That's what they all say afterwards," laughed Travis. "So what's so special about the V2 rocket?"

"It's a liquid propellant rocket, so it can be controlled more easily than a solid fuel rocket. A solid fuel rocket is effectively a giant firework, so once it fires it is difficult or impossible to stop, whereas a liquid propellant rocket can be steered and controlled as an engine, so more accurately directed to a target, as the Germans were able to do on

London. In no time at all we could even have a manned rocket-propelled aircraft."

Marshall clearly had Travis's attention now. He continued: "It seemed his reputation 'took off', excuse the analogy, when Hitler invited von Braun to explain how his rockets worked and what they could do. Von Braun gave a lecture to Hitler and finished with a short movie film of a test rocket taking off. Hitler was totally enthralled and made him a Professor there and then. He committed to a massive programme to develop the V2 at Peenemunde. At the time Hitler could see things slipping away and was looking for a secret weapon which could turn things around.

"At its peak there were several thousand people working at Peenemunde, many of them slaves who were prisoners of war, mainly from Poland and Russia. Many died through unfit working conditions or accidental explosions. The problem was that they were in such a hurry to get these missiles into service that they cut a lot of corners. It's been suggested that more people died in making the V2s than were actually killed as their targets. Despite their setbacks, at the moment the V2 is still the only object to leave the earth's atmosphere and enter the vacuum of space. They are still years ahead of the rest of us."

"Let's get him on board," responded Travis enthusiastically. "And his team. We don't have anything like it at the moment. We could develop rocket powered aeroplanes, nobody would catch them! I'm not so sure about trying to get to the moon, but if we could produce a V2 type of rocket with a longer range and a more powerful warhead, then we'd be invincible. We could even have an atomic bomb as a warhead, that would scare Stalin!"

"I think it would scare us all," concluded Marshall. "Thanks for listening, I wanted to keep you informed. Are you in favour of bringing these people to the USA?"

"You bet, good work, please carry on."

True to his word, Marshall continued his negotiations with von Braun and his team. They had had conversations with the British, but there was nothing firm on the table, whereas the Americans offered everything they could have wanted: excellent well-funded facilities to develop missiles and in the long term a possible moon project. They would also be able to settle with their families as a community, somewhat removed from the more conventional industrial areas and therefore any possible resentment or adverse reaction to wartime Germans coming to live in the USA. Needless to say, they needed little persuasion and gladly accepted.

CHAPTER 4

REDS UNDER THE BED

It may have been paranoia, but US Republican politicians were convinced that prominent members of the left-wing Labour government were in league with the USSR and being manipulated by them. The Atlee-led government planned to create many nationalised industries as they believed this was the fastest way to get things running again and prevent exploitation, since it was effectively bankrupt after the war. The Americans' view was the Labour government was committed to Socialism on a grand scale, being in the process of extending public ownership to include coal, gas, electricity, steel production, the postal system, telephones, broadcasting, the banking system, water supply, railways, air travel and road transport. For them this was bad enough, but when Labour published its ambitious plans for a National Health Service, to be introduced in 1948, this was the last straw for the USA, seeing this as a step nearer to real communism and justifying their worst fears. Within Britain the government's plans for a National Health Service were strongly opposed by the Tory opposition as they regarded a compulsory National Insurance contribution as a form of taxation and predicted the income of doctors and dentists would be significantly reduced.

The Americans were convinced that Britain was modelling itself on a USSR-style government and were particularly concerned as Britain had accrued massive debts to the USA, partly through the updated version of the Lend-Lease arrangement and saw a conflict of interest. Travis met with his closest colleagues in the Oval Office. Like many of his meetings, it was not an official or scheduled meeting and no minutes were taken.

He began, "I'm very concerned about where England is going. This is bad news, I suspected this would happen when they kicked out Churchill. I'm convinced those limeys are cosying up to Stalin. We have to step in, we can't let this happen. At the moment Atlee can do no wrong for most of the British people – is there anything we can do to destabilize their government?"

"Do you really believe they've thought it through that far?" interrupted James Palmer, one of the financial experts. "Surely they're just putting into practice what they've been hatching for years. My guess is they've based their theories on the Soviet model, especially as they felt the capitalist alternative didn't work too well for them in the thirties. But that's not the same thing as forming an alliance with Stalin."

"Perhaps we could get Atlee and his men here and persuade them that their ideals have long-term implications for our relationship. Perhaps make it look as if we're offering financial aid providing they back down on their more extreme ideas," suggested Dulles.

"I doubt if they can be easily bought off," countered Travis. "I think we need to get someone over there who can spread the message through the radio and newspapers to put pressure on the government. We have a few friends who own some of the right-wing newspapers and we could plant a scare story about a secret Russian plot. Maybe say that Stalin is about to visit Britain for talks about 'Anglo-Soviet' cooperation."

"That wouldn't fool many people; everyone knows that Stalin refuses to travel. It was all we could do to get him to Yalta and Potsdam," Dulles replied. "We could put out a story that British officials are to meet their Russian counterparts at a secret venue, somewhere in Europe, with a view to future cooperation. Then we could justifiably send a team to London for talks with Treasury ministers. That would at least look quite constructive. We could easily say this about a financial package and an offer of military support to aid British defence, seeing as we already have US bases on English soil."

"Yes, I think we can do all those things," replied Travis. "Invite Atlee to Washington, make him feel important. And, taking your suggestion, we should also send our guys over to meet with their financial people. Any rumours we can spread will help scare the people who in turn will put pressure on their government to cooperate with us. Ideally, we should be trying to persuade them that they should be tying up with the USA, rather than the USSR. Britain has a lot going for it, it just needs pump-priming. Personally, I would like to see Britain as part of the USA – maybe that's the message we should be trying to get across?"

Dulles answered quickly, "Nice idea, not sure if they're ready for that."

It was now September 1945 and Travis acted immediately to invite Atlee to the USA, nominally to discuss how to plan their future economic relationship and to ask how Britain intended to repay its debts to the USA. Atlee could hardly refuse such an invitation, such was Britain's dependence on support from the USA at that time. He replied promptly, and then set about choosing his team to travel with him. Foreign Secretary Ernest Bevin was an essential choice, but what he really wanted was someone familiar with international law and finance. He decided Lord Drakeford would be ideal, experienced enough to be familiar with the rapidly changing relationships around the world, yet also in touch with those of his own generation, many of whom were returning to civilian life after military service. Atlee had great hopes for Drakeford, possibly influenced by having worked with his father, a fellow barrister, and had closely followed Rufus's career. Ernest Bevin recommended two civil servants who should also be part of the delegation, their diplomatic expertise second to none.

It was a quiet Tuesday morning and Drakeford was working at home, preparing a case due to appear in court in a few weeks' time, when the phone rang. "Lord Drakeford?" enquired a rather terse female voice.

"Yes, speaking," replied Drakeford.

"This is the Prime Minister's office. Would be available to travel to America as part of the Prime Minister's delegation, the day after tomorrow? I assume you have a passport?"

"Why, yes of course," replied Drakeford, a little taken aback.

"Thank you, a courier will deliver some briefing notes to your home later today and we will send a car to pick you up from your home at seven o'clock on Thursday morning to take you to the airport. Goodbye."

Drakeford was stunned by the suddenness of the call. He walked a few yards to the next room where Christine was also working at her desk. "Who was on the phone?" she enquired.

"It was the Prime Minister's office, they want me to be part of Atlee's team to travel to the USA on Thursday. Sounds like I might get to meet Travis."

Christine was equally shocked at the news. "Brilliant, at least you'll get to hear what he has to say first hand, instead of reading about it in the newspapers a day or two later. Maybe he's not as fierce as they say?"

"Yes, it will be good to be in a position to have some influence, although perhaps I'm getting carried away!" He returned to his case preparation, but found it difficult to concentrate now this forthcoming venture was less than two days away.

The courier duly arrived later that afternoon. The briefing notes were indeed brief. There was a list of who would be travelling as part of the delegation, with a short agenda on the next page. Predictably the agenda was more of a discussion document, covering Britain's political aims and objectives, repayment of loans and the future relationship between the two countries. Atlee would be accompanied by Ernest Bevin, his Foreign Secretary, with Herbert Morrison staying in Downing Street, nominally in charge while Atlee was away. There was no information on the American personnel they would be meeting and no indication of when they would be returning home. He suspected this was Atlee's suggested agenda, not one that had come from the White House.

The car duly arrived on time on Thursday morning and Drakeford climbed aboard with his small suitcase. Packing had been a problem because he had no idea whether this may be for a day or two, or for almost a week. He arrived at Northolt airport and was introduced to his fellow team members, Robert McIntyre and Martin Tyler, civil servants whom he had met briefly during his time as a junior minister. It was clear they had no more idea than he as to meeting content and duration. A few minutes later Atlee and Bevin arrived and after brief introductions they boarded the plane. They were booked on a commercial DC-4 which had just entered service as a transatlantic airliner.

Once in the air they settled back and prepared themselves for the long flight. Conversation was difficult as the noise of the four piston engines dominated everything, even though they were in the first-class passenger compartment. Fifteen hours later they arrived in New York and were promptly met by two smartly dressed men from the British Embassy. Drakeford wasn't sure whether they were serious diplomats or trained bodyguards capable of killing with their bare hands. He secretly hoped it was the latter. They stepped outside into two large limousines waiting next to the airport arrivals area and they embarked on the five-hour journey to Washington DC. In all, a full day's travelling.

On arrival they were shown to nearby accommodation at Blair House, situated close to the White House. There was no formal reception or high cabinet member to greet them, but they were met by a senior White House official who made them welcome and made sure their dinner reservations were registered with the restaurant manager. He then bade them goodnight and explained: "We hope you will be very comfortable after your long journey. Breakfast will be available from seven o'clock and we will send a car round to pick you up at nine. The President will then meet you in the Oval Office. Goodnight, gentlemen."

Atlee and his team were somewhat surprised by the indifferent reception, but were secretly relieved as they were exhausted after their journey. The last thing they wanted was to have to make conversation at an official dinner where they might have been honoured guests. They had a quiet evening meal where Atlee gave a brief overview of the purpose of their visit, much as outlined in the agenda.

Next morning, feeling refreshed after a night's sleep and an all-American breakfast, the official car swept into the forecourt and the five men clambered aboard. A few minutes later they were at the White House. A tall man in army uniform greeted them and invited them to follow him to the Oval Office. They followed on, looking around, trying to take it all in. They arrived at the Oval Office and Travis stood up from behind his desk, greeting them with handshakes and gestured for them to be seated in the comfortable chairs arranged in a semi-circle. He introduced Alan Dulles and Joe Thompson, a financial expert he had brought from New York to advise him as he didn't entirely trust the team he had inherited.

"Thank you for coming, and welcome to the White House. We have a long relationship with England and the English, and long may it continue."

Atlee quickly replied, "Actually there's more to it than just England, we have Wales, Scotland and Northern Ireland. Since 1927 it's been known as the United Kingdom of Great Britain and Northern Ireland. But we're pleased that we all share a common language, including the United States, of course."

Travis was slightly annoyed with Atlee's little lecture. He wasn't used to being corrected and his face showed it. "Actually, my father was born in Scotland, that's where the name Travis comes from. I've never been there, but soon I intend to."

He continued: "Let's get down to business. We're interested to hear your plans during your period in government, however long that is. It's not quite what we were expecting, but I'm sure there's some common ground to our mutual benefit."

Atlee began, "I'm sure you will understand the desperate situation we are in and the measures we have had to take to get our economy moving again. Industry was on its knees after the war and our services were operating under great pressure. We need to get as many people back into the workplace as they return from military service…"

He had hardly got started when Travis jumped in. "Yes, we understand that. But was it really necessary to nationalise everything to achieve this?"

"We felt we had no alternative, there just weren't people with sufficient capital to invest and get things moving. Moreover, we were reluctant to invite overseas investors as this would have compromised our status as an independent nation."

"But you didn't need to take this as far as a nationalised health service. That will cost your government a fortune, money which by your own admission you don't have."

The meeting was regularly interrupted by catering staff bringing refreshments. These were welcome in view of the unaccustomed warm weather, but somewhat frustrating as the breaks spoilt the flow of conversation.

Atlee continued: "Our private health system is in tatters. It's just about adequate for those who can afford to pay, but most people can't afford it and we need to get people healthy as quickly as possible so that they can get out to work."

"I'm afraid you'll find it will bankrupt your economy. There's no way we could get the American people to accept such a service. Our people have private heath insurance, mostly paid for as part of their employment package. If that's not available then charities step in."

Drakeford felt he should make a contribution. "We've done our calculations and believe it could work. We need a healthy workforce, whether it be those doing manual labour, right up to teachers, engineers and scientists. What's more, as you know, we have enormous debts to repay after the war."

Travis showed total disinterest in Drakeford's comments. He was keen to get to the issue of his particular concern. "We believe Britain is developing a relationship with Stalin and modelling itself on his regime. My guys have been checking out a few of your people, like Sir Stafford Cripps, one of your cabinet members. You kicked him out of your Labour Party in 1939 because he had Communist sympathies. Then he gets sent to the USSR in 1940 as British Ambassador. Who knows what he agreed to during the two years he was there? Seems highly suspicious from where we're standing, so you will understand why your plan for the National Health Service just confirms our worst fears. Frankly you're off the scale," he declared, showing an element of anger as he spoke.

There was an uncomfortable silence for a few seconds and this was the trigger for Drakeford to respond. In recent weeks he had developed a now well rehearsed short monologue in conversation with political colleagues and this was the opportunity here in the White House to deliver it. It required only the slightest word change to adapt it to the Americans.

"Our plan for socialism is a long way from the USSR model of communism as defined by Marx and Lenin. The Russian mentality is based on 'The State knows best', with a one-party system that rejects democracy as we know it. We don't like Joe Stalin any more than anyone else in the free world; he has a dubious past and is a bully in charge of what is virtually a dictatorship. However, you must appreciate that he has taken up his position because he has a paranoid vision that America intends to invade the USSR, all part of your plan for world domination, using the atomic bomb as a tool to threaten other nations with. He has moved to surround his borders with buffer-zones such as Poland, Estonia, Lithuania, East Germany, Czechoslovakia and Ukraine as a form of protection. Small wonder that he has shown a friendly face towards Britain?

But we have no intention of forming a political alliance with him. We're happy to trade with the USSR, as we might any country within reason, but we intend to remain politically independent."

With his legal background Drakeford was a confident speaker, the equal of any politician. Travis sat for a moment and no one spoke, then he gave a brief response. "I hear what you say and it sounds impressive. Do you agree with Mr Drakeford's comments?" he said, turning to Atlee.

"One hundred percent," replied Atlee. "There's a big difference between our definition of Socialism and that of Communism, as currently practised by the USSR. There may be many issues where we disagree, I would sooner we found areas where we do agree."

"Ok," replied Travis. He could see that views were firmly entrenched and they were a long way off any compromise. "We may have different views on that. Let's leave it there for today, I can see that you're all feeling the effects of your long journey."

* * *

On day two the discussions moved on to Britain's role internationally. Atlee explained, "We have had an important role in Palestine since 1918. We hope this will be resolved by the United Nations in the not-too-distant future; meanwhile, it's a drain on our military resources."

"It's highly likely they will recommend a new Jewish State," responded Alan Dulles. "We understand the USSR is also in favour of that solution. Then it will no longer be your problem."

Atlee continued: "We can no longer justify the structure of the British Empire and we are looking at a plan to transfer all the countries currently in our Empire to have their own democratically elected, independent governments. We are hoping to retain a relationship by forming a British Commonwealth, thereby retaining special trade relationships."

"That sounds a sensible approach," replied Travis. "What about your relationship with non-Commonwealth countries, particularly the 'iron curtain' countries as I've heard Churchill refer to them?"

"We're happy to trade with anyone, within reason, provided we can agree on suitable tariffs and exchange rates. The important thing is we need to export to earn foreign currency. That has to be our priority, even if it means going short on our own domestic requirements, like motor vehicles, aircraft, almost everything we manufacture, because that is one of our strengths. You will appreciate that apart from coal we don't have a lot in the way of natural resources."

"Apart from rain!" joked Travis. Nobody responded, although the brief levity was a relief for all. "And what about the USSR, they have lots of natural resources, do you fear they could hold you to ransom?"

"No more than any other country, even the USA," countered Atlee smartly.

Travis, ignoring this dig, continued, "We're very aware that Stalin is hoping to expand his influence to countries currently outside their USSR boundaries. We believe in a free world and are anxious that as many countries as possible stay that way. I believe that the USA is the most powerful country in the world and people will listen to us. We alone have the atomic bomb and we've shown that we're not afraid to use it."

"I understand that," replied Atlee, "but surely you wouldn't want to use that against Russia? I think the world would be outraged if you did, it would be seen as the ultimate act of aggression. We now know the level of destruction which the bomb inflicts, to say nothing of its after-effects. And rest assured, Russia will have its own nuclear weapon in a few years' time, as will other countries, including Britain. Once in a nuclear age there will be a deadlock as no one will be prepared to use such a weapon for fear of reprisals. A full-scale nuclear war could see the end of the world as we know it."

"I'm not sure if I agree," countered Travis, "it could be ten years or more before anyone else has a nuclear weapon, we're way ahead in the field of nuclear physics. We're recruiting some of the German V2 designers, so imagine a rocket, as big or bigger than the V2 and with an atomic bomb as a warhead. No one's going to mess with the USA in future, that's my ambition. At this point in time we have to exert as much influence as possible in order to keep Stalin in his place. We believe Stalin has his eyes on your country because you have a lot of what he hasn't got, like a manufacturing industry and people with appropriate skills. We plan to keep a substantial military presence in Britain and mainland Europe, just in case he has ideas on expansion."

Atlee felt both sides had stated their position and thought a change of subject was appropriate. "As you know, we're planning to host the 1948 Olympic Games in

London. We think it will send out a strong message to the world that Britain is open for business. It could also bring together many nations who have come through a world war and need to move on, and put difficult times behind us. Sport is a great way to achieve that. Even though we have to take an austere approach, it will impose a difficult financial burden, but we think it's worthwhile."

"I think it's highly commendable," replied Travis. "We support you in this, it will be of great benefit, I'm sure. It's also an opportunity for heads of state to meet informally and I hope to be there myself. What about countries that were against us in the war?"

"We would like to 'bury the hatchet' as far as possible. However, I think Germany and Japan may be a step too far; they will not be invited."

At least the Olympics was something they could agree on. Otherwise it was clear that both sides had different views on the world, clearly stated, and this was a good place to end the day's discussion. It was still early afternoon, but Travis made it clear that he had another appointment. As he stood up to leave one of Atlee's sharp-eared assistants overheard the word 'golf' mentioned.

"Please continue your discussions with my team, we'll reconvene tomorrow," said Travis as he opened the door. "We've arranged for as all to meet for dinner in the White House this evening at eight o'clock."

Shortly afterwards the meeting broke up as both sides realised there was little progress to be made without the President being present. The British contingent returned to Blair House and made the most of their opportunity to shower and change clothes, given that they were mostly travelling light and not expecting a long stay. Drakeford made the most of the opportunity to update his diary, writing several pages to record his impression of events at this level. Around six o'clock they met in the ground floor lounge, with suitable refreshments, to discuss the day's proceedings.

Atlee began. "So what do you make of the meeting so far?"

His team looked at one another to see who was going to lead with a reply.

"He's certainly not holding back," replied Bevin. "He's made it clear that he doesn't want us to go down that particular road, in his eyes it's just a watered down form of communism."

"I don't think he was even listening," countered Drakeford. "He likes to hear himself speak and doesn't like to be disagreed with. He's already formed his opinions and has a plan to put us in our place. I suspect he's saving that for tomorrow."

Their debrief continued for another hour, the general feeling being there were no grounds for optimism. At around a quarter to eight a large limousine appeared outside the main entrance and everyone managed to find a seat, cramped, but adequate for the short journey to the White House. They arrived and were led by a smart young man wearing army dress style uniform to a moderately sized room in the East Wing where the tables were already set and the American delegation was waiting to greet them, apart from Travis. They chatted politely as the waiters handed out drinks, and then at ten minutes past eight Travis appeared with his wife. There was no apology from him, just a "Good evening, please take your seats". No one was surprised to see that place names had been set, carefully arranged so that British and American participants occupied alternate seats.

As they might have expected, a fine meal was served, the turkey being as good as anyone could ever recollect having tasted before. Clearly no rationing in the USA and no need to demonstrate restraint. There was much conversation during the meal, little of it about politics, more about personal and family experiences, then, as the last of the table was cleared, Travis decided it was time for him to hold forth. The relaxed atmosphere became more formal as he stood to address the gathering.

"Gentlemen, it's been a fine evening and we've enjoyed having our British guests with us, and I must remember to say British and not English!" he said with a smile, looking at Atlee. "I think this is something we must do more often, it helps to meet face to face and develop a better understanding of one another. I would like us to work together as we both have considerable talents and complement one another like no other two nations. And I believe we all agree that we have to be strong to resist the threat of Soviet expansion. We are far superior militarily, but I appreciate that may not always be the case."

At this point Drakeford had to contain a yawn, thinking to himself this was all very predictable.

Travis went on: "Tomorrow I will set out my ideas for us to move forward, how we might work more closely together and benefit financially. But let's not get involved in politics this evening. If you don't mind, my wife and

I will excuse ourselves and return to our living quarters. Would you believe, we haven't finished unpacking yet!"

Everyone laughed politely as Mr and Mrs Travis shook hands with Clement Atlee and Ernest Bevin and left by the entrance whence they came. Everyone relaxed again, the noise level increased and more drinks were served. At around ten o'clock Atlee stood up and briefly addressed the gathering: "Many thanks for your hospitality and for giving up your time to be with us this evening. I'm sure you will understand that we are still feeling the effects of the long journey. We look forward to continuing with our more formal talks tomorrow morning."

There was an agreeable response from around the table and the smart man in uniform appeared as if from nowhere to lead the Atlee team back to the waiting limousine. They returned to Blair House and bid one another good night. Drakeford felt he had little to add to his diary, apart from his impression of the East Wing and the quality of the food that was served.

* * *

Next morning the British team met over breakfast, still recovering from the previous evening, with no real appetite for even more food, let alone a traditional American breakfast. As they gathered around the table everyone was aware that Prime Minister Atlee had yet to arrive. "It seems our PM has overslept," announced Bevin. "Let's carry on, I'm sure he'll be along in a while."

Almost thirty minutes had passed and still no sign of Atlee.

"I'd better go and see if he's awake," said Bevin. "He needs to surface quite soon, else we'll be late for our meeting with the President." Bevin stood up and left the breakfast room.

Atlee's room was further along the corridor than his own room and being one of three he was not entirely sure which door he should be knocking. He decided to take a chance on the basis that not all rooms would be occupied, so he knocked on all three. There was no reply from any of them. He decided he needed help, so went back downstairs to the reception desk. He spoke to the large, very important looking gentleman behind the desk. "Excuse me, do you know which room Mr Atlee is staying in? He hasn't appeared and we're worried that he's overslept and we have a meeting with the President in half an hour's time." He then added apologetically, "Of course he may be in the bathroom and couldn't hear me knocking the door."

The man on reception responded immediately. "Hi, I'm Bill Healey, the manager, pleased to be of service. This sometimes happens to our visitors, we make them too comfortable. He has a telephone in his room so I'll try that." He let the phone ring for a full minute with no reply. "That's unusual, perhaps as you say, he could be in the bathroom. Let's go and see." He grabbed a bunch of keys and strode off, followed by Bevin, struggling to keep up as they climbed the stairs.

Bill Healey knocked one of the doors that Bevin had tried earlier, but there was no response. He found the appropriate key, unlocked the door and opened it a few inches. "Mr Atlee, are you ok?" he shouted. There was no reply, so they entered the room. There lay Mr Atlee still in bed and unresponsive. Bill checked that he was still breathing and nudged him gently on the shoulder. "Mr Atlee," he said a few times. He turned to Bevin and said, "This is not looking good, we need to get help. I could send for a doctor, but I think the best solution is to get him to hospital as soon as possible." He picked up the telephone and mumbled quietly to someone on his switchboard.

He turned to Bevin and explained: "They'll send an ambulance right away. With the White House close by there's always an ambulance on standby, hidden discreetly and available at a minute's notice."

Bevin looked around the room. Atlee's clothes had been slung over a chair, but there was no evidence of any other activity. His briefcase and some papers sat neatly on the desk. A few minutes later two ambulance men in uniform arrived with a stretcher on wheels and immediately took control. "Please stand back, leave everything to us." They were calm, but very efficient. They lifted Atlee from his bed and placed him on the stretcher. Within seconds they had gone.

Bevin and Bill Healey went back downstairs. They didn't speak, there was nothing to say. The British contingent was still waiting in the breakfast room and Bevin explained. "I'm afraid the PM's been taken ill and he's on his way to hospital. I guess we'd better get word to the White House, I'm not sure if we can carry on with the meeting without the PM."

They boarded the waiting limousine and drove to the White House, slightly later than planned. They were shown to the meeting room where Travis and his negotiators were waiting, unaware as to the reason for the delay.

Bevin began: "I must apologise for our lateness, I'm afraid Mr Atlee's been taken ill and has been taken to hospital. I assume someone will let us know when he's been assessed by a doctor."

Travis responded, showing little concern. "I guess there's not much point in continuing without your leader. I suggest we suspend our meeting until we hear news as to his condition. It will give you an opportunity to look around while you're waiting. I'll arrange for someone to show you around the White House and the Capitol Building."

"Thanks," replied Bevin, "we would appreciate that. Please let us know when you have news. Perhaps he might recover well enough to be released later today, or if not maybe we can visit him in hospital."

Travis pressed a button on the wall next to his chair and almost immediately a secretary appeared. "Rosemary, could you ask Jim Watt to come along and escort our visitors on the guided tour?"

Off she went and a few minutes later a smart young man appeared, tall, with short-cropped hair and dressed in a dark blue suit.

"Good morning, Mr President. The short tour or the VIP version?" asked Watt.

"Oh, the VIP version," replied Travis. "But make sure you stay in touch, the British Prime Minister has been taken to hospital and we may need to let his colleagues know when we have some news."

Travis turned to his team and said, "We may as well go back to what we would have been doing. I doubt if we'll be resuming this meeting again today. We'll reconvene when we have some news and decide where we go from here."

They dutifully gathered up their belongings and filed out of the room. Bevin and his men left their briefcases on the table and followed Jim Watt out into the corridor. Drakeford felt a little surprised that Travis seemed unconcerned and unsympathetic. They were shown around what was a very large office building with many people hard at work amidst the clatter of many typewriters. After a brief break for refreshments in a café area they emerged into the outside world, for the first time in days, and took the walk along to the Capitol Building. This was very impressive, especially the equivalent to the House of Commons and the Lords, that is the House of Representatives and the Senate, two very large rooms, although both were empty at the time. A commissionaire was busily explaining what went on when a young lady ran up to Jim Watt. "I have a telephone call for you," she explained. Watt followed her to an adjoining office and had a brief conversation before replacing the receiver on its base. He thanked her and returned to his tour party. "I'm told we have news from the hospital, we should return to the White House."

They thanked the commissionaire and quickly returned to the White House and to the conference room where their belongings remained where they had been left. Within a few minutes everyone, including Travis, gathered to hear what he had to say.

Travis announced: "I'm informed that Mr Atlee's condition is related to a heart problem. I'm told he is conscious, so you can go and visit him. However, I think our discussions have reached a point where we should not continue without the Prime Minister. I think we have developed a good understanding and your visit has been well worthwhile. We'll make a statement to the press without going into detail. We'll take you to the hospital and then back to Blair House. Then we'll arrange tomorrow to have you driven back to New York where a flight will be arranged."

Bevin replied: "Thank you for your hospitality, Mr President, I agree that under the circumstances we should bring our meeting to a close. We enjoyed our guided tour and appreciate the arrangements for our return journey."

Drakeford looked on, privately amazed by the President's bluntness. Perhaps this is the way Americans operate, he thought, not the way we British do things.

After handshakes all round, the contingent returned to their waiting limousine and were driven to the hospital, just a short distance away. They were shown to the private room where Mr Atlee was being looked after. He was awake, but not able to communicate.

Bevin spoke: "Hello Clem, how are you feeling?"

Atlee did not reply, just moved his eyes and smiled weakly.

He turned to his colleagues, "I'm not sure if he's aware that we're here or where he is, there's nothing we can do, it's just a matter of time as to how and when he will recover."

Drakeford replied: "I agree. This is very similar to the condition suffered by my father a few years ago. Unfortunately, he never recovered, but there's no knowing exactly what's caused Mr Attlee's illness. Whatever it is, it will take time and there's no point in us hanging around. We've been shown the door by Travis, so we might as well go home."

Everyone nodded in agreement. They thanked the hospital staff and returned to their now familiar form of transport, the black 'limo'. Back at Blair House, Bevin arranged for a transatlantic phone call to alert Mrs Atlee before she heard about her husband's condition on the radio. He went to find Bill Healey and together they went back to Atlee's room. Bevin gathered up the briefcase and a few loose documents as the last thing he wanted was for the Americans to read the contents, even though there was probably nothing there that conflicted with what he had said. He took away the briefcase, while Bill gathered up the clothing and repacked Atlee's suitcase. "I'll get this sent to the hospital, it can stay with him until he's fit to travel," he explained.

Later that day the White House issued a short statement, explaining that Prime Minister Atlee had been taken ill and was being cared for in hospital. It gave no clue as to the reason and concluded by saying that his team would be returning to London forthwith. The press and radio news media duly reported on the PM's illness. Further to the official statement there was inevitably much speculation as to the reason why. There was some suggestion that this could be food poisoning or fatigue brought on by the long flight, followed by the strain of negotiating with the American President. Later that day another official bulletin was issued stating that Atlee had been taken ill with what might be a heart complaint and he would be staying for a while longer under observation. Back in England some newspapers mused that he was effectively under house arrest, suggesting it was a tactic employed by Travis to sabotage Britain's decision making process.

Next day, Bevin and the team were taken back to New York in a large limousine and returned to London by scheduled flight.

Immediately after they had left Travis decided to give a speech to journalists at the White House. Standing at the podium he declared, "Unfortunately, Mr Atlee's health has forced him to take a complete rest and following doctors' strong advice it has been decided he remain in Washington for a while longer, until he is fit to travel. Before Mr Atlee's health scare, his team and I have had a long conversation about Britain's future and his plans to put his country back on an even keel as they recover from the war. I must tell you we have come to the conclusion that the British were not being exactly straight with us. It is our suspicion that the British government *is* negotiating with the USSR with the possibility that a permanent, more formal, arrangement may transpire."

At the side of the room two of his aides looked at each other in amazement. "That's a total lie," whispered one of them. "We were there, the whole time. That's not what Atlee hinted at, and afterwards no one mentioned that as a possibility."

"What are we going to do?" replied his colleague. "We can't just let him get away with it."

"We've no choice. That is if you want to keep your job. So much as a word of dissent and your feet won't touch the ground."

Next day the American newspapers carried the headline "Travis exposes Britain's plans for an alliance with the USSR". The press had a field day, clamouring for more news, speaking to whoever was available. Everyone, of course, was tight lipped, because they had nothing to add; this was totally President Travis's own statement.

The news in the papers and on American TV and radio programmes came as a shock back in the UK. In Atlee's absence and with Bevin still out of the country, Herbert Morrison, an experienced cabinet minister, was temporarily in charge and asked to continue, despite his own reservations. The next day Ernest Bevin and his team arrived back in London, having been isolated from developing news broadcasts during the long flight. They were greeted at the airport almost immediately by news of Travis's press conference and were totally taken aback. They were quickly ushered into waiting cars which sped off, to be met by senior ministers at 10 Downing Street. Bevin was very tired after his long journey, hoping to get home to bed, but this news had set the adrenalin pumping and he was now wide awake.

"We were there the whole time," declared Bevin to his closest colleagues. "At no time was there mention that we were collaborating with Stalin. He's put his own interpretation on the whole thing."

Drakeford, equally shocked and annoyed, was sat next to Bevin. "I would like to endorse the Foreign Secretary's remarks. Travis made comments about the threat of the USSR, but we made it clear that we would not be negotiating with Stalin's regime. I would also add that we only have their word that Mr Atlee is suffering from a heart complaint, it could be any one of a number of possibilities."

Bevin had hardly had time to debrief them when it was apparent that telephones were ringing and the press were clamouring for a statement. He took a few minutes to gather his thoughts and then walked into the press briefing room, followed by Lord Drakeford, where reporters were already firing questions before they had even sat down. As an experienced politician Bevin waited for the room to fall silent before attempting to speak.

"As you know I have only arrived back in the UK less than an hour ago, having been on an aeroplane for the previous fifteen hours where we had a news blackout. On arrival I was briefed by my team and I've just read a press report of President Travis's news conference. I have to say I'm surprised by what he said. He certainly expressed concern that our policies were very radical and somewhat to the left of what the Americans were expecting. Mr Atlee explained the reasons why we had taken these decisions, because our economy was on its knees and we had to get things moving fast. The President certainly hinted that we were a little too close to the Russians, but at no time did he accuse us of colluding with them or being less than honest."

The press began to fire questions. "You may not have actually discussed it, but are there any discussions taking place with the USSR?" Another asked, "Does any member of your cabinet have links with the USSR?"

Bevin answered, "There have been no discussions with the USSR. And no member of the government has links with the USSR. We do have some MPs with strong left-wing views, but that's in no way the same thing as an actual relationship with any communist organisation."

"Are you calling Mr Travis a liar?" one journalist asked.

"I think he's putting his own interpretation forward, and this is not the same as lying. What's more, I've only read a report in the press within the last hour and have not had a chance to hear a recording of his speech. I'm sure things will become clearer in the next few days. If you don't mind, I can't comment any further, because I've told you all I know. I'm now ready to go home to bed."

"What about Mr Atlee, did you see him before you left?" asked a female journalist.

"Yes, we saw him briefly, he was very ill and barely recognised me. However, I'm sure he's in good hands."

"Some people have even speculated that his illness had been induced by underhand means to disrupt UK government," she countered.

"I can't comment, we have no proof and I doubt if we ever will."

Bevin stood up, even though reporters were still hurling questions, and he left the room. As he walked down the corridor he whispered to a colleague, "I've been absolutely honest, perhaps too honest, but I know we haven't heard the last of this."

A car driven by a government chauffeur delivered Drakeford to his home. He was ready for bed, but first relaxed on the sofa, drinking coffee with his wife.

"I heard Bevin on the radio," said Christine. "Was there more to it than he's admitting?"

"No, he was being honest. He said afterwards he might have been too honest, I'm sure he could have easily described Travis as a liar, but after all Bevin is the Foreign Secretary and diplomacy comes with the territory."

"What was your impression of the meeting in the White House? Was it impressive?"

"Yes, it's an impressive building and we were well received. However, I did feel that we had been invited merely to be told what to expect. I don't think they were really very interested in what we had to say. The President has surrounded himself with some very smart people. However, I don't think that Travis himself is really that bright! He's grown up within a business empire that was set up initially by his father and he's spent most of his adult life as the top dog. He's clearly used to being in charge and prepared to fire anyone who doesn't agree with him. I don't think he does detail very well, relying on his team to keep him up to speed. He has a strong personality, a certain presence, and is good with words, hence his rapid rise to the presidency."

"I think we suspected that was the case. It's just that no one messes with a man with that much power," Christine added.

"By contrast I thought Atlee was very impressive. He didn't allow himself to get ruffled, he just made his point quietly and then moved on. It was a pity that Travis wasn't listening. My own theory is that Travis came with his own agenda, and getting Britain as the USA's forty-ninth state is well up that list. Ordinarily that idea wouldn't have got off the ground, but the radical plans of the incoming Labour government have given him the justification to interfere, to save us as it were, from the USSR."

At that point Drakeford stood up. "I'm out on my feet, I really must get a few hours' sleep. It's impossible to get any sleep on a transatlantic aeroplane, the engines are so noisy and there's always vibration. But first, I've just remembered my diary, I have to write this up while it's still fresh."

The mood of the British people did not subside as the days moved on. There was no denial from the White House; indeed, there was no comment of any kind forthcoming at all. The reaction next day in the British press was incandescent. Headlines like '*Who does Travis think he is?*' and '*America makes its intentions known*' were everywhere. The BBC radio carried interviews with both political experts and ordinary people in the street. The BBC always takes up a position of neutrality, but it can project an underlying view by carefully selecting the people invited for interview. All were equally angry. The USA ambassador, John G Winant, was asked to comment, but was unavailable. One of his assistants said, "I suspect President Travis has been misunderstood, I'm sure that's not what he meant, he was just suggesting something that the British people might find attractive."

CHAPTER 5

THE AMERICANS ARRIVE

The following week a team of Americans arrived in London for talks with cabinet ministers. Their journey had been unannounced, quite predictably, as their presence would have inflamed the situation still further. Officially their mission was to discuss financial and military aid, but Britain saw it as an opportunity to question how they might be delaying its repayments on the massive loans. Significantly the American team contained a Republican Senator who specialised in foreign policy, assisted by three financial experts.

The meeting participants were ushered into Downing Street via a rear entrance. Representing Britain were Ernest Bevin, the Foreign Secretary, Lord Drakeford and two other Labour MPs, Jack Lambert and Ted Campbell, together with a small team of civil servants. The American team consisted of Senator Harold B Crosby and his assistants, including Joe Thompson, Travis's chosen financial advisor. They were shown into the cabinet room and Ernest Bevin opened the meeting, welcoming his guests from across the Atlantic, some of whom he had met during his recent trip to the White House.

"Thank you for making this journey," he began. "I had assumed you had not come this far to meet up with us unless you had something in mind by way of an offer of financial aid or at least something to help us in the short term until we can get our economy moving again. Perhaps a delay before the loan payments commence?"

"Well, that's not quite what we had in mind," responded the Senator. "Our briefing from the President is more radical than you might have been expecting. He's anxious that you change course from your left-wing agenda. He's proposing 'subtle' economic sanctions be imposed on Britain by delaying the introduction of trading agreements. As a start we will put a hold on British imports into the USA, including cars and machine tools. This will be introduced with immediate effect. We then want you to suspend your programme for nationalisation, particularly the planned national health service."

There were gasps and ashen faces on the part of the British contingent. For what seemed a few minutes no one spoke, they just couldn't believe what they'd just heard. "You're effectively asking us to suspend normal government," responded Bevin.

"Yes, that's exactly what we're saying," replied the Senator. "The President wants to see an interim cabinet in place consisting of politicians from both countries, together with top military personnel to make sure decisions are implemented."

Geoffrey Anderson, a top civil servant in the Board of Trade, could not remain silent any longer. "This is effectively theft, whatever way you look at it. Britain leads the world in so many areas. Look at our aircraft industry, Frank Whittle invented the jet engine, we have the Gloster Meteor, the fastest jet fighter in the world, we have fifteen top aircraft companies such as Avro, Gloster, Hawker, Armstrong Whitworth……"

"Yes, yes, we know," interrupted the Senator.

"I could go on to name a similar list of car and motorcycle manufacturers, machine tool manufacturers, and…"

"Ok, ok, we get it," said the Senator. "May they go from strength to strength, it's your newly adopted system of government that's the problem. We want to be your friend, not your enemy."

"It's effectively a takeover bid," exclaimed Bevin. "It's as if you want us to be your forty-ninth state."

"Yes, that's our briefing from the President. That's precisely what he has in mind."

"That's exactly what Hitler did with Austria in 1938," responded Anderson. "Just because they spoke the same language, he assumed they should be one country."

"I would dispute that analogy," said the Senator. "Our President is not a fascist, and our presidents have to be elected every four years, that's a massive difference."

"And Hitler refused to hold a plebiscite in Austria," countered Anderson. "Would Travis deny that option to the British people? My guess is he would get less than ten per cent in favour if he held a plebiscite. Would he abide by the decision?"

The Senator chose not to answer that question, as frankly he didn't know the answer, but he might have guessed. The level of hostility in the room was very clear. Some of the minor players on both sides looked embarrassed.

"I suggest we leave it there," announced Bevin. We need to confer with other colleagues, perhaps we can meet again tomorrow?"

"Very well," replied the Senator. "We too will consult and reconvene tomorrow, same time, same place."

Everyone left the room without speaking. The USA delegation left the building by the same way they had entered. The British reassembled in a smaller conference room and immediately ordered suitable refreshments.

Geoffrey Anderson was the first to speak. "At least when Hitler marched into Austria they actually welcomed him, apart from the Jews, of course. It would be all-out war if Travis tried that here, there's no way he would convince us it was in our best interests."

"Maybe that's our best approach," replied Bevin. "It would never be an amicable arrangement, they would spend the next fifty years as an occupying force. That would be in complete contrast to Hawaii where the people are quite keen to be an American state, seeing as there are so many Americans already living there."

"I think they were as shocked as we were," said Anderson. "Americans like to think they're popular and our reaction gave the opposite impression!"

"Sadly, I don't think we've any strong negotiating tactics in our locker, apart from civil disobedience and we can't be seen to be suggesting that," said Bevin. "They have all the high cards. Let's wait and see what they come back with tomorrow. Just keep up a strong exterior, don't let them think we've given up."

Geoffrey Anderson responded, "What's the worst case scenario if we just don't pay our debts? We could try asking the USSR for a loan, that would upset the Americans!"

The meeting couldn't suppress a laugh, relieving the tension somewhat.

"Better keep that one in reserve," countered Bevin. "I suspect they're in a worse situation than we are. But it would be interesting to introduce the idea into our conversation, just to see the reaction."

Next day the same people reconvened in the Downing Street cabinet room, with everyone taking their places in the same seats as before. Senator Crosby opened the discussion. "Overnight we've made a few transatlantic phone calls. The White House is still very keen to proceed and feels in time the British will come round to the idea of being more closely allied with the USA. However, they realise that it would be a mistake to force it without everyone having the opportunity to see what it would mean for them. Nevertheless, they insist that trade sanctions will go ahead, but not as severe as we proposed yesterday. Instead, we will impose limits on your imports to the USA, but not a total ban. Meanwhile we insist you suspend the more radical aspects of your political agenda."

"You might suggest to the President that he comes here to see the strength of feeling for himself," responded Bevin. "I don't think he would have the kind of reception he's been used to, he would need to keep his head down!"

"He'll come when he's ready," replied the Senator. "I think we've come as far as we can for now. We'll let the civil servants work out the details. We'll get back to you tomorrow and hopefully we can issue a joint statement."

The meeting broke up, having lasted for only a matter of minutes.

Back in their private meeting room the British contingent sat down to contemplate what had just been said. Geoffrey Anderson was again first to comment. "If the British people were quite annoyed before they will be apoplectic when they get to hear about this. We're going to have goods earmarked for export stockpiled at the seaports. People will be laid off. It's the last thing we want."

"Hopefully they'll see the error of their ways. This will do no one any favours," replied Bevin. "Right now, we have to go out there and face the press. Yesterday's meeting was almost unnoticed, but they now realise something's going on. I'm afraid we have to tell them like it is. Tomorrow's front pages will be interesting, to say the least."

The delegation broke up, with the civil servants going back to their offices in Whitehall almost unnoticed, but as soon as Bevin and Morrison appeared, the reporters gathered round, firing questions.

Bevin tried to defuse the situation. "As you've realised by now, we've been having talks with an American team about the future. You could say, it was 'talks about talks', but nothing has been decided. There may be a formal announcement tomorrow."

"Will the Americans be deferring our loan payments?" asked a reporter. "Will they be actually reducing the payments?" asked another.

"No," responded Bevin, "I don't think that will happen," trying to prepare them for what was to come later.

"Is the President going to come to Britain to see things for himself?" asked another.

"We've certainly made the invitation, but again, nothing's been agreed."

With that Bevin and Morrison climbed into their ministerial cars and slowly drove away.

After working through the night, the USA contingent appeared at Downing Street with their statement. The two British ministers were there waiting, together with the other ministers who made up the cabinet. The American statement read:

> *The President of the United States of America wishes to emphasise his concern that the political agenda of the United Kingdom is a major cause for anxiety and an impediment to future trade relations. Until a compromise can be agreed the USA intend to impose trade sanctions, thus limiting exports from Britain to the USA, effective as of midnight tonight, GMT. The President is hopeful that this will be a temporary measure, with both sides working in close cooperation to achieve a mutually acceptable solution. In the longer term the President is anxious for Britain and the United States to become equal partners in a completely new political agreement, details of which have yet to be negotiated.*

Bevin's first thought was 'is that the best they can do, after almost twenty-four hours. It was pretty much identical to the verbal version that had been given to them yesterday morning'.

Copies were handed out to the press who had been invited indoors. The Americans departed from the scene by the rear entrance, leaving the British ministers to face the questioning. This time Morrison opened the question-

and-answer session after giving the reporters a minute to read the statement.

"You will see," he began, "that this is not a joint statement. Right now they have us over a barrel; all we can do is to refuse to cooperate, but that could hit our trade even worse. Obviously we will look for other markets, particularly within the British Empire, but that might take some time."

"What's this about us becoming equal partners? Does that mean becoming a US State?"

"Who knows?" replied Morrison. "I can't see that going down well with the British public. In my view it will never happen."

"What about the British Empire? If Travis becomes our head of state he will automatically rule over the Empire. He would then have a USA Commonwealth. That would be a massive feather in his cap."

Morrison countered very quickly: "Let's not get carried away, you're jumping to conclusions. He's not taken over yet, we're still negotiating."

There was a sombre mood with no more questions as reporters were anxious to return to their offices and typewriters in order to get their version into the papers. A BBC news reporter read the statement from the tranquillity of the local studio, unaware of the reaction he was triggering in homes and factories throughout the country. At the same time the American delegation was just returning to their hotel where they were met with a hostile reception from the public and the few reporters who had worked out where they were staying. Clearly their plan was to check out of their hotel and get to the airport as soon as possible.

The first editions of all the major newspapers carried similar headlines:

'Travis wants Britain for his US Empire'
'Travis intends to succeed where Hitler failed'
'Britons must fight for their independence'
'British politicians roll over when faced with Yankee threats'

The more sober headlines read:

'Britain and USA in tense negotiations on trade deals'
'USA restricts British exports'

The mood on the streets was downcast. People wanted to demonstrate in order to show their feelings, but there was no focal point where they could assemble. The American Embassy was under 24-hour guard, surrounded by dozens of armed US soldiers, while London policemen looked on from a safe distance. This was a new low-point in morale, probably the worst since 1940.

Next morning the full cabinet met at Downing Street, with Herbert Morrison chairing the meeting. He began by confirming what by then most people already knew. "The American delegation whom we've just met over the previous two days, when pressed, admitted they had been sent here by President Travis to spell out their intentions. They want us to drop our political agenda, particularly that relating to nationalisation, something which we'd anticipated. However, they were offering no help with our loan payments, contrary to our expectations, and as from midnight they've introduced trade sanctions. But the sting in the tail was the President's ambition for Britain to become another US state. Just what that would mean for the British Empire is anyone's guess at the moment. We pressed them as to whether there would be a plebiscite on this and we received no answer. Probably because we explained that they wouldn't get many votes. To be honest I suspect the people we were dealing with were well aware of their unpopularity. I'm sure the situation looks quite different when viewed from the other side of the Atlantic."

There was a stunned silence for several seconds, then he added: "This is basically what all the papers are saying. There's no point in denials."

Then the questions kept coming, one after another.

"How can we react as a government, is there anything we can do?"

"We clearly have a President who shoots from the hip, but how much support is he likely to get from within his own party?"

"And what about the actual inhabitants of the British Empire, how would they react?"

"We just don't know. Maybe the USA wouldn't want the Empire, they might discard it as a gesture towards independence."

Sir Stafford Cripps then added a new factor into the conversation: "Britain has substantial oil interests in the Middle East, in Iraq, Kuwait and Bahrain. I'm sure he might like to get his hands on those." There was a brief silence, then he continued, "And what about goods we import from the USA, mainly foodstuffs? We could ban them, would that make a difference?" Can we use our influence to affect public opinion in America? British goods are popular in the USA right now, especially our cars, bicycles and porcelain; a trade embargo might not go down too well with the American public."

"Yes, that is an option. I agree, two can play at that game," countered Morrison. "Unfortunately, it would hurt us more than it would hurt them, especially in the short term."

Bevin replied: "I agree that's certainly an option. Of greater concern is how are our own people going to react? They'll probably attack anything they see as American. We could have riots. As a government we can't be seen to be orchestrating public protest, especially violence, against what is at least for now a friendly country."

Hugh Dalton, Chancellor of the Exchequer, responded: "We could resign and call a general election. If the Tories win they'll probably abandon our plans for nationalisation. Would that satisfy Travis? If we win, would Travis agree to abide by the decision of the people?"

"Let's keep that option open for now. By far the biggest issue is the threat to our sovereignty and there's no predicting how he would deal with that," responded Bevin.

He continued, "I think we need to issue a statement pleading for calm, not to overreact and make the situation any worse. We could say that we're looking for clarification, although no further meetings are scheduled. In fact, their delegation couldn't leave quickly enough, they could see what was coming."

With that the cabinet meeting closed, while Morrison and Bevin went off with their aides to draft yet another statement, even though they had nothing new to say.

CHAPTER 6

RESISTANCE

Lord Drakeford had read the account of Travis's victory speech in *The Times*. Now, following Travis's press conference announcing Atlee's illness, this confirmed his worst fears, reinforced by the latest events reported in the press with the government appearing to have no option but to accept the latest demands being imposed on them.

"So now everything we feared is now a reality," he said to his wife. "Look at the reaction on the streets. So where do we go from here?"

Her reply was short and to the point. "We can't stand by and let him walk all over us, we need to organise protests against selected targets. I think we need to get together with a few of our friends, we can't make it easy for him. Let's get on the phone."

Drakeford phoned some of his friends during the day, all sharing his concern. They had all hoped that FDR could still win his fourth term and were distraught at the course of events since the presidential election.

His theme to his friends followed predictable lines. "We need to get organised. I'm not suggesting we get involved in the street protests, but we need to attack this at a higher level. I think we need to meet somewhere, fairly central, and work out how we can talk to the right people and make the Americans think again. I'll be in touch again when we've worked something out."

Time was moving on; it was now January 1946. Lord Drakeford looked on with dismay as normal life disintegrated. He spoke to his friends, fellow travellers of all political persuasions who between them had several contacts in influential positions. "We can't let this situation escalate," he declared, "we have to do something to make the Americans see sense. Travis wants to see us as part of his future empire and we can't allow this to happen."

A few hours later his phone rang. "Good afternoon, this is Colonel Graham Downton speaking. We haven't met, but I understand you are keen to assemble an action group to bring an end to this American takeover. Would you be prepared to attend a meeting with some like-minded people at my home near Goring in Oxfordshire, it's just northwest of Reading? I have quite a large house and can get about twenty people around my table in the basement."

"Absolutely, that sounds ideal," replied Drakeford, "anywhere, any time, I'm ready for it. Are you ok if I bring a few friends who might be useful?"

"No problem, please do. Is tomorrow ok for you?" said Colonel Downton.

"Yes of course, this has to be a high priority, tomorrow it is."

They quickly exchanged details and times and Drakeford suddenly felt a new wave of optimism come over him as he grabbed his road atlas to find out exactly where he had to go.

Lord Drakeford and friends arrived at the rural location in Oxfordshire and they were introduced to a group of mainly former military personnel who had come together to discuss the situation. Among them were former officers, some politicians and experts in various fields including transport. Colonel Downton opened proceedings with some formal introductions. He introduced Lord Drakeford as a Labour Peer and rising star in the Atlee cabinet, with legal expertise in finance and international law. He introduced Bill Johnson, who had recently left the Intelligence Service, a smartly dressed man around thirty, who had volunteered for the service immediately after graduating from Cambridge where he had studied languages. Clearly, Colonel Downton had drawn in an 'inner circle' of people he had known and in whom he had complete confidence, including Major Charles Brown, a commando who had been involved in the D-Day landings, together with a female colleague, Charlotte Joubert, also from the Intelligence Service. He added, much to everyone's amusement, "Charlotte has been parachuted into France a few times, so is not afraid of a few Americans."

Colonel Downton briefly set the scene. He said, "I feel that escalation of the civil unrest could lead to disastrous consequences and a worst case scenario, that is long-term American occupation and Britain being absorbed into the USA regime, perhaps becoming another state."

No one disagreed as to the severity of the situation, it was just a question of 'how'.

"First I will ask Lord Drakeford to explain the political landscape and how things could develop if we do nothing.

As you probably know, Lord Drakeford was recently part of the Prime Minister's delegation that met Travis in the White House. Then I will ask Bill Johnson to outline how we might exploit the current unrest to bring things to an acceptable conclusion; I believe Major Brown also has some ideas to achieve this."

Lord Drakeford began. "I'm sure most of you are already aware of the background, but in case anyone is a little unsure let me summarise what has gone on and where we are today. I think first you should be aware of our financial debt to the USA, a situation that will leave us near bankruptcy for many years to come. You've all heard of the Lend-Lease Agreement. This was a way for the USA to support other countries in the war, without getting involved themselves. They provided ships and armaments to Britain, the USSR, China and others. To a lesser extent Canada also assisted in this arrangement. Obviously, it all changed with Pearl Harbor and the war with Japan, together with America's decision to get involved in the fight against Germany when the U-boats torpedoed unarmed American ships crossing the Atlantic carrying supplies to Britain. The Lend-Lease Agreement was originally for $31bn. It was not intended to be repaid, but the equipment to be returned after the war. After the war, Britain was allowed to keep what it still had for 10% of the original amount. However, the US terminated the Lend-Lease Agreement on 21st July 1945 and this was replaced by an Anglo-American Loan negotiated by the famous economist John Maynard Keynes for $3.75bn at 2% interest, to be paid annually, comprising payments every year until the year 2000. This was intended to be a better deal and was ratified on 15th July 1945. The House of Lords protested strongly, but it went through as we had no choice."

"I didn't know Keynes was a Socialist!" said one of the team.

"No, he wasn't, he was actually a Liberal" replied Drakeford. "As you know, Keynes died recently so we can't ask him what really went on and what threats were made at the time."

He concluded: "This debt will be crippling and something we should shout about at every opportunity. If the public really understood the full implications of that debt they would do more than protest. We might exploit the current unrest to renegotiate the deal."

"How do we do that, we're not in a strong bargaining position?" said Squadron Leader Kevin 'Bomber' Bowman, a successful Lancaster bomber pilot.

"On the contrary," said Drakeford. "A less severe arrangement might help to appease the British public and convince them that the Americans are not all bad. What's more, the longer this goes on, the more it's costing them, and if they end up making us into a US state they would lose out financially as they would be forced to absorb our debts."

It was then Johnson's turn. "This state of civil unrest could continue for months or even years. We could try and influence the American public by conducting a campaign in the USA, pointing out the unnecessary cost, both financially and militarily, and that many thousands of their GIs will be involved in the occupation when they had expected to be returning home.

"Ideally we need to find a way to open a dialogue with the Americans, whether it be here or in the United States. We have several contacts who might bring that about, although Travis himself is going to be a problem; he just refuses to listen. If that fails, we need to fall back on our military experience to disrupt their plans, while remaining aloof from the public protests that are gathering momentum."

Major Charles Brown then added: "If we do need to fall back on our military experience I have some ideas as to how we might go about this. I have some colleagues who have seen recent action and I'm putting a plan together. I'd sooner not say any more for the moment, let's see how things develop. If the subtle approach doesn't work, then I hope to have a plan B at the ready."

Drakeford then added, "I'm sure we'll be meeting again, possibly several times as this proceeds. Should we give our group a name, it will make us sound more credible?"

"I agree," said Downton, "we can admit to our existence as a pressure group, working to relieve the tension. We can issue press releases to give us credibility."

"How about the British Freedom Fighters?" suggested Major Brown.

"I think that sounds a little war-like, how about British Freedom Group, the BFG for short?" countered Drakeford.

"Brilliant, short and to the point. Decision!" replied Downton enthusiastically. He continued: "I take it everyone's happy for Lord Drakeford to be our group spokesman? With his involvement so far, his name is already known to the public, the rest of us can keep a low profile. Let's issue a press release. We can make it clear that at the moment we're looking for an alternative to the on-street protests, to persuade the Americans to listen to us, on the basis that talking is better than fighting. They're certainly not listening to our politicians, but we can always hope."

Drakeford and Johnson drafted a press release and delivered it to the national press later that day.

'In response to recent events a small group of activists, under the leadership of Lord Rufus Drakeford, have formed the British Freedom Group. This is a cross-party ad hoc committee whose intention is to hold meaningful talks with the President of the United States, or his representatives, to explain that the United Kingdom has a democratically elected government and objects strongly to any external interference in this process. We do not intend to become involved in the on-street protests, but have every sympathy with their motives.'

Next morning the papers carried headlines *'New Pressure Group to confront Americans'*, *'British Freedom Group to organise protests'* and *'Labour Peer wants meeting with Yanks'*. Since Drakeford already had a role in public life, he was happy to be identified with the group. Nevertheless, he hadn't prepared himself for what was to follow. Next day his phone never stopped ringing, with offers of help, financial donations and even petrol coupons. He quickly set up a bank account to process the cheques and the cash stuffed in envelopes. Most of all there were offers of vehicles, premises and specialist persons wanting to get involved.

Later that day he received what turned out to be a significant phone call. "This is Joe Cole of the Daily Mirror. We like the way you've presented the facts in your press release. Would you be prepared to speak at a public meeting?"

"Of course, it can only help," Drakeford replied. "Hopefully not too far away, ideally north London. Will you arrange it?"

"No problem. We'll find a reasonably sized hall, then publicise it in tomorrow morning's edition. I'll get back to you as soon as we've found somewhere."

Less than one hour later Joe Cole phoned back. "Hi, it's Joe here again. We've found a suitable hall in Hendon, just off the Edgware Road. I've put a letter in the post with a map and details of the venue, it should get to you tomorrow. I'll book it for the day after tomorrow. Does 7pm suit you? We can send a car to pick you up."

"That would be great, save my petrol coupons!" replied Drakeford.

"We'll pick you up at 6pm if that's ok," said Joe.

"I'm looking forward to it."

The British people were still widely supportive of Atlee and sensed this outside interference by the USA. The Americans claimed that a liaison with the USSR was an ever-present possibility and a change of policy was necessary, together with a show of US support as a visible deterrent. The right-wing British press was anti-Labour and broadly supported the American intervention, while organisations like the BBC as always tried to remain neutral. The left-leaning press was quite prominent in their criticism of America, that is The Daily Herald and The Daily Mirror, who resented the American interference, and their circulation increased. As newspapers were quite cheap (typically one or two pence per paper) almost every home had at least one daily newspaper delivered. Even local evening newspapers were quite common. Newspapers and the radio were the only ways most people were aware of national and international affairs, apart from 'newsreels' at the cinema, although these were often a week or more behind the times, but nevertheless a good way to spread propaganda.

Next day a car arrived to collect Drakeford just before 6pm. He arrived at the hall at about 6.45 and people were already starting to gather. He thanked the driver and as he stepped out of the car a short, smartly dressed man came straight up to him. "Hello Lord Drakeford, I'm Joe Cole. Thank you for coming, it looks as if we'll have a decent crowd tonight."

They went into the hall, where seating for about 500 people had been set out. "I'd envisaged a much smaller venue," commented Drakeford.

"My fear is that it won't be big enough!" countered Cole. "Let's go backstage so you can get prepared. Are you ok with this? Do you need anything?"

"No, I just hope we have a public address system, I don't fancy having to shout to 500 people!"

"It's all been taken care of," replied Cole.

They chatted for a few minutes and then made their way from behind the stage to be confronted with a packed audience. Spontaneous applause broke out, much to Drakeford's surprise.

As the applause subsided, Joe Cole opened proceedings. "Good evening, everyone, thank you for coming. I'm Joe

Cole of the Daily Mirror. Our paper is very much behind the aims of the British Freedom Group and we think it's time they received maximum publicity. May I introduce Lord Rufus Drakeford KC who is the spokesman for the group? He can explain better than I exactly why they came together and what their plans are for the future. Over to you, Lord Drakeford."

Drakeford stood up and took hold of the microphone. With his legal background, public speaking came easily to him; in fact, he rather enjoyed it.

"Good evening. Let me first explain what our group is about and why we formed. Like many people throughout the UK, we became quite concerned when David Travis was elected as President of the United States as we knew he had different ideas to those of the democratically elected Labour government. A number of us got together to discuss how best to counter the adverse publicity which we were receiving from certain sections of the USA, principally the Republican Party. Our group is made up of a range of people of different political persuasions, but we are all agreed on wanting to resist this interference in our affairs.

"We're aware that protests here are escalating and we have every sympathy with the reasons behind the need to show our level of anger. Our fear is that these will become more intense and serious violence could result. It's unfortunate that the Americans have so many military personnel on our soil, following the war, and that makes them an obvious target for our frustration. They remain here because they want to use the UK and much of Europe to provide American bases. They are paranoid about the USSR spreading its wings, perhaps with some justification.

"The problem is we could end up with a war-situation in our own country. The aim of the BFG is to find a political solution and we can only achieve that by sitting down with the Americans and working something out. So far, they haven't listened to our politicians and have enforced subtle measures to prevent our government carrying out its plans as outlined in their manifesto. We believe the Americans, and Travis in particular, have misjudged the mood of the British people who have said that we might not like this particular government, but at least it's _our_ government.

"To summarise, I would say that the aim of the BFG is to persuade the Americans to meet with us to discuss the way forward. Ideally we would like to meet the President face-to-face to present our views, perhaps by inviting him to see things for himself. At this point I'll stop for now and would be happy to answer any questions."

Joe Cole took over to select questioners, of which there were dozens with waving hands. He clearly knew many of the people near the front, fellow journalists and political commentators.

"How do you propose to make Travis listen to you? He will avoid you for as long as possible, until you run out of steam or just get trampled into submission."

"Frankly, we haven't worked that one out yet. One solution is to feed some adverse publicity to our friends in the States. There's the Democratic Party, some newspapers and many fellow travellers who are desperate to expose

Travis's limitations. He loves being the centre of attention, but only as long as it shows him in a good light."

"What have you got to offer even if you do manage a face-to-face? He basically holds all the cards in his hand."

"We would argue that the USA would be better off with an independent UK. We would be more productive and better able to repay those debts that have accumulated through the war. It's been suggested that Travis wants us to become a forty-ninth state. Nobody this side of the Atlantic wants that. What's more, there are implications here for the British Empire. As you know, the Atlee government has plans for independence for these countries, but Travis may have other ideas. I suspect he quite likes the idea of an empire; after all, he is first and foremost a businessman."

"Does the BFG intend to get involved in the street protests, particularly if the political approach doesn't seem to be working? Does the group have the necessary resources to resist being swept aside by the police or military personnel?"

"To a limited extent. We have several former military personnel who are quite smart and could help us in a crisis, but we hope it doesn't come to that." Drakeford stopped short at this point because he knew that Major Brown had a formidable team ready to do whatever may be necessary, but he was not prepared to admit this publically.

"Who else do you have in your group? We only know of you officially, since you're the spokesman."

"We have a range of people, many former military personnel, politicians, lawyers; we have it covered. I'm not prepared to divulge their names or where they're from as we don't want them to be subjected to pressure or intimidation. I volunteered as spokesman because I was already in the public arena as a junior minister in the House of Lords."

"What's your next move, apart from more meetings like this one?"

"We intend to get as much coverage as possible. Hopefully we'll have the opportunity to put our case in newspapers, meetings and perhaps even the radio. We'd like to encourage more people to make banners, flags, badges, etc., so the message is loud and clear. We want there to be no doubt that this is a majority view, not just those of a few extremists. But more than anything, we want to talk to the Americans, those who have been sent over to put a spanner into our political system. As we speak, we have people trying to arrange such meetings."

Joe Cole brought the meeting to a close. He said to Drakeford, "I need to move, I have to get this into tomorrow's Mirror." There was polite applause and people began to file out at the back of the hall. "I'll be in touch, any help we can give, just ask."

"Thank you," replied Drakeford. "How do you feel if other papers want to be involved? I appreciate your paper has set this up tonight, but I feel inclined to accept help wherever it comes from."

"That's ok," said Cole. "But if anything transpires that you can share with us, then perhaps tell us first." At this point he reached into his top pocket and gave Drakeford a business card. "My phone number's on there, just let me know if you have an exclusive!"

They shook hands outside and Drakeford was grateful to see the car that had brought him was waiting there. Off he went, feeling it was a useful night's work, and was duly delivered to his door.

Next morning all the national daily newspapers carried the story of the public meeting, many with Drakeford's photograph as he arrived at the hall. Not all papers were complimentary, although Drakeford had successfully defused the political situation with his description of the cross-party makeup of the group and his comment that it's _our_ government, even if not everyone's choice.

There was some division among ordinary people, particularly from those with wealth, power and influence who had always resented Labour's victory. The Tories warned of Labour's ambitions to nationalise much of British manufacturing industry, describing it as a 'Soviet-styled democracy'. However, over the next few days public resentment at American interference increased and there were several more demonstrations in London, many turning nasty. As the situation escalated, the police couldn't handle this and the army was called in. Since the military top brass were still unhappy with Churchill's removal from office, however democratic, they needed little invitation to support the Americans' view of Atlee and his political intentions, although rank and file soldiers were less enthusiastic.

Until this point the demonstrations were centred around London, or at American airbases. Although there were no obvious targets further north, people began to gather wherever they thought they could attract publicity, choosing newspaper offices, town halls and even some British military bases. To some extent American-owned businesses were suggested, such as Ford, or Vauxhall, which was owned by General Motors, although they were so long established in England and almost totally staffed by British employees that most people did not associate them with America and decided they would alienate the workforce by impeding their progress.

Drakeford felt that although demonstrations and public speaking had their place, it was now time for action, beginning with an attempt to set up a meeting with the President, or in fact anyone who was prepared to listen. His first move was to phone the American Embassy. The operator answered very promptly: "US Embassy, how can I help please?"

"My name's Lord Drakeford, I would like to speak to the Ambassador please?"

"I'm afraid the Ambassador is not available, I'll put you through to one of his assistants."

Drakeford suspected he was going to speak to someone several rungs below the Ambassador. There were a couple of clicks on the line and a ringing tone, a voice, clearly an American, came on the line. "Good morning, my name is Charles B Hampton, I'm a member of the Ambassador's staff."

Drakeford began, "Good morning, my name is Lord Rufus Drakeford, I was a junior minister in Mr Atlee's government. I'm now the spokesperson for a newly formed organisation called the British Freedom Group. You may have heard about us, certainly if not before, but you may have seen articles in this morning's newspapers."

"Yes, I did see something, I believe. Just what do you want from us?"

"You will be aware that the recent interference of the Americans in our democratically elected government has led to protests and it is our fear that these will escalate still further. We have every sympathy with the reasons behind the protests, but we feel it is time for some serious conversation. Our group has a steering committee made up of people with different political persuasions; ideally, we would like to meet the President face-to-face to present our views. If not the President himself, then someone with direct access to the President."

"I'll pass on your request to the Ambassador."

"I'll give you my phone number, perhaps you'll get back to me," replied Drakeford. At least he had been received with some courtesy. He put the phone down and turned to his wife. "I guess that's a start, let's see how quickly they respond."

"Don't hold your breath," she answered. "I suspect we'll need to phone a few times before they take us seriously."

"Maybe a six feet high pile of manure on the Embassy doorstep might help," he replied. "I know farmers who would happily arrange it."

"I bet you wouldn't get within a hundred yards," was the speedy response.

CHAPTER 7

PROTESTS

U S military bases became the main targets for protesters, leading to violent behaviour in some cases. This gave the US reason to take a more overt role in quelling the protesters, particularly as rank-and-file British soldiers were reluctant to take action against their own people. The civil unrest became so severe that cabinet government was suspended, with military personnel taking 'temporary' charge. To reinforce this decision and to calm the public outrage, King George VI was forced to sign an order dissolving parliament, transferring power to the military.

Meanwhile, Atlee returned to the UK, under escort 'for medical reasons', to convalesce with his wife at a 'remote country location' attached to an American Air Force base, with minimum communication with the outside world. The few people that caught sight of him on his arrival said that he genuinely looked very ill, although his American hosts explained that it had been a rough sea crossing at that time of the year, and he was too ill to risk air travel. After a few weeks the Americans gave in to demands that Atlee be allowed to be interviewed by the British press. A meeting was arranged and Richard

Dimbleby, previously a BBC war correspondent, was allowed to visit Atlee's temporary residence along with a BBC sound radio crew. They set up their equipment and Mrs Atlee sat at the other side of the room, together with a couple of US air force officers. Dimbleby began by enquiring as to Mr Atlee's health and what he had experienced after his arrival in the USA.

"I felt fine when we arrived in Washington and we were well received at the White House. We had discussions over a couple of days, although it was clear the Americans were very concerned as to the direction our policies were taking. On the third day I was taken ill and ended up in hospital and my memory from that point on is very vague. I suspect I was delirious for much of the time. I lost all track of where I was and how long I'd been there.

"Eventually, I realised that none of the staff that I had originally travelled with were still there, and I was told that arrangements were being made for me to return to England as soon as I was well enough to travel. It was explained that because I had been taken ill while a guest of the American President, they felt a responsibility for my welfare until I had recovered. I would be taken home by sea as an air journey would be too risky. Then I would be taken to an American medical facility where my wife would be able to stay with me while I recovered. As far as I'm aware, we are still in that American facility."

Dimbleby came straight to the point, "There are lots of rumours that your illness was brought on deliberately by the Americans, possibly by poison, so that your absence destabilised the British government. Did you suspect that might be the case?"

The American officers visibly stiffened at this question. Atlee was very guarded with his answer. He may have been close to death at the time, but now, even though he was feeling physically weak, he was mentally sharp. Before becoming an MP, he had been a barrister and capable of choosing his words carefully, aware that he was going 'live' on national radio.

"I didn't think so at the time, I suppose I was too ill. Obviously, I've had that theory put to me since returning and frankly I just don't know. Whatever was the cause, it's taking a long time for me to recover."

"Have you asked for an English doctor to provide a second opinion?" asked Dimbleby.

"Yes, of course, but so far that has not been forthcoming on the basis that the Americans still feel responsible for my recovery. However, if this interview achieves nothing else, it might bring this about, if they've nothing to hide." Anxious to make the most of his opportunity he added, "I'm very disturbed to see that since I went across to the USA, the British public have drawn their own conclusions, leading to civil unrest and a military presence that I never thought I would see on our streets. Surely the Americans must respect our wish to remain an independent country?"

The Atlee interview further aroused public interest, now more convinced that something underhand had taken place. Richard Dimbleby's reputation as a broadcaster went through the roof, the listening public were convinced all was not right, and the interview had confirmed their suspicions. Public opinion remained firm, with ordinary people so incensed even more joined organised protests. Having seen off the threat of an occupation by Hitler's troops, they were horrified to see armed US personnel on the streets of the UK.

Drakeford received several invitations to speak, ranging from village halls to small theatres. The theme was usually the same, with the questions becoming more and more predictable. However, the increased severity of the demonstrations and the reaction to the Dimbleby interview, added an edge to the questioning. As happens when disagreements drag on, the participants begin to care less about why they are protesting and develop a loathing for the opposition, including anyone who doesn't actually share their views. Drakeford could detect an edge to the questioning, expecting him to announce an escalation in the BFG's activities. He wasn't prepared to commit himself publically, but certainly felt it was time to step up the scale of the BFG's involvement, particularly as he wasn't making much progress with the Embassy.

Next day Joe Cole was on the phone again. "Good morning," he began. "I've been in touch with a few friends who are planning a march and demonstration in London, maybe around Easter weekend. They plan to assemble in Trafalgar Square then march to the American Embassy in Grosvenor Square. They then aim to continue to Hyde Park where the TUC are erecting a platform and have invited a number of speakers from all walks of life. Your name came up, are you up for it?"

"Yes," replied Drakeford, somewhat hesitatingly, as addressing a large outdoor meeting was not something he had contemplated. "Who else will be speaking?"

"They're trying to cover the whole range. There will be politicians of all parties, trade union officials, clergymen and well-known writers and broadcasters. I'll get someone to give you a bell to sort the arrangements."

An hour or so later the phone rang. "Good morning, I'm Mary Martin of the TUC, I work for the General Secretary. I gather you've agreed to speak at our demonstration at the weekend?"

"Yes, I'll help if I can," replied Drakeford.

Mary continued, "We're calling it the British Freedom Rally and it will be held on Easter Monday. We would have preferred Sunday, but the police objected, to say nothing of The Lord's Day Observance Society. I think Joe Cole explained that we aim to assemble at Trafalgar Square and finish at Hyde Park, hoping to arrive about three o'clock. Can you get yourself to Hyde Park for about two o'clock? I'm sorry we can't arrange transport, it's all happened rather quickly."

"That's no problem, I'm quite familiar with the area."

Easter Monday came and fortunately it was a warm sunny day as Lord Drakeford and his wife drove into London. He was able to park his car at the back of the legal firm where he worked in South Kensington, and they strolled along to Hyde Park. They were surprised by the numbers already assembled and they made their way to the stage where they were greeted by the organisers and some of the speakers already assembled. It was about one-thirty as they took their seats behind the stage, or platform to be more accurate. It was canvas topped and had a powerful loudspeaker system rigged up, working off a car battery.

"Good job it's not raining," said Drakeford to his wife, pointing to the wiring of the speaker system. They settled back on primitive chairs as best they could as Christine produced their packed lunch and vacuum flask. One by one, the various speakers arrived, some they recognised instantly, while others were less familiar.

The assembly at Trafalgar Square amazed everyone, numbering many thousands, and was high spirited but well behaved. There were only a few shoppers around, being a bank holiday, although there were many sightseers who had travelled to London expecting the roads and walkways to be quieter than a regular Monday. They looked on, some expressing encouragement, some very confused, others somewhat irritated at having their afternoon disrupted. A tall man with a hand-held loud speaker marshalled everyone as they gathered at the foot of Nelson's Column and they set off towards Grosvenor Square behind a police escort. There was a brass band marching at the head, adding to the cheerful atmosphere of the occasion. The demonstrators had several British flags and banners representing trade unions, local military associations and a variety of diverse interest groups. However, as they arrived in Grosvenor Square they were disappointed as barricades had been erected to keep the marchers well away from the Embassy itself, so they merely walked in one side and out the other, although they made plenty of noise just in case the ambassador was in residence.

The column was about ten people wide and by now about half a mile in length, growing all the time as people joined along the way. Almost on time the phalanx arrived at Hyde Park where they were met by thousands who had already arrived and a way was cleared for them to approach the front near the platform. By now the crowds stretched right up to the park boundaries. Estimates were something exceeding twenty thousand, although there were other observers who tried to play down the occasion and put it at half that number.

The occasion was opened by Sir Walter Citrine, recently retired TUC General Secretary, a post he had held since1926. He had a considerable reputation in the trade union movement and had been President of the International Federation of Trade Unions since 1929 and a director of the Daily Herald newspaper. He had received his knighthood in 1925 and was much respected for his book, published in 1939, 'The ABC of Chairmanship', which had become the bible for people running meetings.

He began, "Welcome to the British Freedom Rally, it's amazing to see so many people here today. I'm sure this will have a big impact on the powers that be, with so many people prepared to travel from all over Britain to show their concern over how their country is being run. We have a number of speakers here this afternoon and while all will have a common theme it will also demonstrate the breadth of feeling and patriotism they all share for our country. I would like to introduce our first speaker, Mr Ernest Bevin, a member of Clement Atlee's cabinet until everything was put on hold by way of interference by our friends across the water."

There were loud cheers for Mr Bevin as he came to the microphone. "Thank you, I appreciate your support. After having attended the meeting with Mr Travis at the White House and forced to return home without Mr Atlee, I was concerned that I might be deemed partly to blame for what happened. Fortunately, that has not been the case, I think everyone on this side of the Atlantic is aware that Mr Travis has his own agenda. Where that will lead us, who knows? But I know that the British people will not surrender, they were determined not to give in to Hitler and they definitely will not give in to the American President."

Bevin could see that he had support from the audience, so decided to fuel their resistance to American domination a little further. "People have short memories. At the beginning of the war, at Churchill's behest, we gave the USA all our technical know-how to aid the war effort. That included radar, a British invention, which was one hundred times more powerful than anything they had, and Frank Whittle's jet engine which no on else had come near to at the time, including the Americans. And this is how they repay us."

Other speakers followed, including Herbert Morrison, another of Atlee's front bench and temporarily acting as a stand-in Prime Minister before the Americans put the military in charge. There were also contributions from Liberal and even Conservative MPs, who were equally united behind the common theme, although they admitted they did have Tory colleagues who were less sure about the confrontation and thought a peaceful solution was available. There was a passionate plea from a Church of England vicar, resplendent in his 'working uniform', encouraging people to demonstrate peacefully and avoid violence against the Americans.

Probably the most radical contribution came from Fred Kinsella, a Yorkshire miner, who was well known for his fiery speeches. "I think people need to ask, what's in it for Mr Travis and his cronies? By ruling Britain it keeps their business interests intact. That's why they stepped in to support us in two world wars. We have a motto in Yorkshire which goes '*If ivver tha dos owt for nowt allus do it for thissen*'. For the benefit of our southern colleagues, I'll translate: 'If ever you do something for nothing always do it for yourself'. The Americans weren't here to help us, they were protecting their own interests. If Hitler had conquered Britain then Britain and the whole of Europe would be under German domination and the USA would have lost all their business interests. What's more, such was Hitler's ambition he would have set up shop in Greenland and moved his battle onto American soil. So what we've seen here in recent months is just another phase in America's commercial ambitions. All this talk about Russian influence is just a good excuse for getting their boots on our patch."

There we cheers and applause from the audience, not to say a few gasps as well. Sir Walter thanked him and said, "Well, I did say that our speakers today represented the full range of opinion. May I introduce our final speaker, Lord Rufus Drakeford, who is the spokesman for the British Freedom Group, or the BFG as we've come to know it."

Lord Drakeford climbed up onto the platform and walked to the microphone. "Thank you, Sir Walter; as the spokesman for our campaign, the British Freedom Group, it's good to be speaking at the British Freedom Rally. I doubt if I can follow the previous speaker with anything like the impression he has created. However, I will do my best."

He effectively repeated the now well rehearsed speech that he had delivered several times at public meetings, although nothing near this scale. However, as there was no option for questions from the audience, just the odd heckler, he ended by adding a few points that would normally have come from the floor.

"We're not advocating violence, we just want to have a proper conversation with the Americans, something they have clearly avoided so far. But, if necessary, we have a few tricks up our sleeve. We want to get all the publicity possible to aid our campaign. We have many friends across the Atlantic who can spread adverse publicity. Mr Travis likes the limelight and likes to be popular. He's good at saying what people want to hear, so criticism will be uncomfortable and will even cost him votes. We're prepared to meet him anywhere, anytime, that is our challenge. So far all attempts have been met with a flat refusal, so we may have to step up our campaign to another level. Believe me, we have some very capable people, but I'm not at liberty to say more at this stage."

He received polite applause and a few cheers, no more than he had expected. Sir Walter Citrine took to the stage to close the meeting. "Thank you all for coming, I think we've made an impact; if only half of what's been said gets reported in tomorrow's newspapers our day will have been worthwhile. Have a safe journey home."

CHAPTER 8

GETTING SERIOUS

U ntil this point in time the US Military wasn't taking the protests very seriously, more akin to a swarm of irritating flies that would eventually die off or move on to somewhere else. However, as the UK and USA top brass met, as they did on a regular basis, the British warned that this was not going to end very soon and tougher measures were required. Protesters could be dissipated, either by water hoses or foul-smelling gas, anything to discourage them from gathering. As a priority they announced a 9pm curfew on the streets of the UK. They made it clear by way of press releases that they intended to take a hard line with protesters and severe penalties would be imposed by the courts.

Many civilians, now demobbed from WWII military service, knew a thing or two about street fighting and how to handle weapons and explosives. Explosive devices were planted in key locations by British protesters, soon to be termed 'terrorists'. Casualties occurred on both sides, including Americans. Chaos ensued as ordinary people were incensed to see army personnel on their own streets and needed little invitation to assist with diversionary tactics. The situation caused some division within families as many young English women had formed relationships with American GIs, and many marriages had resulted. The soldiers had to carry out their duties as directed, trying to keep law and order while attempting to not provoke the situation further as the local population showed their resentment.

Despite his best efforts Drakeford could find no American prepared to speak to him. The best he could get was: "You'll have to speak to Washington, only the President can change things." There was no doubt the situation was escalating and Drakeford decided it was time for the BFG to reconvene, so he called Colonel Downton to arrange another meeting.

"Can we come to your place again, I think we need to step up the action?"

"Absolutely, I was thinking the very same."

Next day the BFG reconvened at the Colonel's house and immediately got down to business.

Squadron Leader 'Bomber' Bowman opened the discussion: "Clearly our peaceful approach hasn't worked, we're just getting the brush-off. We could try something more drastic, like bomb threats or worse."

Colonel Downton was quick to respond. "I understand your level of anger, but fear this may have the opposite effect and destroy any sympathy the Americans may have for us. Ideally, we should separate ourselves from the mass protests, we're looking for a diplomatic solution, and we don't want to be accused of orchestrating riots and street fighting."

Drakeford offered another solution. "We could go to Washington and get to meet Travis there. If we get sufficient publicity in the American press he might not be able to resist a photo opportunity. The press would wind things up, like 'the limeys coming to confront the President'."

Johnson responded: "We have heard rumours, spread in the American press, that Travis may visit Britain to 'crack the whip'. Perhaps we should try and confront him to let him see the futility of destroying our friendship, just because they don't agree with our politics?"

"So how do we confront the President? We don't know when he's coming and where he'll be staying," stated Drakeford.

It was now the turn of Major Charles Brown, recently demobbed, who had been a paratrooper in the D-day invasion. He was well equipped for such an operation: confident, well built, of average height and in his early forties. He was obviously very athletic and looked as if he could easily compete with men half his age.

He began, "We have inside information, I'm not going to say exactly where, let's just say that some of the amorous relationships with our American friends have triggered divided loyalties. I have a team on standby who could bring about a surprise confrontation in whatever form that might take. I have around thirty men of all ranks, including paratroopers, infantrymen and despatch riders, they're just itching for action. We're almost certain that Travis will come, it's just a question of exactly when and where."

"That sounds like a plan," exclaimed Downton. "What do you need in terms of resources? We have a lot of contacts prepared to offer money, equipment and a secret

HQ. And don't forget we have petrol rationing, that could restrict some longer journeys."

"We've thought of that. I have a written list prepared, I'll meet with you afterwards so we can put something into action," replied Brown. "Also, I believe we should keep our operation absolutely secret. The police will be co-operating with the military to round up any plotters or protesters."

After some excited discussion the BFG broke up on a note of optimism and Colonel Downton asked Brown, Drakeford and Johnson to stay on to help put the plan into action. Clearly, Major Brown had been doing some homework since their last meeting. He took a folder from his briefcase.

"First of all we need a secret HQ where we can direct operations and ideally meet the President, whether by mutual consent or not. We've been offered a place near Henley-on-Thames which was a countryside hotel before the war. It was then known as Parkland Hotel, but was requisitioned by the ministry during the war and used to hold high-ranking German prisoners for interrogation. It's ideal, it's three storeys high, plus an attic, has a well-equipped kitchen and even has lots of wiring for phones and the like. It's well equipped with an office, dining room and a lounge. It has good security, with a strong fence, searchlights and wrought iron gates at the main entrance. It also has a back entrance accessed by a totally separate country lane, with a small single storey residence which we can use and have someone on sentry duty round the clock. It's been locked up since the war and is now soon to be returned to its owner, with compensation. The owner happens to be a friend of mine, so he's very willing to help us. We need to devise a name which we can use, but doesn't give any clue as to where it might be. For now I suggest 'Manor Towers', although I think the owner has plans for a completely new name when it reopens in a few months' time, he wants to get away from the old Parkland Hotel image. As a cover for our operation we can say we're part of the restoration team, helping to convert it back from a military establishment to its original condition."

"Sounds just perfect," enthused Drakeford, "and not too far from my house, or from London."

Major Brown continued: "I've assembled a team with a range of specialist skills. Obviously, they all have military experience, I think we'll need them, and there are people like Charlotte, who you met earlier. We have some useful equipment, the odd car, a van, many firearms and I'm trying to get a pair of two-way radios. My two despatch riders will act as couriers and each have their own motorcycles; these are ex-War Department machines, bought legally. They are brand new, just never required once the war came to an end. Like so much equipment, ex-WD sales have proved very popular. I've asked the guys to paint their machines black as they will attract less attention than the original khaki."

"Are the rifles ex-WD as well?" asked Drakeford with a wry smile.

"I'd sooner not say," replied a serious faced Brown. "Let's just say they're on loan."

He continued: "We also have a telephone expert who works for the GPO. I think his skills could prove useful if the phone lines get tampered with."

He then unfolded a sheet of foolscap paper which contained a list of names. "We'll put one man on reception to act as gatekeeper. I have another lady who can look after admin, basically handing out money, cheques, petrol coupons, whatever is necessary. I have two ladies who will look after the kitchen, they used to run a restaurant so they know what they're doing. I have a photographer with a military background, I suspect we'll need him from time to time to provide evidence. And obviously we'll have four or five ex-army soldiers of various ranks who will patrol the grounds, provide security, etcetera, both for us and for the President, assuming we manage to persuade him to join us. That's probably about ten or twelve people who will be staying at the HQ for as long as it takes."

Johnson asked the question no one else wanted to ask: "How do we get the President to listen to us? Are we going to kidnap him or persuade him to come quietly?"

"We think he will come and most likely fly into Greenham Common, one of the biggest American airbases in England. If that's the case, we have people on the inside who will keep us informed as to when it's going to happen. The obvious ploy is a roadblock and for that we can make a black Wolseley look like a police car. We also have some naval uniforms which can be easily adapted to look like police uniforms, together with some police hats. I've had long talks with the men I know can organise things on the ground, so we have a well-planned strategy in place. If he doesn't go to Greenham Common it might be Upper Heyford or Brize Norton, so we do have a plan B, just in case."

Drakeford had some reservations. "We're clearly in breach of the law, once we've started out on this operation. Is that something everyone is prepared for?"

"They're all aware of what's entailed. There's the military operation on the ground, then there's the Manor Towers part, assuming we're successful in the first part. I'm asking Bill to be the manager of the Manor Towers operation. Bill, that means your role at the HQ will also be seen as illegal, so I hope you realise that?"

"I'm ok with that," replied Johnson.

Drakeford added, "We've come this far and nothing's going to happen unless we're prepared to put our reputations on the line. If it all goes wrong at least public opinion could be on our side."

"What happens if bullets start flying and someone gets hurt, or worse?" asked Johnson. "I assume people will have live bullets in their guns and they know how to use them. We'll need to have armed guards at the HQ, twenty-four hours per day."

"We don't intend to fire any guns, but we will if we have to," replied Brown. "The guards travelling with the President will be armed, of course, but we're counting on the surprise element. We don't think Travis himself will carry a weapon; he has people to do that for him. The main thing is that this is the last thing the Americans will be expecting in rural England, so he'll probably not be travelling with the kind of entourage that he would have in Chicago.

"We've been over the ground, checked out the exact place where we intend the ambush to take place and have practised our moves several times."

"Can we go and see this Manor Towers, sometime before the President arrives?" asked Drakeford.

"Yes, I'll get back to you just as soon as I get the keys," replied Brown.

"Ok," said Colonel Downton. "It seems the plan is in place, all we need is for the President to arrive and it all clicks into place. Shall we leave it there? We all have the right numbers if we need to get in touch."

"As soon as he arrives on English soil the plan will start, and we have a chain system so everyone is immediately aware of their part. Don't worry, you'll be hearing from me," Brown responded.

Major Brown got straight on with his arrangements and next day collected the keys to the Henley HQ. He phoned Drakeford and Johnson to arrange a meeting.

"I suggest we meet at your place," he said to Drakeford, "this will mean the three of us can drive in one car to the HQ and attract less attention. Shall we say nine o'clock tomorrow morning?"

"No problem," replied Drakeford, "I'll phone Bill right away and let him know."

Next morning the three boarded Major Brown's Rover and made an uneventful journey to Henley. With Johnson navigating, using a pre-war road map, they found the country lane which gave them access to the back entrance. Brown sorted through the assortment of keys he had been lent until he found one that unlocked the door. The initial impression was favourable, the place had been left clean and tidy, clearly the conclusion of a military operation. As one would expect for what had been a hotel, there was a reception area adjoining the main entrance, with a counter facing the door. Leading off from behind the reception was an office. This had four desks spaced around facing the walls. Brown said, "This could be where Susan Watson can operate from, looking after all the admin. She's a very efficient organiser. Bill, you and Charlotte can each have one of the other desks, while I'll share the fourth desk with whoever else needs one."

They then moved to a well-appointed kitchen, well up to the task of providing meals for anything up to thirty guests when operating as a hotel. Leading off the kitchen was a dining room, with a dozen tables and four chairs per table. There was a spacious lounge across a corridor, with a bar in the corner, although there was a distinct absence of liquid refreshment. One end of the lounge was covered with a well-stocked selection of books, probably contributed by visitors who had stayed at the hotel in the thirties.

They proceeded up the stairs to a landing with five bedrooms leading off and two bathrooms. They quickly looked into each of the rooms, three had double beds, the remaining rooms with twin beds. All doors had numbers and were lockable. Another staircase led to an identical layout as the previous floor. The final staircase led to the attic. This had a landing with five doors leading off. There were three small bedrooms, clearly servants' quarters, and a small bathroom. The remaining door led to a self-contained flat, comprising a lounge with a dining table and chairs, and doors leading off to a small kitchen, a bedroom and a bathroom. There was also a large high-set window with an excellent view of the grounds in front of the building. Each floor had an emergency exit to an external fire escape which looked as if it hadn't been used for years.

"I guess the owner or hotel manager would have kept this flat for himself," said Drakeford. "If we manage to bring the President here this will be a good place for him to stay, whether he agrees or not. However, we'll have to keep his door to the fire escape locked – we can't have him doing a runner during the night."

"Yes, we'll fix it with a padlock and chain, otherwise it's ideal, I'm very impressed," replied Johnson. "Let's get the guys in here as soon as we can, we need to get this place up and running."

The three descended the stairs, checked the lights were working, then carefully locked the door behind them and drove back to Drakeford's village. "All we need now is a President," said Johnson, half jokingly. "If he doesn't arrive it will all have been for nothing."

Drakeford responded: "He'll come, he can't resist a bit of publicity, and likes to be seen as a man of action. I don't think he's been to Britain for some time, if ever, so he'll want to see his newly acquired kingdom."

It was just two days later when Major Brown received the message he'd been waiting for, a tip-off from Greenham Common. His informer said: "The President is on his way, due to land later today." That's all Brown needed and immediately got in touch with his six team leaders who came together for a final briefing and to confirm that everything was in place. They gathered in a disused barn, in a quiet country lane, not far from Henley-on-Thames. He extracted a sheet of paper from an inside pocket and unfolded it to reveal his master list. He checked down the list, looking for a response as he reeled off each item.

"All vehicles ready?"

"Yes, sir," came the swift reply, with a simple nod from the man responsible for organising transport.

"Uniforms?"

Another nod of agreement.

"Firearms?"

A less straightforward answer. "Yes, we have ten rifles and ammunition. We have about a dozen very realistic dummy rifles used for training. They all know what to do."

"Remember, no shots to be fired unless they fire first. If you have to, shoot the guards and not the President," emphasised Major Brown. "And most important, when the deed is done withdraw quickly and carefully so as to leave no trace that we were there. That includes all the vehicles as well. As soon as the President leaves the airbase, I'll receive the signal and the plan clicks into motion from that point on. I'll make the next call and the chain begins. Any questions?"

"No, sir," chorused the team. With that, everyone dispersed and boarded whatever form of transport they had arrived with. All they needed was just one phone call.

CHAPTER 9

TAKING CHARGE

Day 1

Travis was buoyed by his own confidence following the Japanese surrender in August 1945, together with his presence at Yalta and Potsdam; so as Britain descended into chaos he could see a great opportunity to enhance his status on the world stage and decided to fly in and take charge of things for himself. He arrived unannounced at Greenham Common, an American air force base in Berkshire, with little fanfare. It had been a long 15-hour flight, even in the modern Lockheed Constellation, and he was able to take an overnight break in well appointed officers' quarters. The plan was for him to travel to the US Embassy next morning where he would meet the ambassador and stay for a few days, close to key personnel and direct the operation like a military supremo. As soon as Travis arrived, Major Brown received the call he had been waiting for, sitting at home by his phone, poised to make two key calls to set the wheels in motion.

Next morning everyone went to their appointed meeting place, careful not to arouse suspicion. As well as the people involved in the process to abduct the President, another team was preparing to set up the temporary headquarters at Manor Towers. Major Brown had obtained the use of a single-decker bus, driven by one of his team, and everyone had been briefed so that a route and timetable could be followed. A minor problem was most of the personnel had not previously met one another, they just knew where the bus would pick them up and how to identify it. Major Brown had planned this carefully and a large number 1912 was placed inside the windscreen of the bus, the number chosen simply because it was his year of birth. On boarding the bus everyone was to state a password to the driver – this was 'Lancaster'. One by one people were collected, mostly men, but there were four women. Several people had gathered outside Aylesbury railway station. They were all carrying large holdalls or small suitcases, but having not met before no one spoke as they weren't certain who or what they were waiting for. Suddenly the bus identified by number 1912 came round the corner and all but two of them gathered together as the bus came to rest. Those remaining looked confused as the others were all going to the same place, yet appeared to be total strangers. One by one they stepped aboard, each giving the password to the driver, and took their place. As it moved away the atmosphere relaxed since they all knew why they were there and conversation ensued as they introduced themselves.

After several stops the bus driver was satisfied that he had the appropriate number of people on board and made his way through the country lanes – clearly a man with local knowledge – until he reached the main gates of Manor Towers where Bill Johnson was waiting. Everyone got out of the bus and Johnson greeted them. "Good morning, I'm glad to see the plan is working and you all know why we're here. Let's get inside and I'll show you round." He then thanked the driver who then drove away carefully while Johnson closed the gates and turned the key in a hefty padlock. They walked up the drive to the main entrance and went inside.

Meanwhile, the President and his entourage set off for the US Embassy in an unmarked black car, although it was clearly of a size and style rarely seen on British roads. He was followed closely by two other similar cars carrying his advisors and security personnel. Everyone assumed his visit was a well guarded secret, so as the convoy proceeded southwards on a main country road there were no outriders to prepare the route. Suddenly they came upon a roadblock, manned by police – or so it appeared.

A tall man in uniform went up to the driver of the leading car. "I'm afraid there's been a serious accident involving a large commercial vehicle further along, rendering the road impassable. Unless you want to turn round and go back the way you came we'll have to divert you. Could you follow that police car and he'll show you the way to avoid the incident and get you back on the main road."

At this point the entourage suspected nothing and were even impressed with the quiet efficiency. They followed the car as it drove down a quiet country road through a wooded area when they came upon another roadblock as a farm tractor and trailer drove out of a side turning and stopped, straddling the road. No sooner had they come to a stop when around twenty armed men appeared from the bushes on both sides of the road. The surprise element meant that there was little anyone could do to resist these determined, threatening and well organised men. They opened the door of the lead car carrying the President.

"We are freedom fighters," said the leader. "We don't want violence or bloodshed, we just want to take the President away for a serious discussion, but we won't hesitate to use our weapons if there is any resistance."

The President, clearly shaken, slowly got out of the car at gunpoint and followed the man who had just confronted him, with another armed man behind, and was marched off past the police car and the tractor. He was made to climb in through the rear doors of an inconspicuous blue Bedford van which was parked next to the roadblock.

Inside the van, equipped with primitive seating in the loading area, Major Charles Brown introduced himself. "Good morning, Mr President, welcome aboard, apologies for my blunt introduction. Not quite up to your usual mode of transport, but not for long."

Travis looked quite bewildered and somewhat pale. He said nothing as he sat on one of the old car seats which had been screwed to the floor. Apart from the driver and Major Brown, there were two other men sat in the front of the van, carrying rifles, and dressed in workmen's boiler suits.

The tractor was partially moved to allow the van to drive away down the lane, followed by the bogus police car. The armed men disappeared into the trees whence they came. The tractor had suddenly lost its driver, it appeared abandoned, so there was no way the cars could follow in pursuit. Many of the occupants emerged and as they came together much shouting ensued. They quickly realised that they had been out-manoeuvred and got back into their cars, with no alternative but to turn around, although this was not a simple procedure as the cars were too large for a narrow country lane. It took several minutes as they shuffled to and fro, one getting stuck in a ditch requiring around a dozen well-dressed men to help push it back on the road. From a safe distance, invisible to all the president's men, the British team observed the manoeuvrings with some amusement. As the cars disappeared, the tractor driver reappeared and drove his tractor away along a farm track. The President's cars retraced their route back to the main road. Naturally the original roadblock was nowhere to be seen.

The Bedford van continued along the narrow country lane for a couple of miles, then turned left onto a main road where another car was awaiting. The bogus police car stopped and the occupants got out and removed the police signs. The two cars then followed the van, but all personnel were armed and ready in case of an unexpected intervention. As they rounded a bend, they came upon an overhead railway bridge and suddenly realised they had driven into a roadblock, manned by two policemen and three US army GIs. There was one car ahead with a woman driver and she was waved through. The Bedford van driver and his front seat passenger wore overalls, everyone else in the van kept well down. In anticipation of such an event the van carried a ladder on its roof and had written on the side "W G Philips & Son, Plumbers".

The driver, through his driver's window, spoke to the policeman. "Hi mate, just on my way to a job, bit of an emergency, a burst pipe," he said.

The policeman seemed disinterested and waved him on. As they pulled away, Major Brown breathed a sigh of relief. "Just as well," he said, "we didn't really want to shoot anyone, and they were just doing their job as they'd been asked. Probably looking for protesters on their way to a demo!" The following cars were also waived through as the two men in the first car wore police uniforms, the two in the second wearing army uniforms.

About ten miles further on, Travis's captors turned into a country lane and stopped outside a country mansion where the two men in army uniforms got out of their car. This was a pre-arranged photo opportunity, as Travis was ushered from the van and invited to shake hands with a distinguished army officer in uniform who said very little except "Welcome to Britain, I'm Major Sir Rupert Stevenson. We apologise for our strict security measures". They both posed briefly for the camera. Feeling more confused than ever, Travis was helped back into the van and it continued on its way.

At that point Major Brown made some phone calls from a call box; first Bill Johnson, then the Drakeford household as the network kicked in. "Hello Rufus, we've got him, we should be at Manor Towers shortly. Do you want to come and join us?"

"Yes, of course, I'll be right over," replied Drakeford. He turned to Christine. "They've got him! The plan worked. I'm off to meet them."

"I'm amazed it was that easy," she replied. "Off you go, goodness knows when I'll see you again. Make sure you don't get arrested before you've even started!"

The Bedford van, with its rudimentary seating, was plain sided with no windows so the President had no idea where he was being taken. They turned into a quiet country lane and into the side entrance of a large country house, after which the gates were immediately slammed shut. Everyone got out and entered the house by a side door.

"What the hell's going on, where are you taking me?" shouted Travis. "I demand to have my staff and security guards informed and have them join me as soon as possible."

"I don't think that's going to happen," said Major Brown. "For the time being, at least, you're on your own."

He led the President upstairs to a small suite of rooms on the attic floor, or fourth storey by the American definition. It was not up to the standard he had been used to, but perfectly adequate and probably more spacious and comfortable than most English people would have had at that time and better than most hotels. The main room was fully carpeted, contained a settee, a table and four chairs, while there was a small kitchen and a well-equipped bathroom leading off it. He was invited to sit at the table and a meal was provided, served by an attractive young lady in an army uniform. Once the table was cleared, two men entered the room, one in an army uniform, the other a well-dressed gentlemen in civilian clothes. They sat themselves down and invited Travis to join them.

The man in uniform introduced himself. "We've met already, I'm Major Charles Brown. You will recall we met when you travelled in the back of the van and today I've been your personal bodyguard. May I introduce my colleague Bill Johnson who has worked in British intelligence and has extensive diplomatic experience. Welcome to your accommodation; for the time being we'll call it 'Manor Towers'. Until 1940 it was a private hotel, and then it was requisitioned by the British Secret Service. It was used to house high ranking German prisoners for interrogation, so you will appreciate it is very secure."

The young lady in the army uniform reappeared, this time carrying a tray containing coffees and other beverages. Major Brown introduced her. "This is Charlotte, she's a member of our team and will make sure you have everything you need while you're our guest here."

"Good afternoon, Mr President, I've been looking forward to meeting you," she said in a clear English accent. Travis had almost expected her to be French, based on her name and appearance.

Bill Johnson began, "I'm a member of a group of freedom fighters, known as the British Freedom Group, or the BFG, who are looking to restore law and order and remove military personnel from the streets. We're entirely separate from the mass protests, although we totally sympathise with their motives. We're disappointed, to say the least, regarding your comments following your meeting with Clement Atlee, our Prime Minister. That's not what we're about and our personnel who were present dispute that this was ever mentioned. We intend to renegotiate Britain's relationship with the United States and restore government to its former democratically elected status. We're prepared for this process to take as long as is necessary."

Travis replied, somewhat hesitatingly, "I just spoke my mind; it's what I believe even if we may not have used those words at the time."

"At least we understand each other," replied Johnson.

"I could have gone further. Left to me I'd restore Edward VIII to the throne. He got a raw deal, just because he wanted to marry an American woman," countered Travis.

"She had some dubious connections," said Johnson, "and what's more, Edward used to visit Adolf Hitler, where they got on rather well. He had to go."

At that point Lord Drakeford arrived at the top of the stairs, having just driven from his home. Johnson made the introduction: "May I introduce Lord Drakeford. He is a lawyer and until your soldiers intervened he was a member of Mr Atlee's government in the House of Lords, our upper house. He's our group's spokesman, since he's already in the public arena."

Travis looked at him pensively. "I think I recognise you. Weren't you with Atlee's team who came to the White House?"

"Yes, absolutely correct," replied Drakeford. "You must meet hundreds of people, I'm surprised you remember."

Travis just nodded, making no further comment.

Introductions over, Johnson continued: "Everyone assumes that you plan to make the UK your forty-ninth state; that possibility hasn't gone down well."

"I think they might quite like the idea, once they got used to it," replied Travis. "Just think, British people could go to live and work in the USA, I'm sure that might appeal to lots of young people. Your scientists, engineers, teachers, craftsmen, all would get work. And no need for a National Health Service in our wonderful country."

"I suspect it wouldn't be that easy," countered Johnson. "And I suspect your voters wouldn't be too pleased when they realised their jobs were under threat!"

Johnson looked him straight in the eye. "You can see the extent of outrage your comments have caused. I cannot begin to describe the damage to UK-USA relations, such a pity after the spirit of cooperation during the war. Apart from the one-sided meeting with Atlee, you have not been prepared to even listen to us and the level of protest has just escalated, with no prospect of an amicable solution. As the public sees it, we are under USA rule, like an occupied country, and we're being screwed for every penny we make for the next fifty years. Hence, we have you here so you have no choice but to listen and hopefully put the record straight and make some concessions. We believe it's in both our best interests."

"I can't agree anything here alone, I need my team with me before I can even talk about it," protested Travis. "Americans don't do business under duress."

"We'll see what transpires, we don't care how long this takes," replied Johnson. He stood, clearly in charge, deciding the discussion had gone on long enough. "I'll wish you good evening, we'll talk again tomorrow." He and Drakeford then left the room.

Travis couldn't take his eyes off Charlotte. She was in her mid to late twenties, slim, with short red hair. Even dressed in her army fatigues she was a very attractive young lady who turned heads wherever she went.

"I'm being treated like a prisoner," protested Travis, appealing to Charlotte. "Not many home comforts here,

I'll be bored out of my mind. What about a radio? Even prisoners get to listen to the radio."

Major Brown stepped in: "We'll set one up, you are quite welcome to hear what's being said. And you'll be pleased to know there are no commercials on our BBC radio, just three main stations, the Light programme, the Home service and the Third Programme. We have a small library downstairs, Charlotte will find something to suit your tastes. And we'll bring you newspapers whenever we can. Hopefully you will be reasonably comfortable here. We'll make some attempt to obtain your essential luggage. Meanwhile, Charlotte will make sure things run smoothly."

"We'll leave it there for today and talk again tomorrow." They left the room and the door was locked behind them. An armed guard sat outside on the landing.

Travis was quite bewildered by all this. He couldn't believe that a group of British guys had had the audacity or the capability to outwit an American President and his guards. Here he was alone, without an entourage or anyone he could rely on, probably for the first time in his life. He tried to tell himself that it would only be a matter of time before his American military personnel would be along as they must surely have followed him, even if at a distance. It was his first ever visit to Britain and, like most Americans, he assumed it was a small country and all hiding places would soon be exposed.

Meanwhile, in Washington DC, no one could understand the silence. They knew the President had arrived safely and spent the night at the American Air Force base. They assumed he would be moving on the following morning to London where he would be staying at the US Embassy. It was now 4 pm in Washington and 9 pm in London, so Vice President Delaney decided to put in a call to Ambassador Winault.

"What's happening, has anything happened to Travis?" he asked.

"No one's telling me anything," replied the Ambassador. "We know he left Greenham Common this morning and should have arrived here about midday, we were all ready for him as it was a great occasion, being his first visit since he became President. His car may have broken down, but surely someone would have told me by now."

"Then get back to me as soon as you have some news," responded the VP. "Whatever the time of day or night. We need to know before the press do."

The VP contacted his Secretary of State, Alan Dulles, and General William Sykes, his most senior military man. "I'm sure there's a logical explanation," he told them, "but it appears Travis has gone missing somewhere in England between our Air Force base and the Embassy. As soon as I hear from the Embassy, I'll get back to you."

"Perhaps they've had an accident," replied Dulles. "You know how narrow and twisty those country roads are over there. Just keep me posted in case we need to do anything."

Day 2

No sooner had the photograph, taken outside the country home, been delivered to the press when Drakeford received a telephone call from Bill Binder of the Daily Mail. He said, "Lord Drakeford, as spokesman for the BFG, would you like to comment on the whereabouts of the President of the United States?"

"I'm afraid I can't tell you," replied Drakeford. "All I can say is that it's my understanding that he's being well looked after and will come to no harm."

"But it's your group who have abducted him, you have provided us with a photograph of him being welcomed."

"But you're assuming he's been abducted; the public should be told he's arrived for secret talks. That's unless you tell them otherwise, you're well practised in making things up. We want an opportunity to get the President on his own to present our side, to explain that he's out of step. We just want him to listen."

"I can see you're not being very forthcoming. If that's the best you can give me, I'll have to write my own interpretation of what's happening."

"I'm sure you will."

With that Binder put the phone down.

Drakeford was aware that having been part of Atlee's government his address and phone number was known to the press, so calls like this were bound to happen. He was also aware that his telephone line would be tapped, so he had to be careful who he phoned from his personal line. This was uppermost in his mind as he drove to Manor Towers that morning. On arrival he made a suggestion to Bill Johnson: "What we need is a two-way radio between here and my house, the sort of device spies used during the war. I'll talk to Charles, he'll sort it out. I'm sure Charlotte would have used one when she was undercover in France."

"But that would probably have been using Morse code," said Johnson. "We need to be able to hold a conversation. I'm sure Charlotte would have been trained to use whatever was available."

"I understand," replied Drakeford, "I'll leave it to you."

Back on the ground floor Johnson spoke to Major Brown about a radio. "Charles, you mentioned some time ago when explaining the equipment that you were trying to find a two-way radio. In view of the risks involved with using the telephone I think we need to use that two-way radio between here and Lord Drakeford's house."

"I'm sure we have radios in one of those boxes in the cellar. Obviously we'll need a pair to talk to each other. I'll go and look and bring up the units," responded Charles. Ten minutes later he returned with the required equipment. They were still packaged and had never been actually used in a real-life situation. "First I'll test them out, then we'll train up Rufus to use it. We'll put Charlotte in charge of that task, she can be our operator."

Shortly afterwards Major Brown had, with Charlotte's help, rigged up the radios and satisfied himself that they were in working order. He called Lord Drakeford over and invited him to take a seat in front of a radio, next to Charlotte. Drakeford was well aware that she was extremely attractive, and intelligent. He was a willing pupil, happy to be in her company, but told himself that this was strictly business and he must not be distracted. She quickly explained the controls and how to fire-up the radio. She explained, "The radio probably has a range of up to 25 miles, to be honest I'm not sure. It works off a battery, so take this away with you and try it out when you get home. You'll also need to rig up an aerial wire as well."

With that he put the unit into a cardboard box, together with the battery and an aerial wire. "Thanks, Charlotte, I'll give it a try a soon as I get home."

He arrived home and immediately rigged up the radio and its aerial in an upstairs bedroom. His first attempt didn't work, try as he might. He decided that was enough for one day and would try again tomorrow.

Next morning Drakeford was still annoyed with himself and slightly embarrassed that he had been unable to make the radio work, so he took the opportunity to have a second attempt on setting it up. Christine was looking on and studied the sketch he had been given by Charlotte. "Aren't those wires the wrong way round?" she said, pointing to the back of the radio.

He quickly realised his error. "My fault," he admitted sheepishly to his wife, "technical matters are not my strong point."

He reconnected the wires and immediately Charlotte responded. A very short conversation took place.

"I told you it was easy," she said.

"Yes, and very clear, too," he replied. "It took me two attempts, simple when you know how. It was Christine who followed your sketch, I had just connected things up incorrectly, without double checking. Typical male I suppose!"

Meanwhile, the American forces had been caught out by the audacity of the operation. They had no detailed knowledge of the English countryside and were assuming that Travis was being held locally before spreading their net elsewhere, perhaps Scotland or even Ireland. One place they were well aware of was Bletchley Park, which had been used during the war by British and American personnel involved in code breaking. This, they assumed, would be an ideal place to centre the operation and immediately put in place a surveillance team around Bletchley Park. They fully intended to conduct a thorough search, but were aware that Bletchley Park was very well known and would need official clearance to achieve this. Without delay the Americans set about obtaining the relevant documentation.

The photo of Travis taken the previous day had been 'leaked' to the press and it appeared in all the major newspapers with the caption 'President Travis is welcomed by Major Sir Rupert Stevenson on his arrival to England'. There was no such person, of course, this was one of Brown's officer friends in disguise. Until then hardly anyone was aware that the President had come to England, and the US military top brass were very embarrassed to see his picture on the front page of the newspapers. No one was prepared to admit that the operation had been carried out, but a few people recognised the location of the photograph and assumed this is where the President was being detained. There was a quickly organised police raid on the house, much to the amazement of the owner who knew nothing about it.

There was an initial standoff when the Americans denied anything had happened as they had totally underestimated the strength of feeling. The public were never told of the hijack incident, but nevertheless many rumours were circulating. As a cover it was subsequently announced that the President was personally directing operations while staying in a secret country residence for security reasons. In reality, they were too embarrassed to admit they had been outmanoeuvred by a group of largely unknown activists who had proved to be extremely competent and clearly had a military background. As it was clear this was not going to be resolved in day or so, the President's captors made him comfortable and provided him with a few basic necessities.

The picture of the President being welcomed by Major Rupert Stevenson appeared in all the British morning newspapers, so there was no denying he was not staying at the Embassy as planned. For the time being everyone stuck to the cover story, that he was staying at a secret location to conduct the operation. It was 4 am in Washington, but nevertheless the Ambassador decided he needed to speak to the VP before the press beat him to it.

Vice President Delaney was fast asleep when his phone rang. He immediately sat up, wide awake. "It's Ambassador Winault here," said a faraway voice. "It appears the President's car was trapped in a road block and Travis taken away. We've no idea where to, but there's a picture in all the papers this morning showing him being welcomed outside an English stately home. We're currently trying to identify where it is and will be sending in the cavalry later today. At least it appears that the President is unharmed."

"Do we know why he was abducted," asked the VP. "Is there a ransom demand?"

"Not so far. Could be a bunch of small-time crooks out to make a few bucks," came the reply.

"Well get back to me as soon as you have more information," replied the VP and he promptly put the phone down. He immediately contacted Dulles and Sykes. "Meet me at the White House in an hour."

It was now five o'clock in the morning as the three men sat down to discuss their next move. The VP began, "Wherever the President is being held we have to leave it up to the military people to sort it. I would have expected a ransom demand by now, but it's still only mid-morning in England."

"We have to be careful how we approach this," said Sykes with some seriousness. "Having shown us where he's supposed to be staying, they know we'll be descending on them. If there's a shootout we have to be careful not to put the President's life at risk."

"My guess is it's a decoy," said Dulles. "They know we have the numbers and the firepower, so they'll play for time. He's probably somewhere in an underground bunker!"

The VP responded, "My understanding is that the police have already checked out the stately home where the photo was taken. There was no sign of the President, so I suspect you're probably right, he's already somewhere else."

Sykes reacted: "I'm more concerned as to how they allowed this to happen. Whoever was responsible for organising the transport and security deserves to be shot. Americans don't take kindly to such humiliation."

The VP, anxious to calm things down, said, "I think we should put out a statement to the press, more or less on the lines of that issued by the press in London. We don't want to wind things up, it could all be over in a matter of hours."

With that he pulled in the White House Press Secretary and between them set out a single paragraph to be issued at 7am, Eastern US time. It read:

"President David Travis has flown to Britain to deal first hand with their economic problems and the civil unrest which has escalated in recent weeks. For his own security he is restricting his travel and therefore staying at a secret location where he is working with his financial experts and senior military personnel. He is likely to stay there for two or three days and expects to fully resolve the situation to everyone's satisfaction."

CHAPTER 10

TIME TO NEGOTIATE

The BFG decided it was time to make contact with the American authorities, beginning with the American Embassy. Major Brown had recruited Terry Bell, who worked for the General Post Office (the GPO) and known to his friends as 'Tell'. He had been collected from home that morning and driven to Manor Towers. Terry explained how he could assist and the possible problems that might occur.

"Since they know someone, somewhere, has their President, they will be expecting a call to the Embassy, after all, where else would anyone start? When that happens they will immediately want to track the source of that call. I plan to make that difficult for them by tapping into the line remotely. That can work a couple of times before they realise what we're up to and will block our calls, forcing us to use a conventional location which they can track. At the moment they don't know anyone's location, but may have guessed that Lord Drakeford, as the BFG leader, could be involved and may already have his phone tapped, meaning that they can track any number he cares to ring. This will all have been set up at the telephone exchange, so please make sure Lord Drakeford is careful who he rings. He can talk to friends and family as he might do normally, but not members of the group and definitely not this place as it will bring them straight to the President."

With everyone duly briefed, the group comprising a driver, Terry Bell and Bill Johnson set off at 8.00am in the blue Bedford van, now with the plumbing business name removed. They pulled over on a main road next to a large telegraph pole. Terry Bell straightway went about his task, fitting up a ladder against the telegraph pole and climbing to the top. He quickly extracted some equipment from his rucksack and attached it to the overhead lines, then dropped a cable down to the ground. The cable was then attached to a telephone held by Bill Johnson, sat in the back of the van. He rang a number and after some exchange problems he was put through to the American Embassy in London. A receptionist answered very efficiently and he said to her, "Good morning, my name is Bill Johnson of the British Freedom Group, I wish to inform you that we have your President. Could you put me through to someone in authority?"

After a short delay a gruff American voice replied, "I'm one of the Ambassador's deputies. What's this about you having our President? Is this a joke?"

"No, it's not a joke. He's with us and right now he's being well looked after and in no danger. However, we, that is the British Freedom Group, need to have a discussion about our future relationship with your country. If this is not a good number to make contact, perhaps we can find a trusted intermediary for future communication, I'll leave that with you. I'll ring again tomorrow, around this time. Meanwhile the President would like to have his personal belongings. Could you deliver his luggage to a neutral venue for us to collect?"

"Let me think about that?"

"Well, when you've thought about that perhaps you could deliver a suitcase at four o'clock this afternoon to Joe's Café, in the High Street, Aylesbury. I'm sure you can manage that. Please don't try to intercept, the President needs his clean shirts and underwear."

Bill Johnson rang off and emerged from the van, signalling to Terry to come down. Several vehicles had passed while this was happening, including a police car, but no one had paid any attention, assuming it was routine GPO maintenance. "Good job there, Terry," said Bill, "once I got through it was a very clear line."

It was time to see if the American had taken seriously the request for the President's personal belongings. Another member of the team, Andy Price, made the journey by motorcycle to Aylesbury. He parked his bike close to Joe's café at around 3.30 pm and took up a place inside, ordered a large cup of tea and unfolded his newspaper. He looked around furtively to see if anything was happening out in the street. There were a few people walking past, but no one looked suspicious, and four o'clock came and went. Suddenly, just when he felt nothing was going to happen, a grey Ford Pilot drew up outside and a passenger wearing a dark blue overcoat emerged from the back seat with a large suitcase. He entered the café and walked up to the counter and said, "Could I leave this here to be collected by Mr Johnson?"

"No problem, I'll look after it for him," replied the man behind the counter.

The man in the overcoat turned and left without delay, jumping back into the Ford Pilot which had left its engine running. The car roared away, narrowly missing Andy's parked motorbike. Andy, by now on his second cup of tea, continued his surveillance mission. The man behind the counter had been replaced by a woman, he assumed because four pm represented a shift change. There were perhaps half a dozen other people sat around, with two men in their forties at the same table. He noticed that they were getting quite agitated, glancing at the counter and then at the entrance from High Street, as if they were waiting for someone. This went on for some time until one of the men went up to the counter and asked, "Do you have a suitcase to be collected by Mr Johnson?"

"No, I know nothing about a suitcase or a Mr Johnson," she replied. The man, clearly annoyed, leapt over the counter to see for himself. There was clearly no suitcase, so he burst into the backroom where he could see there was nothing there either. He returned to the café and said to his accomplice, "No sign anywhere, they've pulled a fast one, I'm afraid, let's go."

Naturally the BFG had been prepared for such an eventuality. By intercepting the suitcase the President's men thought they could grab the messenger that they anticipated would have been sent to retrieve it, forcing him to admit to where he was supposed to make the delivery. In fact, within seconds of the suitcase's arrival it had been attached to a rope beneath the counter and dragged sideways into the back room by Jeff Davies, one of the team. He then opened the rear entrance and flung the case into the back of the Bedford van waiting in the yard at the back of the cafe. Off they went, driving unobtrusively, before anyone had realised. Having seen all had gone smoothly, Andy Price got back on his motorcycle and disappeared.

In the back of the van, Major Brown got to work on the suitcase. Not surprisingly, on investigation he found the luggage contained a small battery-powered radio transmitter, intended to send signals for around twenty-four hours. He transferred all the suitcase's contents to another suitcase, except for the radio transmitter which was fixed in place in the original suitcase. About ten miles away, on a quiet country road, they stopped in a gateway next to a near empty barn. The original suitcase was deposited in the barn and within less than two minutes they continued on their way.

The Americans tracked the radio signal and assumed it was the secret location. They hurriedly organised a team of US Marines to move in as darkness began to fall. When they arrived they moved carefully and quietly, being unfamiliar with the area, expecting to find a large country home at the very least, if not a castle. They were amazed to find the target was a disused barn and assumed they had somehow miscalculated the location. They burst into the barn with powerful torches and rifles at the ready, to find the suitcase unhidden, there waiting for them. They opened the lid to find the case empty apart from the transmitter and a note on a piece of foolscap paper:

'WELCOME TO ENGLAND. ENJOY YOUR TIME HERE BUT DON'T STAY TOO LONG.'

They picked up the suitcase and walked despondently back to their line of waiting army vehicles. There was some hilarity that they had been sent on a futile rescue operation, but the high ranking men were not amused as they felt they had again been outwitted by some country bumpkins, further inflaming their annoyance.

The van with Major Brown on board returned to the residence where the President was being held. He climbed the stairs, accompanied by Bill Johnson, and handed over the suitcase. Travis was listening to the news on his newly acquired radio.

"At last! I'm ready for a change of clothes," said the President. "The BBC news said I'm staying in a secret location. At least that part is right."

Johnson told him, "We intend to use you as a bargaining tool because you mean an awful lot more to the Americans than you do to us. Given half a chance, the British public would tear you limb from limb. As far as we're concerned you could disappear without trace and no one will ever know. To be honest, that might still happen."

"I doubt it, it's only a matter of time before my guys find out where I am. You'll live to regret this."

"We're trying to make contact. The purpose of all this is to arrange meaningful discussions about Britain's future. So far, the Americans have just moved in and ordered our politicians to stand aside as they call the shots. Perhaps they'll take us seriously now they can see we're not going to stand aside and let you take over."

With that Brown and Johnson departed and the room locked behind him.

Day 3

Next morning it was time to attempt stage two of the communications plan. Johnson boarded the Bedford van with his 'plumber' and they collected Terry the telephone man from a nearby village. They drove to a suitable location on a main road, parked next to a telegraph pole, but a different location to the one they had used yesterday. Terry fitted up his ladder and climbed up; within minutes Bill Johnson was ringing the American Embassy.

"Good morning," he said to the receptionist, "can I speak to your deputy ambassador?"

Immediately the same voice replied that had spoken yesterday. "Hello, do you still claim to be holding our President?"

"Yes, and you'll be pleased to know that he now has his personal belongings. We weren't impressed with your cheap trick with the hidden radio transmitter. What did you take us for? Perhaps you've found a suitable intermediary to help us communicate?"

"Yes, we would like to suggest Michael Millerchip, a Cambridge professor. He's a well known public figure and he's agreed that he can take a neutral position. He can be reached on his home phone on Hilltop 478. He will take messages from you and in turn will relay messages from you back to us."

"Thank you, we'll check him out and be in touch shortly," replied Johnson. He was aware that the telephone engineers were already trying to trace his call, since he had promised to phone at that time. He rang off, gave the thumbs-up to Terry, and they moved on smartly.

Back in the van Johnson explained to Terry what had been agreed. "They've provided us with an intermediary who we can telephone and leave messages for one another. Somehow I'm suspicious that they'll still try and pull a fast one."

"I agree," replied Terry. "I think it best not to use the phone from HQ. I think I know of an empty office in Aylesbury. I was there yesterday and the phone line is still connected. Maybe we can use that?"

"Let's go now and see if it still works. We can then phone Professor Millerchip, it will show willing."

They parked up in Aylesbury, near the town centre. A dark blue van can be very useful in not arousing suspicion. They entered an office block where people were working on the ground floor. They climbed the stairs and sat themselves down in the empty office which had been stripped, apart from a couple of chairs. The telephone was on the floor and Johnson dialled the number he had been given. After a couple of rings the call was answered:

"Millerchip," said the voice.

"Good morning," said Johnson. "My name's Bill Johnson of the British Freedom Group. I understand you've agreed to act as an intermediary between ourselves and the Americans?"

"Yes, that's correct. I'll relay messages. I hope there will be no repercussions for my part in this?"

"No, certainly not from our side. Let's leave it there, maybe we'll be back later today or early tomorrow."

Meanwhile, back at the Drakeford residence, Andy Price, the motorcycle courier, delivered a parcel in the shape of a tube. He recognised the name on the label, it was a journalist friend and as he removed the wrapping paper he found a note inside.

The note read: *Here are a few papers that I picked up in New York yesterday and brought them home with me, just to see what they were saying about Travis's absence. You may be interested in the article in the Post. Cheers, Jim.*

Drakeford quickly glanced at the papers until he came to the New York Post. The headline read 'Is Travis having an Affair?' Alongside the article was a photograph taken with a long range camera of a tall man and a woman in the grounds of Bletchley Park. The picture was not clear enough to identify the persons in the distance, but it could easily have been Travis. The article asked whether Travis had arranged the trip with this in mind, using the crisis in the UK as a cover story. The suggestion was that Travis had colluded with 'a Lord Drakeford, a small-time politician' to invent the idea of the BFG as a distraction.

"Well, that's a new angle we hadn't thought of," said Drakeford. He and Christine both laughed. "I think we both needed a spot of light relief! I was about to drive to the HQ; this will interest them, I'm sure."

At the same time Johnson returned to their secret HQ to report on the morning's activities. By now Lord Drakeford had arrived and they sat over a cup of coffee to plan their next move and Drakeford then revealed his newspapers.

All had articles about Travis's UK visit, and then he pointed to the headline of the New York Post. "Now that's something we hadn't expected," he said. "It's obviously rubbish as we've had him here the whole time."

Johnson quickly read the article. "It could work to our advantage, it might take the pressure off us by diverting attention. Obviously, some opportunist photographer has seen his chance to make a few quid. It's clearly Bletchley Park in the picture, but it could have been taken months ago. With the photo he's been able to invent a suitable story, and with Travis's record it does seem credible."

Drakeford thought for a moment, then responded. "Yes, let's exploit it. Obviously we'll deny any involvement, but no one will be quite sure. Meanwhile, we'll continue with our efforts to set up a serious meeting to get a better deal. I'll contact my man at the Mirror, he'll know how to handle it."

"They've nominated a Professor Michael Millerchip as an intermediary," explained Johnson. "Do you know of him?"

"Not personally, for now we'll have to trust him. Perhaps we'll ask someone to pay him a visit. They don't need to go indoors, just check that he really exists and doesn't have half the US army sat outside."

"Let's test the system," said Johnson. "We'll return to our Aylesbury office and put a call in to Prof Millerchip. We can ask for names of appropriate experts who can advise Travis, assuming he's receptive to advice."

Day 4

As agreed, Johnson drove alone in his black Humber Hawk to Aylesbury. As he turned into the road near to the town centre he was aware of some police activity, so he parked up round the corner from the office and walked along to investigate. He realised that the activity was indeed centred on the office block he was about to enter. There were a couple of policemen stood on the street, but more disturbing for passersby were American soldiers carrying rifles. He approached one of the policemen:

"What's happening? Are they looking for someone?" he asked.

"They've had a tipoff that enemy agents are using the empty office upstairs. Strikes me that someone's winding them up," volunteered the policeman.

"Too true, I thought the war was over, but that's Americans for you!" replied Johnson. "Thanks anyway, I'd better be on my way."

The policemen gave him a cheery wave and Johnson carried on walking, continuing round the block and back to his car. It was a straightforward return journey, but out of curiosity he decided to take a detour to check out an American army base at Tiddington. He was not in the least surprised to find that a group of protesters were lined up near the main entrance, displaying placards with messages such as 'Yanks Go Home', 'We want an NHS' and a picture of Travis with a Hitler moustache. He drove quite slowly past the demonstration which was probably about twenty-strong and was surprised to see a mix of people, from young women to middle-aged, well dressed men. 'Still well motivated,' he thought to himself. He continued his journey and drove straight back to HQ where he parked up under the shelter to hide his car from being seen from the roadside, or from the air.

"You won't believe what I've just seen," he told Drakeford. "Police and GIs swarming all over our office. Clearly, right from the first call we made to Prof Millerchip they had his line tapped. I think we're going to be forced to resort to red telephone boxes in future."

Major Brown responded: "Yes, and never the same box twice, they'll be ready. Or perhaps ask Terry to find some other method, ideally one that doesn't involve climbing telegraph poles every time."

Just at that moment they heard what sounded like a low flying aircraft nearby. Major Brown opened the main door and could see a light aircraft circling above, clearly taking a close look at the building. This was an Auster, a small three-seater, single engined, high-winged monoplane. Austers were mainly used by the RAF for short journeys and observation since there was no low-slung wing to obstruct the view below. Brown could see some British markings, but was not able to identify its origin with any certainty. It was circling at about two hundred feet, much lower than normally permitted for private aircraft, although it was impossible to see how many people were on board. Brown walked about twenty yards away from the door as there was no point in hiding, then gave a cheery wave to the aircraft. Almost immediately the pilot opened the throttle and roared away, as if guilty at being spotted.

Brown walked back inside and declared: "Not sure where that came from, but they're clearly checking us out. They're probably looking at all possible locations, but I don't think there was anything unusual on view to suggest we were up to something. All our vehicles are under cover. We'll just have to wait and see if they send in the cavalry."

Brown continued: "I had wondered how the Americans would go about it, should they identify Manor Towers as the place where the President was being held. They would hardly turn up at the main gate and politely ask to be let in. My guess is that they would drop a couple of dozen marines onto our front lawn. They would guess we wouldn't have the ground force to defend, especially if they utilised the surprise element. We wouldn't have a chance, especially if it resulted in a shoot-out."

Back to the job in hand, Johnson said impatiently, "I think the next move is for us to meet Travis and see how receptive he is to negotiate. If he's reasonably cooperative we'll be able to plan our next move."

Johnson and Drakeford climbed the stairs to the top floor and greeted the guard who was sat on the landing. He stood up, unlocked the door, and the two men walked in to find Travis on his settee listening to the radio.

They shook hands and the three of them sat themselves down at the table.

Drakeford began, "I think Bill has outlined the purpose of this exercise. We want to return to normal peacetime government. We have a democratically elected government and have no wish to be manipulated by any other country, be it the USA or USSR. We do feel the financial constraints imposed upon us will be a major factor in holding back development and we would like to talk about that too. However, if our voters have given us a mandate, including the formation of a National Health Service, then that is what we should do."

As discussions proceeded it soon became clear that Travis was not well versed in the finer details of the Lend-

Lease agreement and its replacement, and what was owed to the USA. He needed to communicate with his colleagues and various specialists.

Travis protested, "I need to communicate with my experts, can't we just pick up the telephone and proceed from there?"

Johnson replied: "Unfortunately we can't trust your people. The latest telephone technology means that the call would be easy to trace. Our attempts to communicate through an intermediary have shown them to be unreliable. We were calling from an empty office and they still raided there this morning, assuming this was where you were staying. However, we'll try again."

"Anything else you need in the meantime?" Drakeford enquired. "The owner has left us a selection of novels downstairs, we'll have a few sent up. Do you have any preference as to genre?"

"Maybe anything to do with America, I'll leave you to choose," replied Travis.

Drakeford then produced his American newspapers. "These came this morning, I'm sure you will find them interesting reading, especially the front page of the Post."

Travis casually thumbed through until he came to the Post. "Holy shit!" he exclaimed. "My wife's going to enjoy that. Just look at what you've done!"

"Nothing to do with us, it's what papers do," said Drakeford. "If there's no news they have to invent it. I'll bet it's sold a lot of newspapers!"

"It's typical of the Post," admitted Travis. "They love stirring up gossip, they've been chasing me for years."

The two left the room and the door was locked behind them. As they walked downstairs Johnson said, "I think I need to find a telephone box."

"Yes, but be careful. If we use public telephone boxes they will be monitoring where they're coming from. If we use them scattered around here, they will home in on us, so we'll need to select our phone boxes carefully to throw them off the scent." Johnson drove off to find a telephone box. He found one in a village about ten miles away, so parked up and made his call. There was initially some delay as the public telephone box required coins to be inserted and buttons 'A' and 'B' to be pressed to make the connection.

"Millerchip," said the voice.

Johnson replied, "Hello again, Professor Millerchip, it's Bill Johnson from the BFG. Unfortunately, our line was tapped when I phoned you earlier, so I'm calling from a public telephone box. Could you ask our American friends to provide the name of an expert or experts with whom we could negotiate? The President doesn't have the detailed knowledge to handle this on his own."

"I'll pass on your message," replied Prof Millerchip. "Although from what you say they've probably picked up this already!"

Johnson returned to Manor Towers and reported his latest telephone conversation. They were thoughtful for a few minutes, then Drakeford said, "I tend to feel the negotiations through Professor Millerchip are going nowhere. I suspect the Americans are just playing for time, hoping they'll find the President sooner or later. Charles, you have lots of military contacts, is there any way we can talk to someone in authority, maybe set up a direct communication?"

Charles responded: "I have a friend high-up in the US military. He doesn't have much time for Travis and would like to see this sorted. I'll make contact with him and see if something can be arranged, ideally in London, there are lots of possible venues there. I'll explain that the President would not be involved in these discussions, he'll understand."

"That would be brilliant. If you could manage that I would at least feel we were making progress," replied Drakeford enthusiastically.

CHAPTER 11

MISSING

Meanwhile, pressure was beginning to mount at the Greenham Common US Airforce base which had become the centre of operations in attempting to find the whereabouts of the President. A small team met, headed by General Howard Thomas.

He began on a sombre note. "There has clearly been a breach in security and our masters in the Pentagon are looking for someone to blame. Someone on this base has let it slip that the President was going to land here and even when he was going to move on. We have a spy and we know what happens to spies."

"To be fair, it was hardly a secret. Everyone on the base knew he was coming and we were all rushing around trying to make sure he would be impressed," responded Major Bill Sutherland. "And a lot of our guys have English girlfriends and even wives. It would be a fairly common topic of conversation, especially as not much else happens. We could interrogate a hundred people who have English connections, but they're not going to admit to having deliberately told anyone and may not even be aware that the leak occurred through them."

General Thomas thought for a moment. "I guess you have a point. So far we've worked on the basis that we're here in a friendly country, but just lately things have turned nasty. Now the natives are not so friendly. I think we should let everyone know we're looking for the culprit and will take action when we find who it is. At least it will tighten things up."

For the time being he wanted to draw a line under this and look at their next move.

"What do we know?" he began. "They've admitted they're holding the President, but we don't know where. Probably not far away, seeing as they asked for his suitcase to be delivered to Aylesbury. They've also made contact through a Professor Millerchip and we've managed to trace their calls to an office, also in Aylesbury, but we found no one there. We approached that rather clumsily through the local police, so I suspect they won't be going back there again. The sad fact is we have vastly superior economic and military power, but frankly we find ourselves in a humiliating position. I'm sure we'll get a good kicking once this is over, someone will have to pay the price, that's how these things work."

Major Bill Sutherland was the first to speak up. "Sooner or later they will make a mistake that will give away their names and where they're operating from. We can put a tail on this Drakeford feller and see who he speaks to."

"Yes, that's a start," replied Thomas. "The alternative is to continue checking out every possible location within a twenty-mile radius of Aylesbury, but that could take weeks."

"What's more, we don't know how much Aylesbury is involved, the President could be fifty miles away," replied Sutherland. "An alternative is to set a trap. Tracing phone calls hasn't worked so far, they're too smart for that, so what else can we try?"

The room was silent, no one wanted to look at Sutherland. Eventually he summed up: "For a start we'll step up the tail on Drakeford and the people he comes into contact with."

Officer Les Harvey came back with another suggestion: "Why not just try to speed things up? We've been playing for time in the hope they'll give in, or they'll make a mistake and we'll stumble on the President. Why don't we agree to negotiate and meet with them as soon as possible? If we get some clever negotiators involved, we may not need to give much away; after all, their main objective is to get the troops off the streets and get their government back in power. That means we get Travis back; after all, that's what Americans want, they don't really care about the numbers. At least when he's back with us we can salvage some credit."

"Might be seen as a climb down," replied Thomas, "but it's an interesting point. Meanwhile, can you all go away and think of some bright ideas. We'll reconvene tomorrow and see where we are."

* * *

Back at Manor Towers the reality of the situation was beginning to sink in. Under pressure and without his bodyguards, the President was proving to be less heroic than when he had previously appeared in public, especially as his captors made it clear that they were prepared to hold him indefinitely, however impractical that might be.

Charlotte had been bringing Travis his meals and looking after his welfare, so he naturally assumed she was a servant. After several visits he relaxed, enabling her to find out more about him and his entourage than he realised. They chatted each time she visited and he thought he could use his charm to find out exactly where he was being kept. Even more, assuming she was there to provide him with room service, he hoped he could use his charm, through her, to get a message to the outside world.

That evening she entered his room, explaining, "Here are your shirts, freshly laundered, I've come to clear your table of used crockery."

Travis was sat on the large sofa. "No need to run away, my dear, have a sit down and tell me about yourself."

She pretended to be a little embarrassed, but took the place he had indicated on the sofa.

"My name is Charlotte Joubert. My mother is French and came to England to teach French and German just after the Great War. My father is German and managed to get out of Germany after the war and came to England. Although he spoke no English he was an electrical engineer and so found it easy to get a job. He married my mother and I was born in 1920. I adopted my mother's name of Joubert as my father's name of Schmidt drew an adverse reaction in those early years. I grew up able to speak all three languages; sometimes we spoke all at the same time! Britain went to war with Germany in 1939 and a year or so later I offered my services as an interpreter."

"Did they not question your allegiance, since your father was German?" asked Travis.

"That wasn't a problem. My father had a Jewish mother and he hated everything that Hitler did to his country. He hasn't heard anything from his parents for over six years."

She gave nothing away, she felt she had said enough to keep him interested. What she said was absolutely true, but stopped short of explaining her true role in the war. As long as he regarded her as a servant, he was more likely to be relaxed. They chatted for a while and he began to boast about his past. He couldn't resist talking about his property business. "I've built a few New York skyscrapers and pulled off some clever deals," he said laughingly, "but when things got difficult I employed the best lawyers. They couldn't touch me."

"The newspapers had a lot to say when you were elected. Your reputation was not just limited to business," replied Charlotte, smiling.

He assumed she was referring to his private life and was only too pleased to expand on her question. "Yes, I've had a few affairs in my time. Women seem attracted to me," Travis declared. He placed his hand on her knee and continued: "Only last year I had an affair which I managed to conceal from my wife. But it does get more difficult when becoming President, everyone knows where you are, twenty-four hours a day; except being here of course!"

She could see he was eyeing her as another victim of his charm. She thought to herself, 'Does he think he's going to have his wicked way with me? He just assumes that he can have anything he wants.' She carefully removed his hand and explained, "You should be careful. You know what this place was used for, they could be bugging this place." She of course knew that the building had been used to interrogate captured Nazi leaders during the war, but was fairly confident that as the attic rooms were used to accommodate the British interrogators it was unlikely there would be a hidden microphone in this particular room. Nevertheless, she felt her comment had been sufficient to scare him, if only for now. She stood up and looked at her watch. "I'd better be getting back, my boyfriend will be sending out a search party."

She gathered up the tray of things she had come to collect. "Goodnight, Mr President, I'll see you in the morning," and promptly left the room and closed the door behind her.

Day 5

Next morning Drakeford had a knock at the door of his home. He opened the door and two large, well dressed men stood there, looking very serious. "I'm Detective Superintendent Clive James and this is Detective Chief Inspector Bob Lindsey. May we come in?"

"Of course," replied Drakeford and they followed him into the lounge.

Sup. James began, "We understand you're the spokesman for the British Freedom Group?"

Drakeford nodded.

"We've been informed that you have the President of the United States in your custody, against his will. If this is the case, we insist you tell us where he's being held."

"On what basis can you insist? Have I broken the law?"

"We could charge you with obstructing the police in the course of their duty."

"The President is a guest of the BFG. He's being well looked after. Since when have the Wiltshire Police been working for the United States?"

"Abducting a person is against the law in the UK, wherever the person's from."

"I should point out that I personally did not abduct the President, I wasn't present when he was invited to meet the BFG for talks, so I'm afraid I can't help you. You can lock me up if you wish, but it won't make any difference. He's actually taking part in high level negotiations as we speak. However, you can rest assured that his stay with us will be quite short, he'll probably be back enjoying the limelight in a few days' time, if not sooner."

The two detectives looked at one another. "You're clearly not prepared to cooperate, but rest assured, we will be back," said Sup. James. They climbed into their large black police car and drove off.

Drakeford's wife Christine had been looking on. "Well, that tells you a lot about the police. I suspect our phone's been tapped, or will be quite shortly."

"I guess they're only doing their job," replied Drakeford, "but I must let Bill know I've had a visit from the police, I'll try the radio." He made a couple of attempts, but had no response. Obviously Charlotte was somewhere else in the building and no one was near to the radio, or weren't sure how to work it.

"I'll go to my brother's place to make the call."

"Just make sure you're not followed, we have to be very careful from now on," she replied.

Drakeford got into his car and drove slowly through the village. He deliberately looped back on himself to check if he was being tracked by anyone. He spotted a Morris 10 a few hundred yards behind. As he turned onto the main road he could see in his mirror that the Morris 10 had also turned in his direction. About half a mile further on he pulled up outside the local post office, and quickly got out of the car and went inside. The Morris 10 carried on past. He bought a newspaper and got back in his car and continued on his way. He had hardly driven a few hundred yards when he came across the Morris 10 parked in a narrow lane with its nose facing the main road. Inevitably as he drove a little further, he spotted in his mirror the Morris 10 pulling out of the lane.

He thought to himself, 'Not very bright, these policemen!' He turned right at the next junction and returned home. As he got out of his car the Morris 10 came past and he gave a cheery wave. He had thought about trying to outpace them to continue on his way, a very real possibility due to his detailed knowledge of the local roads, but thought better of it. He waited for half an hour, drove to his brother's house, with no sign of any following car.

He explained to his brother George the purpose of his visit. "I've just been tailed by the police. I need to make a phone call, but can't risk my phone being tapped."

"Feel free," said George, "any time, it's all in a good cause."

Drakeford picked up the phone and got through to Bill Johnson. "I've had a visit from the police this morning, asking me to divulge the whereabouts of the President.

They went away empty handed, but promised to return. Then I started to drive to my brother's and I was clearly being followed, so I went back home. On the second attempt I think they'd given up. We have to be ultra-careful about where we make phone calls as I suspect they might be listening in. All the more reason to use the radio when calling from home. I think we've sorted it."

"Good thinking," replied Johnson. "However, as you're our spokesman you're probably more vulnerable than the rest of us. So far, they're not aware of the identities of the rest of us, although they probably have their suspicions. Once again it shows that the police are doing us no favours. To be fair I guess they see it as a simple case of kidnapping, which is against the law. Right now we're trying to set up a face-to-face meeting with the Americans, somewhere in London, and obviously you'll be taking the lead on our behalf. Major Brown is working on this right now. It could be a problem if we phone you, so perhaps give us a call later today on the radio and I'll update you."

"Ok, I'll try at 5 pm," he replied; "hopefully Charlotte can be on standby to work the radio."

* * *

Back at Greenham, General Thomas reconvened his group in an attempt to brainstorm some ideas. He began: "Well, gentlemen, we've had twenty-four hours to think about it, any progress?"

Major Sutherland replied, "I think the key to this is through Drakeford. He's a civilian, with no military training, so likely to be less suspicious of what might be going on around him. He's a popular figure in his village and probably trusts everyone. We could, going through the official channels of course, ask the local police to note any people Drakeford meets that they don't recognise."

"How are you going to do that, they don't even have a police station in the village?" asked Jim Dale, one of the officers.

"They probably have a local constable, living in a police house," replied Sutherland. "Let's ask the top cop in the area to have a word. He could insist the village cop does as he's told."

"We could also have someone pay the odd visit to the local pub, someone a little older than our average GI, dressed in ordinary civilian clothes and no obvious US Army haircut," said Dale, looking at Sutherland who was somewhat thin on top. "He could be reading an English newspaper."

"Sounds like a spy out of the movies!" countered Sutherland, "but it's an interesting thought."

Another officer, Les Harvey, a studious, quiet individual by American standards, said, "Let's go for a more technical approach. Could we strap a radio transmitter to the underside of Drakeford's car, then keep tabs on where he goes. We have to assume that at some stage he goes to speak to our President."

"Good idea," replied Thomas. "I'll speak to our technical guys to see if that's possible."

"And meanwhile we could actually try negotiating," said Harvey. "It could still prove faster than the other techniques."

Jim Dale felt obliged to add another comment. "Even if we find the place where the President is being held, what do we do then? Do we send in the marines with all guns blazing? If the President gets hit we could be in deep trouble. A more subtle approach, as suggested by Les, has some merit. If the President walks away unharmed, he'll probably take credit for having charmed his way out of captivity."

"That's a very valid point, we have to keep all options open," replied Thomas. "So, to sum up, we have good old fashioned surveillance, police feedback, a spy in the village pub and a radio tracking device. I guess that's more than we had yesterday. I'll report back to the Pentagon; at least it looks as if we're on the case and not standing around."

CHAPTER 12

THE DEAL

Despite his BFG activities Drakeford was still involved in his legal business, if somewhat restricted. He would regularly walk down to his village post box to beat the daily collection which was about four pm. This day was no exception, it was a gentle stroll of about three hundred yards and he looked forward to it for a breath of fresh air and light exercise. He had dropped off his mail and was on his way home. He turned the corner to see a large black car parked with the doors open, the engine still running and two men stood next to it peering at a map. Drakeford was aware that during the war years the government had issued advice telling people to be very careful when asked for directions by a stranger for fear of 'assisting an enemy agent'. Even signposts had been removed to frustrate an enemy invasion. However, things had now returned to normal and he had no cause to regard these men as suspicious and the threat of enemy agents was a thing of the past.

"We're lost, I'm afraid," said one of the men in a distinctive London accent, "could you tell us exactly where we are please?"

"Certainly," replied Drakeford, and moved to look at the map. Before he knew it the two men had bundled him into the back seat, slammed the doors and the car pulled away. The three of them were in the back seat, while the car was being driven by a woman, sat on her own in the front.

"What's going on, who the hell are you?" he asked.

"Just keep quiet, we'll tell you in due course," replied one of them, a significantly larger man than his colleague, and Drakeford detected an American accent. The car continued for what he judged to be about half an hour along roads he was less familiar with. They came to a built up area and after a few turns they came to a halt in a well established road with fairly large terraced houses. "Where are we?" Drakeford asked.

"Never mind, just get out of the car." They walked in the front door, through a hallway and into a back room. They gestured for him to sit down.

He could now see his captors more clearly. The American introduced himself, "I'm Brad, that's all you need to know. This is Victor and Joan. We're part of the Anglo-American Unification Campaign." He figured Victor and Joan were a married couple and this was probably their home, but the American was clearly in charge. They sounded English, although he could see some American pictures on the wall, together with a framed American flag. Brad was of average height and built like a gorilla.

"I've never heard of your organisation," replied Drakeford.

"Well, we've kept a low profile," said Brad. "However, we've had a new lease of life since Travis became President. Until now we'd been regarded as just another right-wing group, but now we could be nearer to what we've been working towards. We believe that Britain would be better off as part of the United States, possibly as a forty-ninth state."

"So, what do you want with me, I'm the last person you need to be talking to, I couldn't be more opposite to your cause," said Drakeford.

"On the contrary, we intend to exchange you for the President. We know you have him, we don't care where you're hiding him, that makes no difference."

"So where do we go from here?"

"You can give us a contact number, we'll do the rest."

"I don't happen to have a list of numbers in my pocket. I'd only slipped out to post a couple of letters. The best I can offer is to phone my wife. Do you have a telephone I could use?"

"No, we'll make the call, there's a phone in the hallway. Give me the number." Drakeford scribbled a number down on a scrap of paper and gave it to the American. Without hesitation Brad turned and said, "Ok, I'll speak to her, I'll try not to scare her too much."

He promptly disappeared and Drakeford was left with Victor and Joan. Joan went into the adjoining kitchen and returned with cups of tea. He quickly realised this was a somewhat amateurish setup as these people were hardly professional operators. He was tempted to use force to get away, since neither looked as if they would provide much resistance, although Brad was powerfully built. So far he had not seen any evidence of a firearm, but suspected Brad might have one somewhere.

On the assumption he had nothing to lose, Drakeford decided to engage Victor and Joan in conversation. "So why the enthusiasm for the USA? You're clearly not Americans yourselves."

"We lived in America for ten years, in Nashville." Victor replied. "We settled there because it was the centre of the country music scene. I was a furniture salesman and Joan a secretary with the same business. We were very happy there, as were our two children. We came back to England two years ago because of ailing parents, but our children were of an age when they could look after themselves, so decided to stay. We love the American lifestyle, particularly their music, and intend to go back there as soon as we can."

"I can understand that," replied Drakeford, "but why assume that everyone else will share your enthusiasm? The British will take some convincing."

"Our organisation aims to persuade them that they can have the best of both worlds. They don't know what they're missing. Have you ever been to America?"

"Just the once, I was part of Atlee's team to meet Travis at the White House. To be honest we were preoccupied with travel and meetings, surrounded by security guards. Not an ideal way to see a country. I would like to visit again under different circumstances."

A few minutes later Brad reappeared. "I've spoken to your wife. She had been concerned when you didn't come back, but refused to give me any other number, so we have no choice but to use her as an intermediary."

"So what are you going to do now?" asked Drakeford. "Am I staying here for the night or are you going to lock me up somewhere else?"

"I guess you'll have to sleep here. There's a spare room upstairs."

Joan rustled up some basic food for all four of them. They didn't have very much in common and Drakeford figured that they were so far off the scale that there was no point in trying to reason with them. They showed him the ground floor toilet, locked all the doors and then led him upstairs to a small bedroom. There was a bed with a few folded blankets, but little else. He hoped this wasn't going to be a long-term situation as this was clearly the extent of their hospitality.

"Once you've used the bathroom and settled down for the night, I'll fix the bedroom door so you can't get out without waking us. I don't think you'll want to escape through the bedroom window," suggested Brad.

'They clearly hadn't planned this very well,' thought Drakeford.

Back at the Drakeford residence Christine sat quietly to compose herself on receiving this unwelcome telephone call. On the one hand she was relieved to know that husband Rufus was alive and well, but concerned as to where this might lead. Initially she thought she should phone the police, but on reflection had doubts as to what the police could do without any details of his whereabouts. She decided that the priority was to pass on the news to the team at Manor Towers and started to dial the number, then realised she could be blowing their security if the line was being monitored, so replaced the handset. She then spotted the radio which Rufus had brought home and thought she would have a try, having watched him make contact. She went through the start-up routine and immediately Charlotte's voice answered. Having now proved the communication system was working, Charlotte had installed the radio on her desk where she could see the flashing lights on the base.

"Christine Drakeford here, I've just had a phone call from an American telling me that my husband's been kidnapped by an organisation called the Anglo-American Unification Campaign. He said they planned to hold him as a hostage to exchange him for the President. He wouldn't give me any other information and said he would be getting in touch again tomorrow."

"That's unbelievable," replied Charlotte. "I've never heard of them, but they must have a plan. I'll pass on the message to Bill. Thanks for using the radio, that was very quick thinking, and I'm impressed you managed to sort it."

"It was quite easy, having watched Rufus struggle! I'll be in touch again as soon as I hear from them."

Charlotte found Bill Johnson who was in the dining room. "Rufus Drakeford's wife has been on our two-way radio to say her husband's been kidnapped by an American group. They want to exchange him for the President. They'll make contact again tomorrow."

"Thanks," replied Johnson, "that's all we need. Still, nothing can happen until they make contact, they must have a plan."

Day 6
Next morning at Manor Towers Bill Johnson went to see the President.

"I'm afraid there's been a hitch. A group of right-wing nut-cases have kidnapped Lord Drakeford. They're trying to set up a deal to exchange you for him. They call themselves 'the Anglo-American Unification Campaign', I must confess I've never heard of them."

The President laughed. "I've never heard of them either. But sounds as if they could be doing me a big favour, I'm going crazy cooped up in here."

"Well, it's certainly held up our negotiations as Drakeford was our main man. We'll keep you posted. We'll continue with our plan, with or without Drakeford. We're making progress through an intermediary."

Meanwhile, back at Drakeford's temporary place of residence, he was allowed to emerge from his tiny bedroom and shown downstairs. He was provided with tea and toast by Joan, then sat quietly to prepare himself for a possibly boring day ahead. He could just make out a conversation in hushed tones being held in the kitchen, then Brad, who couldn't speak quietly for want of trying, said: "I'll make contact with the base. I'll get on the phone, but it might take some time to get hold of the right person."

As the three of them were engaged in conversation, Drakeford took the opportunity to look around. In the hallway he spotted the telephone and thought about phoning for help. He dismissed the idea, partly because his voice would attract attention and partly because he had no idea where he was anyway. He noticed the wires connecting the telephone disappeared behind a substantial cupboard, stood up against the wall. Without thinking through the implications he grabbed the wires and gave them a strong pull. He heard something crack and he replaced the loose wires in their original position. His instinct was that the more he could disrupt their plans the better, and disabling the telephone would certainly impair their progress.

He returned to his place on the sofa as Brad emerged from the kitchen. He turned to Victor and said, "Ok, I'll make that call now," and disappeared into the hall. He came back thirty seconds later, looking somewhat annoyed. "The damned phone's dead, must be a fault somewhere, typical of this backward country. I'll just have to use a call box. It's not ideal using a call box, so I'll need plenty of loose change." Victor and Joan duly obliged.

Off went Brad, while Drakeford settled himself down for a tiresome, if uncertain, day. He wondered whether Brad was going to phone Christine again, or someone else in their organisation; indeed did he know anyone else in their organisation? However, Brad had a loose piece of paper on which he had a list of names, numbers and telephone numbers, including the American Embassy. He decided to go for plan 'A', that was to phone Greenham Common on the basis that it was their people who had 'lost' the President and would be most anxious to get him back. To do this he had to go through an operator and feed the required fee into the machine. An American voice replied and Brad asked to speak to General Howard Thomas. Brad assumed because he had an American accent he wasn't challenged and was put straight through. He began: "Good morning General Thomas, I'm Brad Lomas representing the Anglo-American Unification Campaign. We have Lord Drakeford, the leader of the group holding the President. We would be happy to carry out a prisoner exchange for a small fee to boost our campaign funds, just for our trouble."

Thomas paused for a few seconds and responded, "Yes we are very interested if you can bring it about. What do you consider a small fee?"

"About a thousand dollars," replied Brad.

"That's a bit steep, but I'll discuss it with colleagues and get back to you."

Brad was surprised that his offer was not dismissed out of hand. Clearly they were desperate to go along with any scheme that might get the President back in their hands. "Whereabouts are you and how can I contact you?" said Thomas.

"I'm in St Albans, not that far away. Unfortunately the phone line's down where we're holding Drakeford, I'll have to ring you from a call box."

"Very well. When I've spoken to my team I'll give you an answer. Ring me again at three o'clock this afternoon."

Brad terminated the call and felt he had made progress, rather better than he had expected. Meanwhile, General Thomas wasted no time in going to see his most senior colleague, Major Bill Sutherland, just a few yards down the corridor. "I've just had this American guy on the phone, claiming he has Drakeford, the BFG leader, as a prisoner. He wants to exchange him for the President. And by the way, he wants a thousand dollars for his trouble."

"That's a turn-up," replied Sutherland. "I'm sure we could find him the money if it saves our skins. Let's keep him in the loop, we could do worse. However, I've been thinking. If we know Drakeford's not at home we could try speaking to his wife, suggesting that her husband's living dangerously and it's time to call it a day. She could use a bit of feminine persuasion to explain to him that he's out of his league. She may even give us a contact number to help things along."

"Good idea," said Thomas. "I think we have an address, let's go straightaway as we know Drakeford won't be at home. If that doesn't work we can be back here in time to speak to this Brad Lomas when he phones again at three." They grabbed their personal items and checked out the address of where to find the Drakefords' residence. Within minutes they were in their car and on their way.

* * *

Meanwhile, back at the house of Victor and Joan, Drakeford suddenly noticed that it had gone very quiet. He suspected Victor was in the bathroom, leaving Joan in sole charge. He thought, "This is my big chance to run for it. However, if I walk out the front door I might walk into Brad coming back." He decided to try the other option, so slipped on his jacket and walked into the kitchen where Joan was washing the dishes. "I need a breath of fresh air," he told her, "just thought I'd step into the back garden." Joan looked rather confused, but was helpless to stop him and assumed the garden was well fenced and therefore secure.

Drakeford opened the kitchen door and stepped into the garden, then closed the door behind him. He noticed a gate at the far end and walked briskly to test if it was open. He noticed a bolt at the bottom, presumably to prevent intruders getting in. He unbolted the gate and found himself in an alleyway which ran parallel to the row of houses. He ran down the alley and found himself in the adjoining street. He noticed a road sign which said Victoria Street, of which he made a mental note for future reference. He jogged a little, although his permanent limp meant he couldn't move as fast as he would want to. He was constantly on the lookout for Brad on his way back from the call box, or the car which had been used to bring him there, but so far no sign of either. He had no idea where he was or where he was going, just intent on putting as much distance as possible between him and his captors.

Back at Joan and Victor's house, Victor reappeared from his bathroom break. "Where's his Lordship?" he asked.

"He went into the back garden to get some fresh air," replied Joan.

"What? Didn't you watch him? How long ago?"

"No more than five minutes, maybe more. Surely he's still there?"

Victor rushed out of the door and into the back garden. There was no sign of their hostage. He checked around to see if he was hiding in the garden, but no sign. He went back inside and slammed the door shut behind him. At the same time Brad reappeared through the front door.

"Where's our man?" he shouted.

"He's escaped through the back garden. I was in the bathroom and obviously Joan wasn't able to stop him. You shouldn't have left him here with just the two of us, you should have had him tied up," protested Victor.

Brad was clearly annoyed, but realised there was no point in arguing. "We need to find him, quickly, he couldn't have gone far. Let's get in the car and drive around." With that the two men ran off and jumped into Victor's car. They drove around the nearby streets, trying methodically to encircle the house, moving further afield. They saw a few people, but no one that looked like Drakeford.

Meanwhile, Drakeford just kept walking until he reached a main road, constantly on the lookout for the black car. He hadn't seen enough of the car when he was abducted, he just knew it was fairly large and was black. Quite unexpectedly a bus came alongside, near to a stop to pickup passengers. "That's for me," he thought. "I don't care where it's going, but at least I'm safe on there." He was the fourth person to step on and sat on the first available seat where he was approached by the conductor. "Town centre, please," asked Drakeford. "You're going the wrong way, mate," replied the conductor. "Stick around and we reach the terminus in three stops' time, so then we'll be going back to the town centre." It was a few years since Drakeford had been on a bus, so he had no idea what fare to offer. "That will be nine pence, please," said the conductor. Drakeford dutifully paid and received a ticket from a noisy machine with a winding handle, attached to a strap hanging round the conductor's neck.

Looking at shop fronts he deduced he was in St Albans. The bus began to fill up as it approached the town centre. After about ten minutes the bus slowed and the conductor shouted, "Town Centre, all change." Off Drakeford stepped, still no sign of the black car. In fact, there were several cars, almost all of them were black, but no sign of the one he had travelled in. He looked around for a red telephone box. He spotted one, next to the police station. The police station was unmistakeable, a greyish brick-built building with a blue light sign outside, as if every British police station had been designed by the same architect. He made straight for the telephone box. After having hardly used a public telephone for years he was becoming quite proficient, having used one several times in the last few days. He rang his home number.

"Hi, it's me, I think I've escaped," he said as soon as Christine picked up the phone. "I'm in St Albans, next to the police station. Could someone come and pick me up?"

"I'll get onto Bill. If he can't find someone I'll do it myself," she replied.

Drakeford reckoned it would be at least half an hour before he could be picked up. He decided the best thing was to loiter close to the police station. If the ominous black car appeared he would run into the police station as no one was going to try and molest him there. He sat patiently on the low wall where he could watch the passing traffic. After some time a policeman approached him: "Waiting to see a policeman?" he asked cheerfully. "You could wait inside if you've got something to report."

"No, but thank you for asking," he replied. "I'm waiting for a friend to pick me up and as we're both strangers here I thought the police station would be a good meeting point."

"A sensible idea. At least you should be fairly safe outside the police station," joked the policemen.

About twenty minutes later he spotted Major Brown in his grey Rover drawing up alongside. "Good morning," Drakeford exclaimed as he jumped into the passenger seat. "Am I glad to see you!" The car pulled away. Drakeford thought he saw the black car coming the other way, but admitted to himself that he was probably becoming paranoid about any large black car with two men sat in the front.

"Why did they let you go?" asked Brown.

"Actually, I escaped. They were quite disorganised, quite amateurish. I suspect they were hoping to extract a fee from the local US base in return for handing me over."

"Nevertheless, it's something we hadn't thought of," Brown responded. "We can protect ourselves, but it doesn't rule out the possibility of hostage-taking by a bunch of real professionals. The Americans could deny all knowledge, of course, but it could happen and there's not much we can do about it. All the more reason to get this project done as soon as possible."

He drove carefully, backtracking the route he had taken out of St Albans. "It will take about half an hour to get back to your place, so I suggest you go and see your wife to put her mind at rest. I'll drop you off, then I must get back to Manor Towers."

Meanwhile, back at the Drakeford residence, Christine was feeling somewhat relieved following her husband's phone call and had just settled down to catch up with some of her research work when the doorbell rang. She realised it was much too soon for her husband to have returned and anyway, he had his own key. She opened the door to be confronted by two large gentlemen in US Air force uniforms. "Mrs Drakeford?" enquired Thomas.

"Actually it's officially Lady Drakeford, but I wouldn't expect you to know that," she answered impatiently. She felt instantly that they were trying to intimidate her and was determined to maintain her composure.

"My apologies, Lady Drakeford. I'm General Howard Thomas and this is Major Bill Sutherland. Is your husband at home?" he asked.

"No, he's away on business, I'm not sure when he'll be back." She felt a little uneasy, being confronted by these unexpected visitors, and didn't feel inclined to be too helpful.

"May we come in and have a little chat?"

"Yes, I suppose so, but I don't know if I can help you if it's my husband you want to speak to." She turned and indicated that they should follow and with a hand gesture offered them a seat in the lounge. Her mind was buzzing and she felt she needed to play for time to get her thoughts clear. "Can I get you tea or coffee?" she asked.

"Yes please, we rather like your English tea, much better than we get in the States."

Christine retreated to the kitchen, filled the kettle and placed it on the stove. As she laid out the teapot and cups she stared at the wall, deep in thought. Why are they here? Do they know more than they're letting on? Do they take me for a docile wife, unaware of my husband's activities? The kettle boiled and she filled the teapot, placed everything on a tray, and carried it into the lounge.

"You have a beautiful home," said Bill Sutherland, "typically English, you must be very proud."

"Yes, we feel very lucky to be living here, it's a beautiful setting and the house is probably approaching two hundred years old." She poured the tea and then waited for them to make the next move.

General Thomas began: "I'm sure you're aware of your husband's involvement with this BFG organisation?"

"Yes, of course."

"I'm sure you know that his group claim to have taken our President. Do you realise Mister, sorry Lord Drakeford, could be in great danger? If nothing else it's against the law to kidnap someone and for that he could end up in prison. And if anything was to happen to the President while he was in your custody the outcome would be catastrophic. That must concern you, surely?"

"Yes, of course we've discussed it. After all, he is a lawyer. We just felt we couldn't stand by and let the Americans walk all over us. We wanted to open a dialogue, but we were met with total rejection. At least now someone has to listen."

"We understand that, we've been in contact with the White House and we've now changed our position, we're prepared to negotiate."

"Well, I'm pleased to hear that. So did you come here expecting that we had your President locked up in our guest bedroom?"

"No," laughed Thomas, "but it would help if you gave us the name or a contact number of someone who could set up a meeting."

Christine thought quickly. The crafty devils think I'm going to give them someone's telephone number so they can track them down and blow the whole operation. She thought it was time to fight back. "I don't have that information and I wouldn't give it to you if I had. I think you know where my husband is and you came here, thinking I could be easily persuaded before my husband gets back."

"No, that's not the case," responded Thomas, somewhat embarrassed to be found out.

There was a stunned silence which was suddenly broken by the sound of a key turning in the front door. Christine sprang to her feet to meet her husband as he opened the door. They hugged briefly before she said: "You've got visitors." He followed her into the lounge to be met by the two large gentlemen in US military uniforms. They both stood and offered their hands to greet him.

"Hello Lord Drakeford, this is Major Bill Sutherland and I'm General Howard Thomas." They were clearly confused as they assumed he was still in the custody of the group headed by Brad Lomas in St Albans. They were curious as to how he had arrived home unexpectedly, but trying not to admit that they knew where he was all along, or so they thought. His appearance was definitely not that of a man returning from a business meeting and he was not even carrying a briefcase, dressed as he was the previous day when walking to the post box.

"We came here on the off chance that you may be at home, but instead have had an interesting conversation with your wife. I'm sure she's relieved to see you."

"Yes, I was the unexpected guest of some people in St Albans, although I'm not sure if guest is the right word. I think they wanted to use me as a pawn in some deal."

"May we ask what was their motive? Presumably, they approached you as the leader of your freedom group, wanting to do a deal?"

"Yes, they called themselves the Anglo-American Unification Campaign, if I've remembered it correctly. They assumed I knew where the President was and that they could exchange me for him. I think they wanted to make some money at the same time. However, they weren't very competent and when their leader, a big American guy, went out to make a phone call, I escaped. I hadn't realised until that point I was in St Albans."

"That was a fairly clever idea, it might have worked," responded Sutherland. "In a sense, we're here for much the same reason. We want to know what you've done with our President. We think you've made your point, it's time to get serious. I don't think you realise what the implications might be."

"I'm aware of all that," replied Drakeford. "But we felt something constructive needed to happen. The protests were getting bigger and more violent, and no one was listening. As you know, we've been communicating through an intermediary to try and arrange talks to achieve a political solution, but that doesn't seem to be getting anywhere. Meanwhile, you Americans have tried every trick in the book to catch us out. Frankly, we just don't trust the Americans to make a deal."

"You realise we could take you into custody at any time. We could even make you just disappear."

"What would that achieve? You could take half a dozen of us, if you could find us that is. At the moment only rumours circulate about the President's situation. If you sabotage our efforts we'll make damn sure that everyone knows about it and we'll tell them how a bunch of British part-timers managed to snatch the American President in broad daylight. That would be very embarrassing for the American news media to report. I'm sure heads would roll at all levels."

"So you're not prepared to cooperate," replied an annoyed Howard Thomas.

"Yes, we'll cooperate, but on our terms. We're not going to be bullied. You've come here offering absolutely nothing, apart from threatening to arrest or kidnap me. We realise the President can't make decisions in isolation, so we want to sit around the table and have a rational discussion. That's what we've been calling for all along. But we're not prepared to be another state, or be manipulated from Washington. Most of all, we want our democratically elected government to be back in control and to get your GIs out of our country. You can threaten all you like, but we have Travis and will keep him for as long as it takes. Right now he's in a comfortable place, well fed and watered, but we'll hide him in a barn if necessary."

These high-ranking officers were not accustomed to dealing with non-military people, and negotiating was not one of their skills. "I'm disappointed with your attitude," countered Thomas. "You'll live to regret this. We were hoping that we might make you see sense, once we had explained the seriousness of the situation."

"You mean you had come to threaten me, even scare me," replied Drakeford. "Just let us get around the table with the right people to sort something out. I'm quite serious about going public with the facts and causing maximum embarrassment. If we were to deliver the President into the middle of a group of protestors he'd be lucky to escape with his life. Believe me, there are plenty of people who would cheerfully empty a rifle in his direction."

The Americans didn't respond, pretending it was all a bluff and Drakeford couldn't be that serious. Nevertheless, it was clear that their attitude was beginning to change. Initially they had not been unduly concerned that their President was being held somewhere in England, they were confident that he would soon be found. It was only a matter of time, and Travis would be able to resume his plans to remodel Britain on USA lines. But now they were no nearer to discovering their President's whereabouts and they began to suspect that the British authorities were in no great hurry to assist. Clearly the President's captors had kept themselves in a small, close-knit group so as few people as possible knew the location.

Drakeford was enjoying seeing these top-rated military men squirm, so decided to step it up a level and continued with his theme of going public. "We could end his presidency by exposing him to the American public, he would have no credibility in the USA. You would be surprised at what's been suggested. For instance, he has a reputation with the ladies, so one idea was to use the old spy's trick, I believe they call it 'the honey trap', that is to have a lady of ill repute visit him and then photograph him in an uncompromising position. He wouldn't be able to resist such an opportunity. The media, to say nothing of his wife, would make a lot of that. Of course we wouldn't want to do that, but our patience has limits and it would be quite easy to arrange."

"You wouldn't dare," Thomas retorted, but not entirely convinced. "We've heard enough, so we'll report back to higher authority, probably the VP's office in the States.

We fully intend to get tough, we're not going to take this lying down."

"Well, your media is doing the job for us, you've obviously not seen the article in Tuesday's New York Post," replied Drakeford.

The two Americans looked confused. They clearly weren't aware of the article and not interested in any explanation. They stood impatiently and left the room, barely acknowledging their hosts and walked briskly to their car which had been parked around the corner. "That didn't go as we'd hoped, I guess Brad won't be phoning us this afternoon," mumbled General Thomas. "I think our heads are on the line, we need to sort something out." They got back into their car and sped off, quite understandably, on the wrong side of the road.

Once he was satisfied that the Americans had gone, Drakeford was on his way to take a bath and change his clothes when his wife handed him another parcel. "This came for you this morning," she explained. Again, he recognised the writing on the label.

The note read: *Here are a few more papers that a colleague picked up in New York. The Bletchley Park story is certainly gathering momentum. Cheers, Jim.*

Drakeford thought very briefly. "I'll get washed and changed, perhaps have a bite to eat, then I'd better catch up with things at HQ." He dumped the papers on the dining room table and headed for the bathroom. Suitably refreshed, he then decided to fire up the radio to inform everyone that he was safe and report that they'd had a visit from the Americans.

Charlotte replied: "Charles has just arrived. I'm sure the last thing you wanted was to have unwanted American visitors. You've had an eventful twenty-four hours, I'll pass on your news, but probably not worth coming over here now, we'll see you tomorrow."

CHAPTER 13

A VISIT FROM THE POLICE

Major Brown returned to the headquarters and parked his car undercover where it couldn't be seen from above. It was around three pm and all was quiet at Manor Towers when suddenly the bell rang in reception. Harry Mitchell was the man on the desk where he was reading a newspaper. He jumped up in surprise as he was not expecting visitors. He peered out of the window and could see two men, one in police uniform, stood there at the main gates.

At Manor Towers the main gates were kept padlocked, but there was a large bell-push beside the main gate, connected to the reception. There was also a telephone installed in a wooden box attached to the gate post, with a hinged door, obviously left there by the wartime interrogation team. The gates were around fifty yards from the main house, so anyone waiting there could be seen easily from a window next to reception.

He used the internal telephone to ring the phone at the gate. Once they had discovered the source of the ringing they opened the door of the telephone box and picked up the receiver. "This is Police Sergeant Dixon here. We believe a crime has been committed in this area and we would like to inspect your premises."

Harry Mitchell replied: "There's been no crime here. What authority do you have?"

"I have a warrant signed by a magistrate," replied Dixon.

"Ok, I'll come down to unlock the gate."

Harry Mitchell replaced the telephone receiver and immediately moved into emergency mode. He used the internal telephone to alert Bill Johnson. "Bill, we've got the police at the main gate. They want to inspect the premises as they believe a crime has been committed."

Bill was quick to respond. "Ok, we'll have to let them in, else they'll suspect something. Take a slow walk down to the gate with the key and I'll put the team on red alert. Clearly, they're not local police else they would have gone to the tradesmen's entrance."

Everyone had been briefed in case something like this was going to happen and a procedure had been rehearsed. There was an alarm system installed from the time when Nazi prisoners were detained there and a bell push under the counter in reception activated a buzzer in practically every room in the building. Harry pressed the button three times, the signal for operation 'Hideaway' to be activated. Everyone knew they had to appear busy with the restoration work. The guards in the outbuilding moved quickly, the three-man team generally known as Tom, Dick and Harry since those names applied to two of them, pulled on their orange boiler suits and took up working positions in the main building.

Meanwhile, Sergeant George Morgan, the chief guard, together with Charlotte, ran up the stairs to Travis's room. They burst in, Charlotte ordering the President to put his book down. "Stand up, get your jacket on, we have to vacate this room quickly, we've got unwelcome visitors. Follow me please."

She beckoned him to follow her. He normally wouldn't have taken orders from anyone, but he dutifully followed her; in fact he would probably have followed Charlotte anywhere. Sergeant Morgan unlocked the door to the fire escape at the rear of the building. Charlotte led the way. "Are you sure this steelwork is safe?" asked Travis, quite bewildered by this sudden burst of action.

"Yes, we checked it before you arrived. Just needs a lick of paint," replied Morgan as he slammed the door behind him. The three descended carefully, Charlotte leading the way, followed by Travis, with Morgan bringing up the rear. Travis was suddenly aware that Charlotte had transformed from a simple servant girl to a confident woman of action. Within a few minutes they were at ground level at the rear of the building, then crossed the lawn to an outhouse containing lawn mowers and hedge trimming equipment.

"So, who are we hiding from?" asked Travis.

"We're not sure," replied Sergeant Morgan. "You heard the buzzer sounding, that is an alarm system to warn everyone that we have unexpected visitors. We have a well rehearsed plan where everyone just responds, we don't ask questions, we'll find out later. It could be the US Army or even some opportunist criminals, who knows? Just in case there might be bullets flying around we thought it safer to remove you for the time being. We'll stay here until Major Brown tells us it's ok to go back inside."

Emerging from the front entrance Harry Mitchell walked steadily down to the gate and unlocked the padlock which was attached to a hefty chain securing the pair of wrought iron gates.

"Good afternoon," said Mitchell, trying to appear casual and unruffled. "Please follow me and I'll introduce you to Mr Johnson, the man in charge of the operation."

"What operation is that?" asked Sergeant Dixon.

"It's a restoration project, Mr Johnson will explain."

They arrived at the main entrance and Bill Johnson was waiting. "Good afternoon, I'm Bill Johnson. How can I help?"

"I'm Sergeant Dixon and this is Detective Thomas Baldwin. We're visiting places like this to carry out an inspection. We believe a crime has been committed and we're looking for evidence."

"Well, I can assure you that you won't find any gold bullion hidden away or even escaped convicts for that matter!"

Dixon was not amused. "So what do you do here? Is it so secret that you have to keep the main gates padlocked?"

"We still have some valuable equipment here. During the war this place was requisitioned by the War Department and used to lock up high ranking German prisoners for interrogation. We're stripping out the equipment used by the secret service so the building can be returned to its owner and restored as a country hotel. The army prefer to keep their use of this place secret, as if it never happened. I assume you have the appropriate authority to enter the premises – you appreciate there could be a security issue here?"

"We have a warrant to search the premises of the Parkland Hotel," replied Dixon. "We would like a conducted tour, it shouldn't take long."

"That's fine," said Johnson. "Let's start with the cellar and we'll work our way up."

At this point Major Brown appeared. "Let me introduce Major Charles Brown," said Johnson. "He's representing the army's interest in this operation, making sure all their equipment is carefully extracted."

The group of four comprising Johnson, Brown and the two policemen started on their tour, descending the stairs down into the cellar. There were WD boxes in the well illuminated cellar confirming Johnson's description of the wartime operation. The policemen could see there was nothing concealed in the cellar and they followed Major Brown back to the stairs. Susan Watson was waiting at the top, holding some official papers and engaged Major Brown in quiet conversation, as if asking his advice. In reality she was just delaying their emergence from the cellar until she received the signal that the three descending the fire escape had made ground level and were about to reach the comparative safety of an outhouse.

The officers checked the ground floor with its spacious dining room and a large kitchen where two ladies were busily preparing food. Leading off the reception was the office, large enough for four people, where Susan Watson was now back hard at work. As they moved around from floor to floor there was military equipment in evidence, together with materials for redecoration, confirming Johnson's cover story. On each floor some of the doors were locked and Johnson readily unlocked them, revealing more equipment, or bedrooms occupied by the team working on the project. Eventually they reached the top floor where their prestigious guest had been staying.

"This is a better room than all the rest," commented Dixon. "I'll bet this is your room," he said. Johnson didn't answer, but smiled and shrugged his shoulders, as if he's been rumbled. Baldwin said very little, but looked around the room. He spotted some of the newspapers left on the table, one of them the New York Post, together with an open book. He made no comment, but raised his eyebrows, a little surprised. Their inspection complete they turned and walked back onto the landing and Johnson closed the door behind him.

Back down in reception Johnson addressed the policemen. "I think you've seen all the rooms. Is there anywhere else you would like to see?" He was aware that Baldwin had hardly said a word and he just shook his head.

"I think we've seen enough," replied Dixon. "Thanks for showing us round. It will make a fine hotel once your work's complete. When will that be?"

"It depends on the owner, but probably a couple of months at the earliest. Harry will take you back to the gates and lock up again; we have to observe strict security procedures," explained Johnson.

Harry escorted his visitors back to the gated entrance and locked up. He was very relieved to see the police car driving away. He acted casually as he walked back, wanting to dance and skip, but managed to contain himself.

Once satisfied they had departed, Major Brown went over to the outhouse to let everyone know they could return. They crossed the yard, entered the door at the rear of the building and Charlotte led Travis back up the main staircase to his attic apartment. "Fortunately, we don't need to return via the fire escape," she commented.

He sat down again and continued reading the book he had left open before the interruption, a book about American history. Charlotte glanced out of the window which had an excellent view of the main gates. "Just as well Travis didn't look out there, he might not have been so cooperative had he seen the police car," she thought to herself.

"I'll be back later with your evening meal," she said cheerily and promptly left the room, reverting back to servant mode.

Everyone was feeling elated as the plan had worked, at least for now. Johnson explained to the group who had assembled in reception. "We're ok for now. Just as well they didn't look in the yard at the back, they might have spotted the Bedford van and put two and two together. Charlotte and George, you both did brilliantly, your timing was absolutely perfect. Luckily, they didn't ask to look outside, they probably didn't realise that we had outhouses, else we could have had a problem, but I don't think Dixon suspected anything. However, the detective spotted the American newspapers and may have put two and two together. I recognised him from my time in Military Intelligence and he may have recognised me. Once they've filed their report someone's going to realise it's not what it appears to be. Hopefully if they check with the army no one will have a clue what's going on, they'll just close ranks because they can't admit they don't know."

Major Brown responded, "My concern is what triggered their enquiry in the first place? Have they been tipped off by someone? I don't think we have a spy in the camp, but someone might have let something slip about this place, unintentionally. Maybe the Auster surveillance aircraft triggered something? Perhaps they assumed the place was empty and it raised suspicions when someone appeared to see what the fuss was about."

"I agree," replied Johnson. "They've probably guessed we would be using an isolated place in the country, although there are dozens of possibilities. Are they going to check them all?"

"Maybe they've started nearest to London and are working outwards. I suspect our use of Aylesbury gave them a clue as to direction. Let's hope this business is done and dusted before we get another visit. Next time they'll probably come mob-handed, possibly assisted by the US army."

After a few seconds' thought, Johnson responded. "I think that's a very real possibility. They might realise it's a perfect location, and as you say, confirmed by the Auster visit. The more I think about it the more I'm convinced Detective Baldwin will make the connection. If they come back, as you suggest, it's all over. We'll finish up behind bars! The only solution may be to carry on as we are, but remove the President, if only temporarily. They can carry out a full inspection, but without the President they can't touch us, we have the owner's permission to be here."

Charles Brown, as practical as ever, responded with a plan. "I have a friend with a farm, about twenty miles away. I'm sure he will help; after all, where do you think the tractor came from that we used for the roadblock? If we take Travis there, escorted by a few of our guys, they could lie low for a day or two. If we get raided here and they find nothing, then we can bring them back. Or we just keep him there until we make progress on the diplomatic front. Shall I make the phone call?"

"Brilliant," said Johnson, "yes, please speak to your friend."

With that Major Brown disappeared for a few minutes. He returned, looking confident. "All set, they have an upstairs bedroom. Our guys can take their own kit with them and sleep where they can. I'll organise the troops and we can move within the hour. Can you get Travis packed and ready?"

"I'll go and speak to him straightaway," replied Johnson.

With that everyone dispersed and went back to their jobs.

CHAPTER 14

A PRESIDENTIAL HOLIDAY

Johnson went upstairs to speak to Travis. "Change of plan," he announced. "Can you pack your kit; we're going to have to move you. We think the secret service people may have guessed where you are, so we need to take precautions. If we get raided there will be some resistance and we don't want anything to happen to you. At this stage we don't know if we'll be coming back here."

"Do I have a choice?" responded Travis.

"Frankly, no, but it won't be any less comfortable. And I guarantee the food will be better! I'll be back in ten minutes."

Downstairs Charles went to organise his men for this assignment, led by Sergeant Morgan. They responded enthusiastically, having spent the previous three days playing cards, apart from their part in operation 'Hideaway'. They packed in double quick time and waited by the side entrance, carrying their rifles. A few minutes later Johnson appeared with Travis, carrying Travis's suitcase.

"I'm afraid it's the luxury of the Bedford van again," Charles announced as they clambered aboard, apart from Bill Johnson. Charles took over the driving as he was the only one who knew where they were going. The van took off gently down the lane, then turned onto the main road and headed toward High Wycombe. Everyone was silent, understandably so, as the soldiers and the US President had very little in common. After about forty minutes, Charles took a side turn and made his way through country lanes and came to rest in a farmyard.

"This is it, guys, everybody out," announced Charles. "They're expecting us, I'll go and let them know we've arrived." He disappeared for a couple of minutes and returned with a large middle aged gentleman by his side. "This is Bill Jackson, he owns this farm, as did his father and his father before him."

"Pleased to meet you," said Travis as he shook Bill Jackson by the hand.

"Pleased to meet you too," responded Jackson, "I've never met an American President before, it's quite an unexpected honour."

The group entered the farmhouse where Mrs Jackson was preparing food in the kitchen. "Meet my wife, Lizzie," said Bill Jackson enthusiastically.

"I'm just preparing an evening meal," she announced. "How many guests do we have?"

"There will be just the four, plus the President," replied Charles. "I'll be heading back to our HQ. If there's any problem, just contact me by telephone; so far your line's not been tapped." He scribbled down the Manor Towers number on a scrap of paper."

Bill Jackson turned to the President. "Let me show you to your room, follow me, I'm afraid the stairs are a bit steep and narrow, but this farmhouse is at least two hundred years old."

Travis followed on dutifully, this time carrying his own suitcase. They arrived on the spacious upstairs landing and Jackson turned to his right and opened the door of his spare bedroom. "Maybe a little smaller than you're used to? But I think you will find it comfortable." He then showed him the door opposite. "This is the bathroom. I'm afraid you will have to share with us, we don't have any spare bathrooms."

"That's fine," Travis replied. "I've stayed with friends on a few ranches in my time, some of them can be quite primitive!"

"I'll let you unpack. When you're ready come and join us. As we have our own farm we're able to bypass some of the rationing restrictions, so we eat well most of the time."

"Thanks," responded the President, "I'll be down soon." For a brief moment Travis was beginning to convince himself that this was a holiday venture, until he remembered the four large ex-commandoes downstairs were there to make sure he couldn't escape.

Charles felt everything was as good as it could be. "Thanks," he said to Bill and Lizzie. "I really appreciate this. I just hope they don't eat you out of house and home!"

"No fear of that, we're well stocked. It's quite an unexpected experience for us; they can stay as long as they want," replied Bill.

"I'll be in touch tomorrow morning," shouted Charles as he climbed into the Bedford van. The engine sprang into life and off he drove back to Manor Towers.

With Bill Jackson's cooperation the four guards spread themselves around the rambling farmhouse and placed their equipment, including sleeping bags, on the floors, including the landing outside Travis's room. One of the luckiest of the four made the lounge his chosen billet where there was a large settee. They were careful to retain possession of their rifles; the last thing they wanted was for Travis to pick up a rifle and hold everyone at gunpoint.

A little while later Lizzie called everyone together as she was ready to serve an evening meal. All seven people sat down around the large kitchen table. She produced a dinner consisting of roast pork and fresh vegetables.

Bill was anxious that everyone should relax – they were where they were and may as well communicate on the same level, at least until Charles returned with further orders. He was first to break the uneasy silence. "Well, when I got up this morning at five o'clock to milk the cows I never expected we would be having the American President here for dinner this evening!"

Lizzie was quick to add her comments, "I quite agree. Life on a farm can be quite mundane sometimes."

"I think I'm as surprised as you," declared Travis. "This is definitely the best meal I've had for a week, possibly several weeks. I must send our White House chef over for some lessons!" He then turned to the four military men, probably in their early twenties, as they sat there looking rather awkward at finding themselves in a quite unexpected setting. "Why don't you introduce yourselves?"

The most senior of the four was first: "I'm Sergeant Morgan," he said in a very formal manner.

"No, to hell with the ranks and all that," interrupted Travis. "Just relax, none of us are going anywhere, I need to know what to call you."

Each gave his first name. "I'm George," said the Sergeant. "And I'm Tommy," said the next. The other two responded similarly. "I'm Dick." The last one was a little more friendly, "I'm Mike. You thought I was going to say Harry!" Everyone laughed.

Bill explained a little more about farm life. "We've run things down to a level we can manage. Hopefully as people get demobbed we can recruit some extra help to look after the land and more animals. We have two sons in the navy, still out in the Far East. Hopefully they'll be home soon, although we have doubts whether they will want to stay in farming."

"I think we will have the same problem," replied Travis. "As our guys return home the money in the factories will be so much better."

"Same here," agreed George Morgan. "All four of us are technically on leave. We're about to be demobbed in a matter of a week or two, we're waiting to be told. We're doing this as a favour to Major Brown, he was our leader in the D-Day landings and the fight through France and Germany. He was amazing, we'd do anything he asked."

"That's loyalty," declared Travis. "I admire you for that. I must admit he made a good impression on me within minutes of our first encounter, even if the circumstances were not as I would have wanted. He's very decisive, clearly knows what he's doing."

They finished their meal and chatted for some time, the atmosphere clearly less tense than when they first sat down. As if from nowhere, Mike produced a pack of cards. To everyone's surprise Travis needed no invitation. "Can I join in?" he asked.

"Sure," said Mike. "We don't always play for money as we don't have that much. Sometimes we just play for pennies or even play for matchsticks."

With that three soldiers and Travis became embroiled in a card game, as if they'd been buddies for years. Morgan kept a safe distance, keeping an eye on proceedings while checking the surroundings, probably quite unnecessarily, but it just came natural to him. After all, you are actually responsible for the President of the United States, he told himself.

Mr and Mrs Jackson read for a little while, then at around nine pm stood up and declared, "We're off to bed, we have to be up very early in the morning, the cows will be expecting us. Please stay up as long as you like, it won't affect us."

Off they went and the others played cards until around ten when they decided to call it a day and organise themselves into their apportioned sleeping places. While being superficially relaxed with Travis, they were nevertheless keeping him under close observation. There was no way he could escape, although he seemed quite content with his new accommodation.

Meanwhile, Bill Johnson's nose for trouble was absolutely correct. No sooner had Sergeant Dixon and Thomas Baldwin returned to their car when Baldwin said, "Something's not what it appears to be back there. There was an American newspaper in the large room on the top floor and a book left open. I couldn't catch the title, but it appeared to be about American history. I also recognised that guy Johnson from wartime service – why would he be there supervising a refurbishment exercise? I think we should take a second look, this time with reinforcements."

"You were very observant," replied Dixon. "We'll go straight back to the station and telephone the authorities."

Back at the police station they were shown to a back room where Baldwin could make a private telephone conversation. He was given the number of the Greenham Common USA airbase and the name of Major Bill Sutherland. He picked up the phone and asked the operator to be connected. After a short delay he was put through and Major Sutherland answered.

Baldwin began: "Good afternoon, this is Detective Thomas Baldwin, formerly of the Home Office. We've just carried out an inspection of a large mansion, formerly a hotel. It was called Parkland Hotel. I noticed in one of the rooms there was an American newspaper spread out and a book about American history. I also noticed that the man in charge was someone I recognised from my military service and he just didn't fit their cover story."

"But did you actually see the President?" asked Sutherland.

"No, but they could have been hiding him away. They had plenty of notice after we arrived. He could even have been in an outhouse or somewhere."

Sutherland responded enthusiastically, "It's the best lead we've had so far. We'll take a look, I'll organise some of our military police." He opened up a well-thumbed map and asked Baldwin. "I have a map in front of me, quite detailed with a scale of one inch to the mile. Could you give me some idea of where this place is?"

Baldwin, working from memory, tried to picture the map. He said, "If you can find Henley-on-Thames, then about five miles to the southeast you should find the Parkland Hotel."

Sutherland pondered for a while as he scanned the map. After a minute or two of total silence he exclaimed, "Yes, I've found it, more or less exactly where you said."

"Well, it was the best I could do without a map in front of me," replied Baldwin. "At least you have it now, the rest is up to you."

"Excellent," responded Sutherland. "We'll arrive there first thing tomorrow, unannounced of course. Thank you, Thomas, good work."

CHAPTER 15

UNWELCOME VISITORS

Day 7

E arly next morning all was quiet at Manor Towers when suddenly a loud clanking noise was heard outside, near the main gates. Always on the alert, Major Brown looked out of the window to see a large group of people at the main gate. He made two quick presses on the alarm button below the main reception desk to alert everyone in the building. A policeman had an enormous pair of bolt cutters which had just severed the chain securing the gates. About a dozen men in military uniforms and helmets, carrying rifles, spread quickly around the grounds surrounding the house. A further dozen armed men marched up to the front door, ready to do whatever necessary to gain entrance. Just as they reached the steps leading up to the door, the door opened and Major Brown stood there, looking surprised.

"Good morning, you didn't need to break our gates to get in, you only need to have asked," he said.

"We need to make a full inspection," replied the leader of the group. Major Brown did not recognise their combat gear as being anything he had worn when on active service, so assumed they must be American.

"Do we have any choice? You haven't even introduced yourself. We had a visit only yesterday by a Sergeant Dixon. What are you looking for?"

There was no reply. Clearly this boarding party hadn't come prepared to make conversation, having expected to make a forced entry. They just pushed past and spread through the building. Clearly their priority was the top floor which had been occupied by Travis. This time they left nothing to chance, they opened every door, checked under beds, inside cupboards. There was also a trap door in the ceiling leading to a large loft space. One soldier lifted up his colleague who then stood on his shoulders to displace the trap door. Another handed up a torch. After a few minutes the man dropped down from the loft, shaking his head and cursing under his breath.

They insisted on seeing every room as well as the cellar. Charlotte had used the radio to make sure Drakeford was not likely to appear. She had just switched off as three hefty soldiers appeared in the office doorway. They were taken by surprise when confronted by an attractive young female, not what they were expecting. Down in the kitchen the ladies were preparing breakfast, the smell of food providing a further distraction.

Brown broke the silence. "We told Sergeant Dixon yesterday that this was previously a hotel, then used as a secret wartime interrogation centre. Our job here is to decommission the building so it can be returned to the owner. Would you like me to give you the owner's details so you can speak to him yourself?"

"No need," said the group leader. Clearly conversation was not his strong point. His team left via the front door and called for his men checking the grounds to gather round. "All clear? Anything suspicious?" he asked. There was just a general shaking of heads and low level muttering.

"Are you going to make good the damage to the main gate?" shouted Major Brown.

There was no answer; the team marched back down to the main gate, clambered aboard through the back of their khaki truck and drove away. They ignored the policeman with his bolt cutters and he got back into his police car, did a U-turn and followed on. The chain and padlock were left on the floor, discarded.

Major Brown went back inside where Bill Johnson was waiting.

"Charles, I think we might have got away with it," exclaimed Johnson. "Your move to the farm was an inspired decision, and just as well we didn't wait until today."

"Yes, just in time," responded Major Brown. "Equally this wouldn't have happened if you hadn't spotted the ex-secret service guy and what he may have seen. That's definitely what triggered their action this morning. The question is, will they come back again? Perhaps we leave Travis where he is for now, he's in a safe place as far as we're concerned."

Charlotte stepped into the conversation. "Yes, we had a phone call from Sergeant Morgan this morning. Everything's fine back at the farm. In fact, Travis is appreciating the wholesome farm food and is getting on well with his guards, enjoying playing cards with them."

"Excellent, let's leave them there. We might need to bring Travis back here if we get into serious negotiations with his advisors," replied Johnson.

"Just as well that Lord Drakeford wasn't here when they arrived," added Charlotte. "If they'd seen him they might have made the connection and realised we were up to something and not exactly as we described."

"You're assuming too much," laughed Johnson. "I doubt if those guys would have recognised Rufus. They were only looking for one person, their President."

* * *

Later in the day a refreshed Drakeford drove to Manor Towers to show he was none the worse for his ordeal. He climbed into his wife's Morris 8, clutching his latest American newspapers, but first thought to collect his copy of the *Times* from his local newsagents. It was a busy little shop, he was second in the queue, so paid for his paper and headed for the door. He noticed two young American GIs behind him in the queue, but wasn't surprised as they were by now a common sight in the area, especially away from busy towns and cities. The newsagent had all the daily papers neatly aligned on the counter. On the front page of at least three of them was the face of Lord Drakeford, now becoming a familiar sight to those interested in current affairs.

"I recognised that guy," whispered one of the Americans to the other. "Look, that's his picture on the front page of the newspapers, I reckon he's that Drakeford guy who's part of the crew who kidnapped the President."

"Perhaps we should follow him, might lead us to the President," said the other. They quickly paid for their paper and made for their car, a pre-war Ford 8 which they had borrowed for the day from an officer colleague.

They saw Drakeford pulling away and followed on, albeit two cars behind. Drakeford enjoyed driving the Morris 8 around the country lanes; on this occasion he had left his SS-Jaguar on the drive at home. What he didn't know was that his SS-Jaguar had a radio transmitter strapped to a cross-member on its underside, a result of a clandestine midnight operation carried out by a US security expert. However, that car was going precisely nowhere.

Drakeford turned off the main road, but had a lot on his mind and hadn't noticed the Ford 8 had followed. They made sure they kept a long way back, occasionally losing him on the bends. The Ford, with its three-speed manual gearbox and transverse suspension struggled to keep pace on the twisty road, apart from the handicap of its driver being unused to a right hand drive car. After some time Drakeford turned off into a narrow country lane, then into an even narrower lane, wide enough for just one car. He had reached the rear entrance of Manor Towers and turned in, and the gate opened as the gatekeeper recognised him without hesitation. It was just at that moment that he spotted the Ford in his mirror. He realised he had been followed, but it was too late, the lane only led to one place, so clearly he was the target. He saw the Ford stop and pull over on the verge, then lost sight as he drove into the parking area. He parked his car and went straight up to the guards at the gateway.

"Sorry, guys, I think I've been followed. They've parked up in an old Ford 8, just down the lane. They will have to turn round as the lane is narrow and a cul-de-sac."

"Leave it to us, we'll check it out," replied the first guard. Not knowing what to expect he signalled for two other guards to follow him as they walked out into the lane. About one hundred yards from the entrance they could see the Ford 8 parked on the verge with no one inside. The soldiers had obviously gone to explore, or possibly hide to evade capture. There were plenty of trees either side of the lane and after a few minutes one of the guards spotted something in the undergrowth. He fired a shot from his rifle, deliberately high, but showing his intentions. The guards split up and advanced stealthily. They quickly came upon the unarmed Americans who hadn't realised the significance of what they were looking for, so quickly raised their hands when confronted by guards pointing rifles at them. The American uniforms hardly concealed their identity.

"Not exactly a day in the English countryside!" said the guard. "You'd better come with us," he instructed, waving his weapon in the direction of the house. The group walked silently back to the house, heading into a small room off reception and gestured for the GIs to sit down.

"I'd better find the Major," said the guard. "Could you empty your pockets and hand over your car keys?"

"It's not even our car," they protested. "We just borrowed it for the day. It belongs to one of our officers."

The GIs were carrying nothing of significance and had no guns. It was clearly an opportunist moment when they had seen the chance to relieve their boredom. One of the guards took the keys and went off to retrieve their car and hide it inside the compound.

Meanwhile Drakeford went into the office occupied by Bill Johnson and Major Brown who were still de-briefing on the morning raid.

"I'm afraid I might have fouled things up," he admitted sheepishly. "I was followed here, they saw me turn in. Your men have gone to follow it up."

"Nevertheless, good to see you back in circulation, you've been quite busy. Charles has updated me on your escape from St Albans!" said Johnson, with a wry smile on his face.

"Yes, and when I got home I had two US army top brass waiting for me," Drakeford replied.

"That's a coincidence, we've had the heavy mob here today, carrying out a search of the building, following a police visit yesterday. Fortunately, Charlotte played a blinder and managed to hide the President when they checked his room," Johnson explained. "Then last night we moved him to a farm owned by a friend of Charles. We plan to keep him there until the coast is clear."

Back in the guards' room Major Brown confronted the two American GIs. "So, what are your names and what's your explanation for being here?" he asked.

"I'm Paul Green," said one, "and I'm Ian Ryan," said the other. Paul Green continued: "We're from the local army base. We recognised your man that's been in the news recently, we just thought he might lead us to the President. We expected to find an old country cottage but we hadn't expected to find a closely guarded English mansion."

"You're saying that you weren't sent out on a mission?"

"No, we're off duty, it's our day off, so we're just checking out the scenery."

"It does seem a convincing story," replied Brown. "But we have a problem. If we just let you go back to your base they will insist that you explain where you've been. Next thing is we'll have the US Cavalry here, and that could turn very nasty. Right now they will have no idea where you might be, so let's keep them guessing. We'll get a message back to your base, explaining that you're staying with us and are unharmed. I'm afraid we're going to have to keep you here for now. We expect this will be all over in a couple of days or so, but until then you'll be our prisoners. However, we don't have any prison cells here, so you'll have to share a hotel room. It could be worse."

Brown turned to his chief guard. "Make sure you have their details and put their belongings in the safe." He was aware that he needed to think quickly, as this was a distraction he could do without.

"We have a spare twin-bedded room. We could keep you there under lock and key, just let you out to use the bathroom, and bring meals to you. However, I'm going to suggest that we take your clothes away and make you wear orange boiler suits. These are what would normally be used by our painters and decorators. Within reason you can move around indoors and have meals in our dining room. You will of course be locked in your room at night and you will make no attempt to communicate with the President. Should you try to escape, our guards will be on the alert, but you won't get far in orange boiler suits – or just your underwear for that matter, should you try to remove the boiler suits. It should be easier for all of us, we hadn't planned on having unexpected guests."

"I guess we have no choice," replied Ryan. He turned to his colleague. "Seems terribly British, being allowed to move around so long as we promise not to escape!"

"I'm afraid we'd just have to shoot you if you try running away!" snapped Major Brown. The GIs weren't quite sure if he was serious. They realised his men had rifles so assumed they would use them if necessary.

Charles went back to his meeting with Drakeford and Johnson. "We've got two GIs staying with us, they accidently strayed into our country home, but for now we can't let them go. They'll be wearing orange overalls, just to identify them. The US army will realise they're missing, but won't have a clue where to start looking because I don't think they were acting under orders. Hopefully we can let them go, once we've got rid of the President."

Drakeford then revealed his latest American newspapers. By now all had updated their articles about Travis's UK visit to include his alleged Bletchley Park affair. One paper carried an article where two Republican Senators had said in an interview: "If Travis has been kidnapped then just pay the damn ransom. If we offer enough money, they'll just take the money and run!" The interviewer had tried to explain that this wasn't about money, these people can't be bought that easily, it's about a principle. However, the Senators dismissed his response, saying, "So they might say, but everyone has their price."

Meanwhile Joe Cole had responded to Drakeford's exclusive with an article in that morning's Mirror, reporting on the headline in the New York Post alleging the affair tied in with Travis's cover story about travelling to England to head the negotiations. Drakeford declared: "I think it's time we moved to stage two of this story by issuing a denial. It's diverting attention away from the main issue. With any luck we could use this to make him more cooperative. Methinks it's time for another photo-opportunity. Let's pay him a visit with our Anthony Jones and his camera."

"Ok," responded Major Brown. "I was planning to drive over to the farm later this afternoon to check on things. You, Bill and Anthony could come with me."

"Is it really necessary for me to come?" asked Johnson.

"I think you should know where the President is staying," replied Major Brown. "We don't want to be in a situation where I or Rufus may be unavailable and we need to get in touch with the President."

Drakeford walked to the end of the corridor where Anthony Jones, the group's photographer, had rigged up a darkroom. "Could you come with us to see the President?" he asked. Anthony gathered his equipment enthusiastically and followed on. The four men climbed into Brown's Rover and off they went to the farm. When they arrived, Bill Jackson met them at the front door and Major Brown introduced his passengers. "This is Lord Drakeford, our group spokesman, this is Bill Johnson and this is Anthony Jones our photographer."

Bill Jackson couldn't resist a smile. "We have an American President one day and now a real live Lord. Whoever will we get tomorrow?"

"Be careful what you wish for, could be the King!" responded Drakeford. "And just call me Rufus, no need for the Lord thing here. Can we see the President?"

Bill Jackson led them to the garden at the rear of the farmhouse, where Travis was sat with a large soft drink, flanked by a couple of his guards. "I could get used to this," he declared. "I hope you've not come to take me back to that dreary flat in the attic?"

"No, not for now, at least," replied Brown. "We've come to take your photograph."

They sat in spare chairs next to the President, with Drakeford clutching his roll of newspapers under his arm. "I'm afraid the Bletchley story has really taken off, it's become headline news in the USA," he announced. "However, I think we have a plan, assuming you're willing to cooperate."

"Fire away," responded Travis.

With that Drakeford invited the President to stand next to him with a blank fence and trees behind them. He then produced today's copy of the *The Times*. "Here. You hold one end and I'll hold the other. Is that ok, Anthony, can you see the paper clearly enough? Is it clear that it's today's edition?"

"Yes, it's quite clear. I'll take a close-up, just to be sure," replied Anthony.

Anthony took a few pictures, adjusting his camera as he did so.

"What will that prove?" asked Travis.

"Well, you may not realise this," replied Drakeford, "but as BFG spokesman my picture has appeared in most newspapers in the last few days. Hopefully, when people see you and I holding what is clearly a recent copy of the *Times,* they will realise that you couldn't be at Bletchley Park at the same time. That is of course unless you want to keep everyone guessing."

"No, no," came the quick reply. "I don't even want to be here, but I can certainly do without the publicity of an extra-marital affair." Then a smile came over his face. "Especially when for once it hasn't actually happened!"

Drakeford then turned to Anthony. "Could you print me about two dozen large copies by tomorrow morning, big enough to fit into a foolscap envelope? I'll then hand them to the press."

"No problem, I'll go for size eight by ten," replied Anthony, obviously quite keen to have something to do.

They stayed for a short while as Lizzie arrived with a tray of soft drinks and everyone chatted, as if it were some social occasion. After about ten minutes, Major Brown, always thinking ahead, stood up. "We must be getting back, we've set Anthony a deadline, we don't want to be handing out dripping wet photographs tomorrow."

With that everyone rose to their feet. "Thanks for what you're doing," Drakeford said to Bill Jackson and Lizzie. "Hopefully we'll catch up some time when things have returned to normal." Even the guards had become part of this friendly gathering, although their rifles were never out of their possession.

The group said their goodbyes courteously and the four returned to Major Brown's car and set off back to HQ. On arrival Anthony disappeared to get started on his project.

Back in the ground floor office, Drakeford turned to Major Brown. He said, "Have you had any luck with your US military contacts? Are they up for direct communication?"

Charles responded: "I've managed to speak to my friend high-up in the US military. They're definitely up for a meeting so long as it's in secret. They want no publicity, so not even the local police would be aware it's taking place. I've provisionally found a meeting place belonging to a friend, it's somewhere just north of London. I'll speak to him later this evening to confirm, then I'll get back to the Americans."

"That would be ideal," responded Johnson and Drakeford in unison. "Shall we meet in my local pub later this evening, it's called 'The Stag'. It will make a change from meeting here, it's a very quiet place, usually only used by locals. By then hopefully you'll know if it's all arranged?"

This was agreed, a welcome change from meeting at Manor Towers. Drakeford drew a little sketch to help them find it. He drove home, but continued to receive calls from journalists, asking for more information as to the President's whereabouts. He was becoming annoyed that some British papers had been putting their own interpretation on the situation, reporting that the President's life was in danger and that a ransom had been demanded for his release. He decided that if he was going to London first thing tomorrow morning, he could hold a press conference to explain the BFG's position before meeting the Americans in Charles's secret meeting place. He decided it was again time to contact Joe Cole of the Daily Mirror.

"Hello Joe, I think some British papers have been putting their own interpretation on the situation, reporting that the President's life is in danger and that a ransom has been demanded for his release. I think I need to hold a press conference to explain the BFG's position. Could you arrange something?"

"No problem. I have the very place in mind, probably in the back of a pub in Fleet Street. I'll use the local bush telegraph to let a few friends know. Let's say nine o'clock in the morning."

CHAPTER 16

TALKS ABOUT TALKS

At last Drakeford felt they were making progress. The three of them arrived at 'The Stag', to confirm arrangements. Such a meeting looked perfectly normal, three men meeting for a drink, as they sat round a table in the corner. All three confirmed that they had not been followed.

Drakeford began. "I think Bill should stay here to act as our point of contact. Charles and I should go to London. I've arranged with my man at the Mirror to hold a short press conference in Fleet Street, we need to dispel rumours and get the press back onside. We can then move onto the meeting with the Americans. Will that fit in ok, Charles?"

"Yes, we can go in my car, just the two of us," replied Major Brown. "Rufus can cover the press conference at nine am and then we can drive to meet the Americans at eleven. I've arranged with a friend who rents out an office block in Uxbridge for us to use it for as long as it takes. I have arranged for a few of my team to attend to make sure the Americans don't try anything too clever. I've also got two despatch riders on standby to convey any messages between us and Manor Towers – we don't want to use the telephone; even at this stage they could be tracking us. Assuming there's no problem with the Americans refusing to negotiate and walking out on us, the meeting will probably go on to the next day and probably one after that. Rufus can stay at my house which is about ten miles north of Uxbridge."

"That all sounds good," replied Drakeford. "I've contacted some of our team of researchers in the House of Lords and they're very keen to help. They've been twiddling their thumbs since the Americans took over. Can you give me details of the venue and I'll contact them to let them know where to go."

As they had been deep in conversation they hadn't realised that they had been spotted as more people began to enter and advance towards the bar. The local village policeman, PC Bob Stephens, came over. It was clear they were old friends as both had lived in the village for several years, long before Rufus inherited his peerage.

"Evening, Rufus," said PC Stephens. "You've certainly become a national celebrity in the last few days!"

"I hadn't expected quite the publicity," admitted Drakeford. "I'm sure it will all die down as soon as it's all over. That's assuming I don't end up in jail!"

"Well, I've been asked to keep an eye on you," replied the PC. "Including people you are seen to be talking to. I'm sure these two gents are just old friends, I'll pretend I haven't noticed! As far as I'm concerned I'm with you, you're doing a good job. I've known you a few years now and I hope we can be friends for a few years more. My bosses should know better than to expect me to snitch on you, it's my job to keep you safe."

As the pub began to fill it was clear that Drakeford was a well-established member of the community. Many had known him for years and addressed him by his first name. However, there was one man sat in the opposite corner sitting quietly with his English newspaper. It was clear that no one had recognised him. "I spy stranger," said one of Rufus's friends. As they chatted and downed a few beers they kept a discreet eye on him. Eventually he stood up and picked up his newspaper and moved towards the exit. At the same time a group of three followed him out the door. A few minutes later the three returned.

"Bloody Yank," one of them announced. "But don't worry, he won't be coming back here again, we've seen to that."

"What happened out there?" asked Drakeford. "Sounds like you threatened him, possibly worse?"

"You don't need to know," came the reply.

Drakeford smiled to his colleagues. "They're not giving up, are they? Good to know when you have friends, sometimes they can be very useful when you least expect."

Like so many old English villages the local pub is a focal point for everyone to meet, even if they're not avid drinkers, and 'The Stag' was no exception. Everyone knew Rufus Drakeford on a personal level and his recent activities had elevated him as a public figure, even if they did not agree with his approach on this issue. Prominent among that group was the Reverend Phillip Caruthers, the local vicar, and he would often drop in for a shandy and a pleasant chat with whoever was prepared to listen. He approached Lord Drakeford and shook his hand. "Well, Rufus, you've certainly put our village on the map!" he said cheerily. I've been following your case in the papers. Have you really captured the US President and are holding him prisoner? Or are they blowing this up just to sell newspapers?"

Drakeford looked at his colleagues before answering; they held deadpan expressions, not giving anything away. "Well yes, it's true that the President is staying at a secret location, away from the gaze of the media, where he's involved in negotiations. You have to admit, whatever your political views, that his interference with UK affairs was unacceptable. Someone had to do something. We don't have the military power to kick the Americans out, while they just ignored us when we tried to negotiate. Remember, I was with the Prime Minister in Washington when this was discussed, and I know how Travis's mind works."

"Yes, but what you're doing is illegal, you can't just kidnap someone whoever he is and whatever he's done," replied the vicar.

"Let's not use the word kidnap, that usually implies a ransom, a financial motive. However, I think there's a provision in English law where you can detain someone you believe has committed a crime. President Travis has ordered an illegal takeover of our government. You can't get a much bigger crime than that, short of assassinating the King. When someone is prepared to listen, we'll hand him over. Somebody had to take a stand and our group decided enough was enough. A few hundred years ago he'd have been in the tower for less!"

"But couldn't you have tried a different approach? If he thought you were doing a deal with Stalin, why try and change his mind? He might have backed off if he thought it might trigger a war with the USSR."

"I doubt it. If he thought that he would have had every excuse to keep his troops here permanently," countered Drakeford. "His ambition is to make the UK part of the United States. If he achieves that, where does he stop? We have a British Empire, at least for the time being. Surely Canada, Australia, New Zealand, India and so on, are not going to stand for that. Until this came about the Atlee government had planned to grant those countries independence. How else do we get Travis to change his ideas?"

"I don't know, I'm not a politician."

"Exactly, that's the standard response. We could see a worsening situation that might get out of hand, and someone was going to get hurt, or even killed as protests mounted. Our group came together and decided we can't stand back, somebody had to do something."

"I can sympathise with your motive, I just can't condone your method. Nevertheless, I'll visit you when you're in jail," responded the vicar, trying to defuse the situation. He could see that Drakeford and his colleagues were unimpressed by his case for appeasement.

"If we'd taken your approach Travis would have got exactly what he wanted, he would walk all over us. At least, he's talking to us and we're not threatening to shoot him, at least not for the moment."

"That's good to hear," replied the vicar, not entirely sure whether Drakeford was joking. "I just hope you can use all your legal training to stay out of trouble."

"Thanks for listening," replied Drakeford, "at least you've heard it from the horse's mouth, as it were. Nevertheless, I'd be grateful if you would keep our conversation between ourselves, especially if the press come snooping round. We must be on our way, I'll bid you goodnight. Maybe next time we'll meet when you visit me in the 'Scrubs'!"

Drakeford glanced at his watch, they had an important day ahead. They stood up and glanced at the assembled villagers, some seated, some standing. "Good luck," they shouted as they made their way to the door. Outside they stopped briefly. "If this is typical, I think we have the support of the ordinary people, even though we're pushing our luck," said Drakeford. With that they went their separate ways to make final preparations for tomorrow. Drakeford's SS Jaguar still remained on his driveway.

* * *

Back at the White House it was time to take stock. The VP called another meeting for his top team, and explained: "We still haven't found the President, we're no nearer. All they'll say is that he's alive and well. However, after consulting our experts at the Pentagon they're recommending a dual approach of surveillance to track down the President while entering into secret talks to find out what they're asking for, assuming it's not just a ransom. I understand that a meeting is to be arranged tomorrow between our top military personnel and this British Freedom Group. I've nominated General Gus O'Donnell to lead the talks. He's our top man on the ground, short of asking the US Ambassador to get involved. We suspect The President intends to replace John Winault shortly, so best to keep him out of it. These are exploratory talks so at least we'll be clearer as to what they're asking for.

"Just to complicate things I've just heard that two of our GIs have gone missing, but as yet we don't know if that's connected. Our GIs are pretty bored, so often get distracted; need I say more?"

"Just let us know when you have some firm information," said Dulles.

CHAPTER 17

TIME FOR NEGOTIATIONS

Day 8

At around eight am Charles Brown picked up Lord Drakeford from his home. It was to be a busy day in London: first they had the hastily arranged press conference at nine o'clock, to be followed at eleven o'clock by the first meeting with the American team. They drove carefully to the venue in Fleet Street and managed to find a parking space nearby. They had decided that Brown would not attend the press conference, just in case they were being followed and his identity was still unknown to the press, and would wait nearby and observe the flurry of activity as busy Londoners made their way to their offices.

A public house in Fleet Street had been chosen, one very popular with newspaper reporters, but the drinking area remained closed as under UK licensing laws this could not open until later that morning. Instead, a function room at the rear had been reserved for this gathering. When he entered the room Drakeford was taken aback by the reception, where about twenty journalists were already waiting for him, all but two being male. In addition, there were about half a dozen photographers standing at the back of the room. He also noticed a BBC recording system at the side of the room, connected to a microphone placed on the top table. He took his place at the table and sat himself down. He could have remained standing to address the audience, but felt it better to remain relaxed and appear a little less formal.

As in previous meetings Joe Cole introduced him. "Good morning, everyone. I'm sure by now you're aware of Lord Drakeford and his role as the spokesman for the British Freedom Group. He's agreed to come here today to end speculation about some of the group's activities and why they were formed. Over to you, Lord Drakeford."

Drakeford began: "I'll make a short statement, and then answer questions. As Joe said, I'm here as the official spokesman to represent the British Freedom Group. We formed as a group because we were concerned that the situation in the UK was becoming untenable, something approaching civil war, with increasing wrath directed towards the Americans. This had stepped up noticeably after President Travis had made his public statement following his meeting with Clement Atlee, our Prime Minister, when he accused the UK government of colluding with the USSR. Believe me, I was there at that meeting in Washington and Travis might have thought it, but that was never said. We don't condone the behaviour of some protesters, but have sympathy with their concerns. Our aim has been to seek an audience with the President to put the UK side and point out the futility of his intentions to influence the British democratic system. To that extent we have been successful in that we have had meaningful discussions with the President and these are ongoing. I can't say anything about the outcome as yet, but at least he is listening."

The questions started reigning in. "So where is the President now?"

"He's in a secret location, and being well looked after."

"Why secret? Why can't we, the press, interview the President? How about a press conference?"

"I'm afraid, once his location is known, the Americans will close in and whisk him away. They've tried every trick imaginable to outwit us in order to find him. Initially they refused to have any communication until we made it very clear that we were serious and prepared to take whatever time was necessary to have meaningful discussions."

"How did you manage to abduct him?"

"It was a very well-planned operation, carried out by a team with well practised military skills. I wasn't involved, so I can't comment on any details, but I can assure you that no one was hurt during the operation."

"So how can meaningful discussions take place when the President is isolated from his team?"

"We have been working through an intermediary. Believe me, this has not been easy as all phone lines have been tapped in order to trace our calls."

"So what's the next stage in these negotiations? Are you speaking to other Americans?"

"That's what we intend to do, I can't give you any more detail, I'm afraid. Meanwhile, I would like to appeal to the public to calm their protests; I believe we are making progress."

"Is it true that you asked for a ransom; after all, that's usually what kidnappers do?"

"I've no idea where that came from. Certainly we intend Britain's financial affairs to figure in any negotiations, but none of us are looking for personal gain from all this."

The questions kept coming, but mostly on the same theme.

"What about the articles in American newspapers about him meeting a woman at Bletchley Park? They're suggesting the whole thing you're saying about his abduction is just a cover story. You have to admit no one would be surprised."

"I agree it's a good story, but there's no truth in it – I can show you the proof," replied Drakeford. "I have some photographs taken with the President and myself, holding a recent copy of the *Times*. This demonstrates he was with me and not at Bletchley Park with an unknown lady."

At this point Drakeford stood up and addressed the room, "Thanks for listening, I've said as much as I can for the time being. If there's any progress I would be happy to do this again in a few days' time. Meanwhile I'll hand these photographs to Joe to distribute as he knows just about everyone!"

He handed the envelope to Joe, thanked him, and left the room. He could hear excited clamour as Joe Cole distributed the photographs. As he emerged onto the front street he could see Major Brown looking into a shop window a few yards along. He turned and looked the other way and across the road spotted a tall man wearing a raincoat, peering over an open newspaper. Drakeford walked slowly towards Brown and said, "I think I'm being watched, I'll keep walking."

Brown replied, "Yes, I've seen him too, couldn't be more obvious, perhaps that's the intention. Just keep walking and I'll go and get the car. When the opportunity presents itself I'll draw up next to you and you can jump in, hopefully before our spy has noticed."

They went away in opposite directions. About five minutes later Brown drove along the road, quite slowly, as he was in a traffic queue. He wound down the passenger window and just as he came alongside Drakeford the traffic stopped. "Rufus," he shouted. Rufus had already prepared himself, appearing to do up his shoelace to make him appear inconspicuous. He leapt into the passenger seat and off they moved, made a sharp left turn down a narrow alley way and then another left onto a main road. Brown kept checking his mirror. "I think we've got away with it," he said. "I can't see anyone following."

The meeting with the Americans was to be held in an empty, three-storey office block in Uxbridge. Major Brown had set this up, since he knew the owner. He was aware of the risk that the BFG team could be walking into a hostile USA reception committee, but had planned to avoid this by moving his own team in there overnight. His only concern now was whether the Americans would actually turn up.

Drakeford and Brown arrived in Brown's grey Rover and parked on the forecourt. Already waiting in the hallway were three younger men, dressed in smart civilian clothes, carrying briefcases and looking very studious, together with a well-dressed middle-aged lady.

At 10.55 am a large American station wagon pulled onto the forecourt. Four men got out, with one much older and larger and clearly in charge. They were followed by a similar vehicle containing four men carrying arms, dressed in American uniforms. They stepped out of their vehicle and were immediately met by Major Brown's men, also in uniform.

"Good morning," said Major Brown. "I'm sure we're all here for the same purpose, to make sure things run smoothly and keep the press at bay. Hopefully, they've not been told that this is taking place."

"Thanks for arranging this," responded the senior American. "I can assure you that no press people have been informed by us. Let's get down to business."

The negotiating teams immediately went upstairs, while the British and American soldiers mingled around the entrance and in the hallway. Someone produced a kettle and produced welcome refreshments, clearly left over from the building's most recent occupants. They chatted casually and someone even produced a pack of cards.

The meeting participants sat themselves down and made their introductions.

"Hi, good morning, I'm US General Gus O'Donnell and I've been asked to lead the American delegation." He was a very big man in every respect, and he was supported by three younger officers in uniform. "Let me introduce Captain Alan Oliver, Lieutenant Robin Brady and Lieutenant James Cleaver."

The British contingent sat on the opposite side of the table. Drakeford introduced himself: "Good morning, I'm Lord Rufus Drakeford and this is Major Charles Brown who worked in the British Commando service during the war. We are assisted by Robert McIntyre and Martin Tyler, who were part of our team that met President Travis in the White House. We are all here today as we support the aims of the British Freedom Group. Also, we've invited Jo Brindley, our stenographer; she will make sure that our conversations are recorded in writing. She's performed this duty in cabinet meetings."

O'Donnell began. "We object in the strongest possible terms to your illegal abduction of the President of the United States. We're here to inform you that we are not prepared to concede anything and it is only a matter of time before we find the whereabouts of the President, a relatively simple task in this small country."

Lord Drakeford responded coolly and clearly. He said, "You think because you came to our assistance in the war you can call the tune. We collaborated with your nuclear programme in 1941 and now you have shut us out. We gave you our radar and the magnetron invention which was years ahead of anything you had in the United States. We gave you our jet engine patents and practical assistance in its development as part of the war effort. You have overrun us with your soldiers, occupying our country as if *we* had lost the war. We now want to see you out of our country and let us run things the way we want. Furthermore, we have your President and are prepared to keep him for as long as it takes."

The American response was predictable: "We are very concerned that Britain is misguided and going in the wrong direction. Your plan to expand state ownership is not something we approve of. We never intended to bring in our troops to occupy your country, but the way things were going we felt it was necessary to put a brake on things. We just don't trust your Labour politicians who we feel are in awe of Joseph Stalin."

Drakeford shook his head, meeting O'Donnell's stare. "We think it is the Americans who are misguided. At the end of the war, Britain was bankrupt and many essential industries and services were on their knees; in many cases the owners had given up or had disappeared. We had to get things up and running very quickly and avoid any exploitation or black market racketeering. Our plan for socialism is a long way from the USSR model of communism as defined by Marx and Lenin. The Russian mentality is based on 'The State knows best', with a one-party system that rejects democracy as we know it. We don't like Joe Stalin any more than you do; he has a dubious past and is a bully in charge of what is virtually a dictatorship. However, you must appreciate that he has taken up his position because he is paranoid that America intends to invade the USSR as part of your plan for world domination. He has moved to surround his borders with buffer-zones such as Poland and Ukraine as a form of protection. Small wonder that he has shown a friendly face towards Britain? And remember that your President invited Churchill to deliver his now famous speech at Fulton, Missouri, where he declared that 'an iron curtain' had descended across the Continent. Hardly an olive branch? What's more, you have 'the bomb'. It's only a matter of time before the Russians have their own, but right now they're expecting the worst."

There was no reaction from the Americans, just a few glances.

Drakeford continued. "As things stand, the relationship between our two countries is at an all time low. You are seen as an occupying force imposing your political will without any mandate. We have enormous debts owing to the USA and these will take over 50 years to repay. Some relief in this area might help to restore goodwill, along with a return to our previous democratic status. But you have to appreciate that the bottom line for us is that Britain will not become a part of the United States, there is no question of that. If that is enforced you will have a long and bloody civil war. Otherwise, everything else is negotiable."

The bluntness came as a shock to the Americans and after a brief pause O'Donnell responded. "To be frank, we never anticipated this would escalate as it has. Our President was very concerned that Britain was becoming far too close to Russia, with its raft of socialist policies. He intended to put some pressure on your politicians, hence the invitation to Washington. What we hadn't predicted was the reaction of the British people. From just a few flag waving demonstrators it spread to the whole country and a full confrontation. Maybe because we happened to have thousands of military personnel still on British soil our President overreacted, thinking we had the upper hand. He thought the British people might even welcome the American influence. You will appreciate that once our soldiers were under threat we were bound to retaliate."

"I'm pleased you acknowledge that," replied Drakeford. "We're a very proud nation and don't want to get pushed around. But you have GIs on our streets and have a 9pm curfew. You've taken our best technology, you've taken over our government and we're about to get screwed for so-called loan repayments. From our position that's effectively an occupied country. Maybe it's symbolic, but we do have your President and intend to keep him until we get out of this mess. It would be very humiliating for you if the American people find out what's really happening in their name. What's more, we've found something we hadn't expected. Mr Travis does like to dominate a conversation in order to impress people, especially pretty young ladies. He's told us a lot about his previous commercial activities and his private life. I'm sure the American people would be delighted to hear some of the recordings we've managed to arrange."

The Americans weren't sure whether this was a bluff, but they were well aware that their President had a murky past. General O'Donnell responded, "That's as may be. However, we hear what you say and I would like to hear what my team has got to say. Could we adjourn to another room?"

"I'm sure that's possible, the place is empty," replied Drakeford.

Half an hour later they resumed their place at the conference table. General O'Donnell sat back in his chair and carefully chose his words. "We accept that this situation cannot continue indefinitely so we have a few suggestions as to how we move forward. Subject to our President's approval and our colleagues in Washington, we would be prepared to reduce the level of payments Britain must make to the USA, but we want something in return. We can appreciate why the government has had to take over many essential services and will hopefully hand them back to the private sector when they have recovered. However, a major sticking point is the plan to introduce a National Health Service. This will be difficult to reverse and goes against everything we stand for; that is liberty, low taxation and the freedom to choose. What's more, we don't think it would work, it's a crazy scheme and the cost to the taxpayer would be beyond the means of the British economy."

"Our economists have done their calculations and they believe it's quite feasible," countered Drakeford; "in fact, we believe in a few years' time other countries will want to adopt something similar, it's just a question of priorities."

They were never going to agree, but after more discussions General O'Donnell said he was prepared to listen to a compromise, something quite out of character.

"Ok," said Drakeford, "let's say in return for reduced payments we agree to suspend the NHS plans for the term of this parliament. If the Labour government is re-elected then we can revisit our plans for an NHS. If a Conservative government is elected, you will probably get your way."

The General thought for a while, because his brief had been to not reinstate the Atlee-led Labour government. He came up with a response. "As parliament is currently dissolved we would like to see a general election as soon as possible in order to make a clean start. At the same time, we would demand that the NHS plans are delayed for a minimum of five years, whoever is in office." Clearly in his mind was that a Labour government would not be re-elected, either now or anytime soon.

They had reached a point where both sides needed to consult, so it was agreed that they would withdraw for the day and reconvene in the morning. A transatlantic telephone call was quickly arranged to allow the General to consult with the Secretary of State over in Washington.

The British were reluctant to allow any telephone contact with the President for fear that the line could be traced, so a summary of the day's outcome was quickly typed by Joe Brindley and the British agreed that this would be passed to Travis later that day and any response would be returned in a sealed envelope.

Major Brown turned to Lord Drakeford and whispered, "Just as well we left Bill at HQ. He knows where the President is being kept, so when he receives the package from the motorcycle, he can then drive over to the farm and hand it to the President. We'd better get a message to warn him as to when and what will be coming. We can ring HQ from a call box in a few minutes' time; that should be safe enough."

The package was passed to a motorcycle courier, a member of the team known as Ben Godfrey, who sped off into the London traffic and out through the London suburbs. At a prearranged point he stopped under a railway bridge and handed the package to a second motorcyclist, Andy Price, who was already waiting. Both were former despatch riders and their machines had been legally purchased from the War Department as 'Army Surplus' and repainted black so as not to stand out as ex-army machines. After the briefest delay Ben continued on his way, while his colleague remained stationary for some time before proceeding with care in the opposite direction by a roundabout route to arrive at the headquarters. The plan was intended to confuse anyone who was trying to follow, either on the ground or from the air.

Ben, the first motorcyclist, carried on for about ten miles before turning into a side street, having now arrived home. He dismounted in front of a small terraced house and pushed his motor cycle into the short front garden and parked it on its rear stand. He had barely got inside the front door and removed his helmet when there was a loud knock on the door. He opened the door to be confronted by several policemen who held him against the wall while others forced their way past him. Ben, a recently demobbed despatch rider, still lived with his parents. They were terrified when they saw they were being raided by policemen, especially as they ran upstairs to continue their search, while two other policemen appeared in the back garden.

After a few minutes the policemen came back downstairs and without a word they left the house, leaving Ben and his parents totally bewildered. Within minutes they had disappeared, leaving no sign that they had visited.

"What's going on? What have you been doing?" shouted his father.

"Nothing, I think it's just a case of mistaken identity," replied Ben. "I'm going off to make a phone call." He went for a short walk, a couple of streets away and entered a red telephone box. He inserted his money, dialled his number and pressed buttons 'A' and 'B' to speak to his contact, Major Charles Brown.

Major Brown had just arrived at home, to be met with a ringing telephone. He picked up the phone, half expecting a call, although not the one he was expecting. "They've been following me, the bloody police, all the way from London," said Ben. "They raided my parents' house, scared them to death. Did they expect the President of the United States to be hiding in our spare room? Fortunately, I'd made the handover to Andy, so they're none the wiser."

"Don't worry," replied Brown. "You did well. It just shows whose side they're on, we can't trust the police, and you have to wonder who's pulling their strings. One day you'll be able to explain to your folks what happened. They'll be proud of you, I'm sure. Meanwhile there'll probably be another trip tomorrow morning. We'll be in touch."

Major Brown then phoned Manor Towers to speak to Bill Johnson. He was fairly confident his home phone was not known to the police. "This is getting messy," he explained to Johnson, "now we're in touching distance of an agreement. I think if we're ferrying messages back and forth we need to have Travis back at HQ. We have to take this extra link out of the chain and I don't think we'll get another visit from the US army."

He continued, "A motorcycle courier is on his way now with a package for Travis to view. Can you take the package over to the farm this evening? Let him take his time, then return in the morning to retrieve it, with any comments he might want to add. At that point tomorrow morning bring them all back to Manor Towers. You'll need to take the van to get everyone in."

"Yes, of course," replied Bill. He was slightly annoyed at being told the obvious, but was aware that this was Charles's style and why he was highly respected. It was his attention to detail to ensure that everyone under his command was aware of what he wanted them to do.

It was almost dark as Andy, the second courier, arrived at Manor Towers. Bill Johnson was waiting in reception for him. "Many thanks, can you be here for about nine o'clock tomorrow morning. Hopefully there will be a reply to take back."

Bill grabbed the package and drove over to the farm. He was a little hazy as to the exact location, especially in the dark, but found his way without too much drama. Bill Jackson welcomed him and led him to a back room where the President was relaxing, having made himself quite at home.

Johnson announced himself: "Good evening, Mr President, your negotiating committee have been meeting today in London. Here's a summary of what's been discussed so far. Please read through and add your comments as you wish. I'm going to leave it with you this evening, so take your time and I'll be back tomorrow morning to take it back and our courier will make sure it gets there in time for the meeting. The bad news is that tomorrow we'll be going back to Manor Towers."

"That's disappointing, I was beginning to feel quite at home here," replied Travis.

He opened the package, read the typed pages carefully and thought for a few minutes, staring at the ceiling. By now he was getting very irritable, and he was beginning to lose track of how long he'd been in captivity. His patience was running short and he was prepared to agree to almost anything. He said, "Let me sleep on it and I'll give you my reply in the morning." He was trying to give the impression that it was not a foregone conclusion, as if he had the power, or capacity, to offer an alternative.

Johnson retuned to the kitchen where Lizzie was preparing yet another of her delicious meals. He explained to Mr and Mrs Jackson, together with Sergeant Morgan, the next stage. "I'm off now, the President has some reading to do. I'll be back around eight o'clock in the morning with the van and will be taking everyone back to HQ. Hopefully we're getting somewhere, so this should be all over in a few days."

"It's been a pleasure having everyone here," said Lizzie. "Perhaps you'd like to stay and have dinner with us? There's plenty of food to go round."

"Why not?" replied Johnson, the smell of roast pork being more than he could resist. "Just don't let me get too comfortable!"

Everyone gathered around and Lizzie brought out the evening's feast and placed it on the large kitchen table. Johnson was impressed with the atmosphere, a contrast to the tension he'd experienced at Manor Towers where everyone was aware of their rank and particular role in the operation.

When everyone had finished and at a suitable break in the conversation, Johnson stood up. "Many thanks, Lizzie, that was the best meal I've had for some time. I could get used to living on a farm. I must get back, but I'll see you all in the morning with your favourite mode of transport."

There was polite laughter, then Johnson bade farewell, slipped back into his car and drove away slowly down the country lane, adjusting to the pitch dark conditions.

CHAPTER 18

A DEAL AT LAST

Day 9

Early next morning Johnson explained to his team at Manor Towers what was planned for the day. "I'm off to the farm now and will bring everyone back here. Hopefully the President will have read through the document I delivered yesterday evening and will have written his response. Andy will be here about nine o'clock and I'll pass the package back to him, so hopefully the President's reply will be back at the negotiating table by about ten."

He clambered aboard the trusty Bedford van and set off to the farm. On arrival he could see that Travis was already packed, as if his release was imminent.

Johnson hadn't seen the actual document which had been handed over. "Did you read through it yesterday evening?" he asked.

"Yes, it didn't take long. I've just added a note saying, *'I think you have reached a reasonable compromise and I authorise you to put this into a formal document which I will sign'.* Let's get this over with. Do I get to go today, now we've reached an agreement?"

Johnson replied, "Not yet, this is just the start. Your decision will be taken back to London and the guys around the conference table will decide on the next step. I imagine they will have to contact a few people in high places. I'm sure there were some transatlantic phone calls yesterday evening."

Everyone collected their belongings and said their goodbyes to Mr and Mrs Jackson. "Thank you for having us, very much appreciated," said Morgan.

"I've enjoyed staying here," said Travis, "just a pity about the circumstances. Maybe one day when this is all over we'll meet again?"

"Perhaps," replied Bill Jackson. "It's certainly been an interesting couple of days." He then turned to Johnson. "I was thinking, have my wife and I been breaking the law, harbouring an American President?"

Johnson was quick to reply. "I'm sure that's not the case. You were descended on by four men carrying rifles, with the US President as their prisoner. You didn't have much choice. Just don't let on that it was a pleasant experience!"

Off they went, it was a warm sunny morning and they even passed a police car going in the opposite direction. Johnson checked his mirrors anxiously, but there was nothing to fear. Before long they were back at Manor Towers and everyone dispersed, with Travis being escorted upstairs to his now familiar apartment.

Andy was already waiting in the yard outside. Johnson handed him the package. "We'll probably see you again this evening, there's bound to be a follow-up. Have a safe journey."

About twenty miles down the road he pulled into a wooded area where the package was handed over to Ben, who then continued in a slightly roundabout route, arriving at Uxbridge about nine-thirty.

He handed over the package to Major Brown, then right on time the meeting reconvened and the envelope containing the President's response was handed over. General O'Donnell read it and announced, "We can soon get that knocked into shape for the President to sign. Of course, you realise that in the USA this has to be approved by Congress before it can happen?"

Drakeford replied, "Surely when the world has seen the outcome of our negotiations, which can be shown as something the President has achieved, then Congress can hardly throw it out. He has a Republican majority in both houses so he will get all the support he needs."

"Are you going to bring him down here for that?" asked the General.

"No that's too risky on many levels. We'll take the formal document away with us and arrange a photo opportunity to show the President signing." This will be forwarded to the press, and then once it's become public we will bring him to London for a press conference where he will be free to go. That could be the day after tomorrow."

"That's taking far too long," protested the General.

"I'm afraid you're in no position to negotiate," replied Drakeford. "If you want your President back without public humiliation, then this is how it's going to be. Ideally this should be a PR exercise where neither side will be shown to have conceded." By now Drakeford was feeling more confident, given that the Americans had accepted that a compromise was the only way this crisis would be resolved.

The British team realised that if a document was to be signed it needed appropriate personnel from both countries. That posed no problem for the USA, but since Britain was effectively under American rule there was no equivalent person to sign for Britain. Since the Labour Party had been elected in 1945, they were effectively the government in waiting, but that was never going to happen under American occupation. After some discussion it was agreed that two people should be invited, MPs Herbert Morrison for the Labour Party and Winston Churchill for the Conservative Party. They were quickly contacted and asked to join the meeting later that day, although neither knew why they had been invited. Nevertheless, both were told that this was confidential and they should not tell anyone of the arrangement. Transport was speedily arranged so as few people as possible knew what was happening.

Later that afternoon the meeting resumed with its two extra participants, Winston Churchill and Herbert Morrison. They had been totally unaware of the proceedings of the last few days and the whereabouts of the President. They were quickly brought up to date, much to their surprise, and immediately took part in the discussions.

After several drafts the wording was finally agreed. It read:

Negotiations have been held between teams representing Britain and the President of the United States. It was admitted that the tension between the two countries had reached an unacceptable level. Accordingly, the following ten-point policy document has been agreed.

1. The 9pm curfew will be lifted with immediate effect.
2. USA military personnel will withdraw from the streets and arrangements will be made for as many as possible to return to the USA as soon as practicable.
3. All trade sanctions will be lifted and business arrangements restored to those which existed in the immediate post-war era.
4. The USA will not proceed with any plans for the United Kingdom to become part of the United States or a US state.
5. Britain will continue to trade with the USSR but has no intention of forming a political or economic alliance between the two countries.
6. Britain recognises that its plans to introduce a National Health Service are beyond its current means and agrees to defer such plans for a minimum of five years.
7. The USA acknowledges the British contribution in sharing technical information to our mutual advantage to enhance the war effort.
8. The USA recognises that the financial liability arising from the lend-lease agreement, and its replacement, is an unreasonable burden on the British economy as it recovers from the cost of the war. The USA therefore agrees to reduce repayments to 50% of the level previously agreed.
9. A British General Election will be held as soon as practicable and normal democratic government will resume immediately afterwards.

10. Both sides recognise that the relationship has suffered during the last 12 months. Together both nations are stronger and our diplomats will begin immediately to forge a 'Special Relationship' which should endure for many years.

Churchill had no problem with the document and as leader of the Conservative Party agreed to sign on their behalf. Morrison was somewhat reluctant as his plans for the NHS had been taken off the table, at least for the time being. He said, "I can't sign this without consulting my colleagues, it's a sell-out to my Party and its principles." At this point a heated conflict arose between the other British participants and an adjournment was agreed to enable them to consult. Churchill stayed in the room with the Americans, while Morrison and the rest of the British team went off to a separate room close by.

Drakeford laid out the facts. "If we can't sign, then we have a stalemate where American occupation will continue. What's more, despite what we've said, we can only hold the President for so long, eventually they will work it out, or someone will accidently let on where he's being held. The fact is that Churchill will sign whether we do or not and that could be good enough for the Americans."

"That's because he sees it as a way of refighting the election and becoming Prime Minister," countered Morrison."

"But we had argued that both major parties should be invited," said Drakeford, "we felt it would be a better public relations exercise to have leaders of both major parties represented, especially as Atlee was just not available."

Morrison thought for a while, stood up and walked to look out of the window. The British delegation looked at one another, one of them indicating with a hand gesture that Morrison should be dumped. Suddenly, Morrison turned around and said, "OK, I'll sign, it's probably the end of my political career, but if that's what's needed to unlock the situation and get the Yanks out, then so be it."

They returned to the meeting room and the two British MPs signed two copies of the agreement. Drakeford said that these would be taken by courier for Mr Travis to sign.

"We could help with that," said the General. "Or bring him here?"

"No," said Drakeford, "I'm sorry, but I'm afraid we still have reservations about the Americans and their recent record. We don't want any last-minute hitches or clever moves to avoid him signing."

The two pieces of paper were carefully rolled inside a cardboard tube and handed to Drakeford who immediately took it downstairs and handed the package to Ben, the motorcycle courier who had been waiting patiently downstairs with the two military contingents. He quickly kick-started his ex-WD Triumph 5S and sped away though the traffic before anyone had realised. Drakeford returned to the meeting room and interrupted the conversations to say: "Assuming the President signs this evening, a photograph and text of our agreement should be in tomorrow morning's newspapers. Then we need to organise a press conference in Downing Street as soon as possible to make the most of the occasion and to show that all is well between our two nations."

"That sounds fine," said the General. "We can arrange that. Just keep us informed."

The convoluted courier system clicked into place, but with a different handover location, and the package arrived at Manor Towers just before dark. The President duly signed the documents with Anthony Jones in attendance to record the occasion on camera.

Photo opportunity over, his smiles reverted to his more morose expression. "Can I go now?" he asked briskly.

"First thing tomorrow morning," replied Johnson. "We'll be going to Downing Street for a press conference."

The photographs were duly processed that evening and later that same evening Andy Price was despatched, carrying several prints and a press release setting out the agreement. He delivered his packages to a prearranged address on the outskirts of London where they could be distributed to all the major newspapers in time for the press deadline of just before midnight. Next morning the photos of the President appeared in the newspapers, showing him smiling broadly as he signed the document.

The newspapers carried a statement issued by the Buckingham Palace press officer. "The King is delighted to hear that an agreement has been reached, with plans to return to democracy and he looks forward to receiving whoever is appointed Prime Minister."

Later the American negotiating team spent some time on the transatlantic telephone line talking to the Vice President and his team and dictated the words of the agreement. There had been much speculation in the press, mainly as to whether Travis was still in his 'secret' place and what might be the outcome. The papers were still taken with the idea that Travis had arranged a secret affair. Eventually the VP's team agreed a press statement:

After some tough and lengthy negotiations President Travis has agreed with representatives of the British government that certain changes will be implemented with immediate effect. Britain has agreed to discard its plans for wholesale nationalisation on Soviet lines and will return to a more conventional free market economy. This includes their plans for a nationalised heath service which have been put on hold and may not proceed at all. The President understood that the government had embarked on their program to avoid possible bankruptcy, a short-term consequence of its war debts. To avoid this outcome and provide an initial boost to the economy the President has agreed to remove the trade sanctions recently imposed and also negotiated a modest reduction in the loan repayments to the United States. It was further agreed that an interim coalition government will operate until a general election is held, thereby providing an incoming, democratically elected government to start afresh. It is our intention that the majority of our US army personnel will be returning home as soon as practicable, although we will retain a basic military presence to assist the British forces in maintaining security. The President will leave the UK on good terms and it is hoped that our 'Special Relationship' will have been reinforced as a result of his visit.

Day 10

Travis was already packed and waiting as Johnson appeared. They descended the broad, winding staircase to reception where most of the team were waiting. It was a strange relationship; the President had been extremely annoyed and frustrated at his being imprisoned, yet he had developed some respect for his captors who had treated him well. He spotted the two men in boiler suits. He could tell by their haircuts and healthy complexion that they might be American.

"Have they got you working here?" he asked. "You're not part of this team, surely?"

"No, Mr President," replied Green, "we strayed here by accident and got captured. Hopefully we can go back to base after you've gone."

Travis replied: "That's a poor excuse. You shouldn't have gotten captured, I expect better of Americans, you're just losers and I've no time for losers."

The two GIs looked at each other with embarrassment. Ryan said to his colleague, "Probably the only time in our lives that we'll get to meet the President of the United States and he calls us losers!"

Travis turned and looked at one tall man in an army uniform. "I recognise you! Aren't you the guy who welcomed me when we posed on the way here for a photo opportunity?"

"Yes, I was Major Rupert Stevenson," he admitted with a smile. "I think I'd been promoted by a couple of ranks, just for the day!"

"Goodbye," said Travis, somewhat cynically. I hope you feel this has all been worthwhile?" He gave a wave to the assembled entourage, with a special smile and a hug for Charlotte.

As he headed for the door, Johnson addressed his team: "Many thanks, you've all done a brilliant job. Please help restore this place to how we found it and hopefully we'll be back this evening to round things up and have one last evening meal together." He turned towards the GIs. "I guess we can give these decorators their own clothes and their car back to them, but not too soon, give us a couple of hours to get to London first."

Johnson led the President to the waiting black Humber Hawk – no more Bedford van this time. Johnson and Brown sat in the front, with Drakeford and the President in the back. Another car led the way, Major Brown's Rover, driven by Sergeant Morgan accompanied by two of his trusted officers, and a motorcycle following.

Johnson explained: "We have an armed guard with us, we can't take any chances. After all, we are transporting an American President and we don't want any dissidents interfering along the way!"

The President failed to see the irony, instead burying himself in a copy of *The Times* which had been collected from a village store along the way. He was anxious to see how the press had reported the latest situation. He had been provided with copious newspapers during his enforced stay and was generally satisfied that his reputation was intact. Initially he was happy that the press had been under the impression that he had been directing the operation from a secret location, assumed to be on a US airbase. More recently the papers had reported on his abduction and the mischievous allegation that he had arranged the whole thing as a cover for a duplicitous affair. He was pleased to see the picture with him and Drakeford holding the copy of the New York Times. "You did me a big favour there," he commented. "I just hope Mrs T appreciated it too."

CHAPTER 19

ALL ROADS LEAD TO LONDON

The journey to London was uneventful; no one took any notice of just another black car on the roads and still less expected to see the American President sat in the back of a Humber Hawk. However, as they drove nearer to the centre the police had clearly spotted their car. As they drove slowly along Whitehall the police waved them down and signalled for them to turn into Downing Street, while their accompanying car was ordered to carry straight on. They ignored the motorcyclist, assuming he was not involved with the President's party, so he continued along Whitehall. He stopped a few hundred yards further on where the Rover had parked. Sergeant Morgan wound down the window. "I think our job is done, the President has been delivered to Downing Street, we might as well return to HQ." They moved off smartly, just as a policeman was about to admonish them for illegal parking.

The Humber Hawk pulled up outside Number 10 and was immediately surrounded by police. Drakeford and the President were ushered through the front door, amidst flash bulbs and lots of shouting. Johnson and Major Brown stayed in the car and a policeman came over immediately and, pointing to a waiting police car, gave the driver a short and direct order: "Turn around and follow that police car waiting over there. Ignore reporters and other people asking questions." They had no choice but to oblige.

"I guess we hadn't thought this through," admitted Johnson. "Perhaps we might have thought of a less public way to deliver the President. Hope Morgan's going to be alright, he's got your car!"

Johnson followed the police car back along Whitehall and they turned into Scotland Yard. The police signalled for him to park and get out of the car.

"Your names please?"

"William Johnson."

"Charles Brown".

The Custody Sergeant then addressed them both. "You are under arrest for the kidnap and internment of David J Travis, a citizen of the United States of America. Come with me." They were quickly escorted to a windowless interview room where they were left alone, with no explanation. Just complete silence.

* * *

Meanwhile at 10 Downing Street Drakeford and the President were welcomed and offered refreshments. Drakeford recognised the Chief of Staff from a previous visit and handed him a large envelope containing the agreement signed by Travis, Morrison and Churchill.

He explained, "I'm not sure who wants this, but I guess it should be kept here. Could be useful evidence if things go wrong!" The envelope was handed to an aide and it quickly disappeared.

After a few minutes to gain their composure, they were led along a corridor to the largest available room, to be met by several dignitaries and US military personnel. This was effectively the 'handover' process, although only a few people appreciated the significance. At the top table sat Herbert Morrison, Ernest Bevin, Winston Churchill and Clement Atlee, looking genuinely ill. The two men made their way to the table where two vacant seats had been left for them. There were many journalists, photographers and a film crew in attendance in the centre of the room. Television had only just reached the London area before the start of the war and was in the process of starting up again; consequently, there was no room to accommodate the bulky outside broadcast TV cameras. Nevertheless, BBC radio was well represented and a live broadcast was possible.

The conference started with Travis shaking hands with the British politicians, together with military personnel and other well-known dignitaries. Without waiting for any introductions, Travis stood and opened the meeting.

"Good morning," Travis began. "As you can see I'm very much alive and well, despite rumours to the contrary. I came here more than a week ago with the intention of sorting out the stalemate and the dreadful situation that was beginning to exist between our two countries. True, we were concerned that Britain was modelling itself on a Soviet system, with its massive programme for nationalisation, one which we felt would put Britain on course for disaster. Our concern was that such an economic strategy would lead to an irretrievable position, eventually requiring a massive bailout by the USA. We have always had a 'Special Relationship' between our countries and long may that continue. A few months ago we had talks with your Prime Minister, but before we could reach an agreement he was taken ill. I'm pleased to see that he is here today and on the road to recovery. Nevertheless, we decided that urgent action was required. We sent over our economic advisors, but if anything that merely aggravated the situation, massaged by your left-wing press I might say, leading to mass demonstrations, particularly against US military personnel.

"I decided this could not continue and decided to take charge personally, determined to bring this escalating level of protest to a halt. In the absence of a functioning government it was difficult to start meaningful negotiations because demonstrations were everywhere, but they clearly lacked leadership. Fortunately, the British Freedom Group stepped up as intermediaries and over a period of days we arrived at a reasonable compromise. I believe by now you have all seen the agreement which I proposed and we gladly released this to the press. It is our intention to restore a functioning government operating from this very building as soon as possible. We believe this will be best served by appointing an interim coalition government, with Winston Churchill at the helm. This will be loosely based on the World War II government, until we can hold a general election as soon as practicable.

"I'm happy to take questions, if anything needs clarifying."

Questions rained from the press. "You speak as if you chose to negotiate with the BFG, but surely that was not your intention? Everyone knows you were abducted."

"Not at all. I joined them of my own free will. It may have looked like a confrontation, but my guys could have easily gunned them down, had I given the order."

"Why did you allow yourself to be taken to a secret location?"

"Because we didn't want the press camping outside, it would have been a distraction. My team knew I was in good hands, so I was never in danger."

"Why were negotiations conducted through an intermediary?"

"Because we were all too aware that phone lines can be tapped, we didn't trust the press, so we needed to protect the security of the telephone system."

"Are you sure there was no story in the dual purpose of your visit, that is the alleged extra-marital affair? Surely it was a good opportunity if no one knew your whereabouts for several days?"

"Absolute rubbish! Thanks to Mr Drakeford we were able to demonstrate that I couldn't be in two places at once. I've never been to Bletchley Park."

"What are your immediate plans?"

"I'll spend tonight at the USA Embassy, then I'm straight back on a plane tomorrow morning. My work here is done; mission accomplished, the 'Special Relationship' is intact."

"Question for LORD Drakeford," the questioner emphasising the Lord. "Do you agree with the President's account of how your business was conducted? Earlier reports suggest things were rather different."

Drakeford replied with a smile, "It's a close approximation! The President may see things differently, but I don't want to spoil his day. The fact is he's here now, nobody got hurt and we have an agreement."

Joe Cole of the Daily Mirror stood to ask a question. "I have a question for Mr Atlee. Mr Atlee, apart from the interview with Richard Dimbleby we've not heard very much from you. We have a formal procedure in our country to decide how a Prime Minister is appointed and for many of us, until that has taken place, we still regard you as our Prime Minister. How do you feel about a return to a coalition government, however brief, led by Mr Churchill?"

Atlee answered, his voice still subdued, "In the short term I believe we have to do what's best for the country. Frankly, my health is still not up to the exacting role of Prime Minister. More to the point, I think you are aware that the decision is out of my hands."

"I think we've said all there is to say," interrupted Travis.

No one else from the top table volunteered to say anything and the meeting broke up without any pleasantries. It had taken less than ten minutes. As they stood up, Drakeford was immediately approached by reporters, while Travis and the other politicians slid away through a side door without Drakeford noticing. As he walked forward and mingled with the assembled journalists he could sense a mixed reaction, but everyone was surprised by Travis's contempt for his audience and for Lord Drakeford. He was especially puzzled as to where his colleagues had gone as he had expected them to have been in the audience. He walked out of the room, dodging questions, and found a policeman in the corridor. "Where have my colleagues gone, the two men who travelled in the car with me and the President?"

"I believe they've been taken to Scotland Yard," answered the policeman. "Possibly for their own protection, but apart from that I've no idea." As he stepped outside he was confronted by reporters and photographers hovering around the doorway to Number 10. The policemen on duty kept the watching public across the street, but were quite relaxed about the press gathering in front of the door. He could see no sign of Johnson's Humber Hawk, so assumed that the report of them going to Scotland Yard was probably correct.

"What's happening inside Number 10?" he was asked. "Will the President be coming out soon?" Another reporter asked, "Is the President free now?" and "Will you be charged with kidnapping the President of the United States? That's a pretty serious crime!"

Drakeford replied, "I'm sure he'll be coming out soon. Personally, I didn't kidnap anyone, we've completed our business with him, so I imagine he'll be going to the USA Embassy. Thank you, gentlemen, I've nothing else to say."

He had to walk around a large black American limousine which had been sent from the Embassy to collect the President from Downing Street. He made his way through the crowd, many waving miniature British and American flags. Once he reached Whitehall he found himself suddenly alone and hurried to Scotland Yard.

On arrival he could see reporters and photographers near the main entrance, but no sign of his colleagues. He was recognised by reporters.

"Lord Drakeford, have you come to give yourself up? You can't just kidnap the President of the United States and expect to get away with it."

"No, I've committed no offence. I'm told my colleagues have been taken here," responded Drakeford.

"Yes, we saw them being taken away. They could be away for a long time!" laughed the reporter. Drakeford ignored them and went up to the reception desk.

"Good afternoon, my name is Lord Drakeford. I believe you have a Mr Johnson and a Mr Brown here, do you know if they'll be long?"

"Yes, they're in police custody," said the sergeant behind the counter. "I have no more information. If they're charged you won't be seeing them for some time. I suggest you take a seat in the waiting area and I'll update you as soon as I'm able."

* * *

At Scotland Yard Bill Johnson and Major Brown had been left for several minutes in an interview room before being led into a large conference room where they were confronted by five high ranking police officers, all male and distinctly middle aged. They were asked to sit down facing the interviewers across the table and asked to confirm their names.

"I'm William Johnson."

"And I'm Major Charles Brown."

The man in the centre introduced himself. "I am Chief Constable Perkins." He didn't bother introducing his colleagues, but continued without further ado. "We have three important questions to which we want answers," said Perkins, clearly the most senior of the officers. "Firstly, what was your role in the plan to kidnap the President of the United States? Secondly, who else were you collaborating with, and thirdly where was the President being held captive?"

Johnson took the lead in replying. "We were just two of a number of people involved, most with a military background, right up to Colonel. We were chosen to conduct the negotiations since we had a military background and experience in logistics and cross examination. Since the US forces were occupying our major towns and cities we regarded them, at least for the time being, as an enemy of our country and therefore a legitimate target. As far as we were concerned, they had occupied our country illegally, despite our citizens having democratically elected a government. Moreover, I should emphasise that at no stage did our group carry out any act of violence and even during the operation to detain the President no one was killed or injured. In fact, it's perfectly possible that our team had imitation firearms."

The police officers were clearly taken aback as they had not realised that this operation had involved some high ranking military personnel. Brown scanned down the row of police officers confronting him, mostly Superintendents, and felt distinctly unimpressed; they were mostly overweight, quite a contrast to the military people he had previously worked alongside.

"So where was the President being held?" asked Perkins.

He felt he needed to play for time by not revealing the secret location where the President had been held as many of his colleagues were still in the building.

Johnson responded: "As far as I'm concerned that is still a confidential matter. The location no longer has relevance to the operation. The President is back with his fellow countrymen, completely unharmed, and feeling rather pleased with himself. Until I see the US army off our streets and on their way back home, I will still regard them as an adversary and an occupying force. If you insist on extracting answers then both I and my colleagues will regard you, the police, as part of their operation."

"It's still an offence to abduct someone," responded Perkins.

"Then I assume you will also be looking for the people who abducted Lord Drakeford. There can't be many couples called Victor and Joan, living in St Albans, in the vicinity of Victoria Street. Just give me the electoral register and within a few minutes I'm sure I can find them for you. What's more I'm sure, if asked, the President will say he came willingly."

The police officers had no immediate response to Johnson's comments. "We need to discuss this between ourselves," said Perkins. He indicated to the police sergeant at the back of the room, "Take Mr Johnson and Mr Brown to a safe place. Please offer them a cup of tea." The 'prisoners' stood up and left the room with the sergeant and were led back to the interview room.

Back in the conference room Perkins kicked off the discussion. "Normally I would discuss a matter of such importance with the Home Secretary. However, we don't have a functioning Home Secretary at the moment. Clearly the law has been broken; you can't just abduct someone and keep them against their will."

"The fact is this was a well organised operation", countered his colleague. "Johnson or Brown were by no means the only senior people involved, they just kept the President under lock and key and carried out discussions with him. What about this Lord Drakeford, he was the official spokesman and held a government position in the Lords until this all blew up. Are we going to arrest him as well? Public opinion is on their side, if we detain them we'll be seen to be supporting the Americans. A lot of people just witnessed us arresting them and will be watching to see what we do."

"Perhaps we should release them on bail," replied Perkins. "I'm sure they have home addresses. It would give us time to find a solution without causing too much unrest. Now they've released the President we're never going to find the others who were involved, they will just melt away." Everyone agreed this was the best short-term solution. The police sergeant was asked to bring them back to the conference room.

The prisoners were sat drinking tea, prepared for a long session. "I suspect we could be detained overnight," speculated Johnson. "Either that or the Tower of London! I guess they'll want to show who's in charge."

"I'm not so sure," replied Major Brown. "A lot of reporters saw us arrested and I definitely heard a lot of camera shutters. I think you made a very good point about the police being identified as backing the Americans. With the UK government virtually non-existent, people will ask who's pulling their strings?"

They had hardly finished their tea when the Custody Sergeant reappeared. "Gentlemen, they want to see you again. Please follow me."

The two detainees followed and resumed their seats in front of the senior policemen.

"We've decided to release you on bail," explained Perkins. "You're being charged with abducting an adult against his will and you will be required to appear in a magistrate's court in due course. Do you have any questions?"

"Only one," replied Johnson. "Does that mean we're free to go?"

"Yes, just as soon as the Duty Sergeant has processed the paperwork."

He looked at the sergeant. "Please take them away and deal with the formalities, then you can release them."

Neither man said anything, they just ignored the senior police officers and left the room with the sergeant. He took them back to the interview room and produced a sheaf of forms from a cupboard. There was much form-filling, just standard procedures, and they were given carbon copies to take away with them. The task completed, he took them to a side exit. "It will be easier if you slip out this way," said the sergeant, who clearly had some sympathy for his detainees, "You'll see that a sizeable crowd has gathered near the front entrance. Your car should be where you left it. Good luck!"

They made their way unnoticed towards the side exit when they spotted Drakeford waiting anxiously. "What the hell's going on?" he asked. "Surely they can't charge you with anything, there will be a public outrage."

"That's what we told them," replied Johnson. "I don't think they had anticipated that possibility. Someone else is pulling their strings and they were too blinkered to realise. The problem now is that Charles and I could become public figures, something we hadn't reckoned with, we just wanted to fade away and get on with our lives. The photographers were all over us on the way in, and I suspect they'll recognise us anytime now."

As expected, they walked out of Scotland Yard and were confronted by photographers and a crowd of reporters who hurled a barrage of questions at them. "Have they charged you with anything? Have you got to come back again? What are your names, you've clearly been working undercover."

Johnson replied, "We've been talking to the police, explaining how we looked after the President in a secure location and how he willingly took part in the negotiations with the British Freedom Group. We've nothing else to say." Despite more questions they insisted on moving on, with heads held down, and walked briskly to where Johnson's Humber was parked. They climbed aboard, with Johnson at the wheel and slowly manoeuvred through the melee to find a way through the London traffic.

Drakeford was probably the only one thinking straight after the events of the last few hours. "Once we get out of London, we should find a phone box and let everyone know that we're on our way," he said, "I'm sure they've been listening to the news and are wondering if they're going to see us any time soon."

"Good idea. It's been an interesting day," said Johnson. "Let's get back to Manor Towers. I need a good stiff whisky."

Meanwhile, at Manor Towers things were moving on. Harry Mitchell had had a phone conversation with Colonel Downton and it was agreed that a celebration was appropriate. Everyone involved with the operation was invited, including those operating on the outside such as the motorcycle couriers, Ben Godfrey and Andy Price, Drakeford's wife Christine, who along with Charlotte had taken over the organisation of the 'homecoming'. In fact, it was the first time they had met in person, having previously only communicated via the army surplus radio. At around six pm the Humber Hawk arrived and the three men got out, to be met with rousing cheers, much to their surprise.

They entered the main dining room where it was clear that a party was underway. There was food on the table and plenty of drink available. There were more than twenty people, including Colonel Downton and several that they did not recognise, possibly those working on the outside recruited by Major Brown, and maybe a few partners as well. Even Mr and Mrs Jackson had been invited. Charles Brown was taken aback as all his security measures appeared to have been jettisoned, then he began to relax as he knew the mission was over and by tomorrow everyone will have dispersed.

Charlotte was first to speak as they entered the room, all three looking slightly bewildered. She began: "We've been following everything on the radio today, we heard Travis speaking in Downing Street. Then later we heard that you'd been arrested at Scotland Yard, but no one knew your names, which we found quite amusing! They later reported that you'd been released, so the BBC reporter speculated that it was probably a case of mistaken identity and the real culprits were still at large!"

The three were presented with drinks and they gradually wound down. They mingled with their colleagues and chatted about the somewhat unexpected course of events their day had taken. After a while, it was clear that Lord Drakeford was being persuaded to make a speech.

He stood on a chair at the head of the table where he could be seen. "What a day!" he began, causing some laughter. "We expected some activity as we entered Number ten, but once inside Travis totally ignored me. I wasn't aware that Bill and Charles had not even made it into the building, but had been whisked off to Scotland Yard. You may have heard Travis's speech on the radio, he certainly put his own interpretation on things, and he has a gift for turning adversity to his advantage."

He continued: "The police were up for slamming Bill and Charles behind bars. Unless they had been tipped off beforehand, the only evidence they had that they had been involved was that they were driving the car that delivered the President. Bill explained what had happened when interviewed and it's clear the police hadn't grasped the significance of the occasion and why we had set out to achieve what we did. I think they realised the public were right behind us and any action would probably have started a riot. I suspect it will all go very quiet when the dust has settled and we won't hear very much more.

"The President was everything we had expected, difficult to work with and quite arrogant. However, the week he spent with us was probably the first time in his life when he wasn't surrounded by people responding to his every beck and call. He was initially quite uncooperative, but over the days I believe he actually mellowed and actually enjoyed being able to relax alongside normal people who were not in awe of him. I suspect that won't last long!

"Finally, I will keep it short, I just want to thank you all for your efforts. Charles recruited a brilliant team with many specialist skills. Everyone did a magnificent job and we managed to achieve our objectives without a shot being fired and no one getting hurt. One day we will have a reunion, I'm sure, perhaps we should call it 'Our Special Relationship', as I think we might have changed history, just a little."

Everyone cheered and applauded. Drakeford was clearly feeling elated as he grabbed some food and another beer. He turned to find Bill Johnson, and to his surprise found Bill and Charlotte in an emotional embrace.

"You've taken me by surprise," he exclaimed. "I didn't know you felt like that about one another."

Bill replied, "Actually we've been an item for some time. We met while working for the British intelligence service about three years ago. We felt our relationship should not get in the way of this operation and to keep it completely professional. Hopefully now we can sort our lives out and plan to get married in a few months' time, particularly as we're fairly confident the Americans won't be putting us in prison!"

"Congratulations!" said Drakeford. He half turned to the people in the room who could not have failed to notice their encounter. "Did anyone else know about this?"

"No, we had no idea," volunteered one of them, somewhat unconvincingly, "but we're very pleased, nonetheless."

"Could be a few extra wedding guests," said another.

They drank a toast to the happy couple; it was just what was needed to top off the evening. Anthony Jones, ever the professional photographer, took several pictures as the atmosphere became even more relaxed. By late evening some people went on their way, like Lord and Lady Drakeford, others went back to their rooms where they had been staying for the past nine or ten days.

The next day it was all hands to tidy up the accommodation, with lots of cleaning, washing of bed linen and kitchen equipment. Anthony Jones had developed his photographs from the previous evening and handed out prints to grateful friends. Fortunately, he still had copious supplies of photographic paper for which he had no further use.

Around midday a single-decker bus arrived to take people to their nearby homes or railway station; clearly Major Brown was as efficient as ever. He was satisfied that the building was more or less in the same condition as they found it.

He stood as everyone stepped up onto the bus, carrying their luggage and saying their goodbyes. Inevitably he was the last to leave, being the key holder, so after one last check he climbed into his Rover and drove away, another project completed. Having left the army, he was already looking for his next challenge, he was never one for a conventional lifestyle.

CHAPTER 20

REPAIRING PUBLIC RELATIONS

Back in London Travis had arrived at the US Embassy in Grosvenor Square, his car having been escorted by four police motorcyclists through the streets of London. He entered the building where the Ambassador and many of the staff were assembled and they greeted him with polite applause.

"Good afternoon, Ambassador Winault, it's the first time we've met, I believe. Thank you all for staying on, I'll be staying overnight, but I must get back to the States tomorrow. First of all, I need to phone the White House."

The Ambassador led him to a well-appointed office and invited Travis to sit down and pick up the telephone. "Just ask for the White House, the operator on the reception will connect you."

Travis had waited less than a minute when he heard a female voice: "This is the White House, good afternoon, Mister President, the Vice President is ready to speak to you. I'll put you through."

"Hi there, Mister President," said the VP. "You've had quite a time over there. Are you feeling ok? Did they give you a hard time?"

"Nothing I couldn't cope with," replied Travis. "I hope to be on the first plane out of here tomorrow. I've had enough of this country for the time being. Could you transfer me to the residence, I need to speak to my wife."

"Sure," replied the VP, "I'll see you later tomorrow. I'll get you transferred to the East Wing."

The phone rang there for at least a minute until it was picked up and a female voice came on: "Hello, this is the President's residence," she said.

"This is the President," shouted Travis. "Can I speak to my wife?"

"I'm afraid she's not here, sir, she left two days ago, I'm not sure where she went."

Travis slammed the phone down. "Show me to my room," he barked to the Ambassador.

That evening he dined with Ambassador Winault, but was in no mood for easy conversation.

"How come you allowed this to happen?" demanded Travis. "Couldn't you have sent one of your bullet-proof limos to collect me from the airbase? To be kidnapped by a bunch of peasants was so embarrassing. Look what I've had to give away to get a satisfactory outcome? Not a word of this, mind, the USA's reputation is on the line."

"It was down to Greenham Common," protested Winault. "They were confident it was an easy one-hour journey. They tried to make your transport as inconspicuous as possible. I would have done the opposite, I would have had military vehicles front and back, no one would have dared interfere. We'll know another time."

"You bet we will, there will be changes," replied Travis. "Rest assured, heads will roll when I get back."

Next morning he was up and ready. The suitcase which had followed him from Manor Towers was already packed and the car ready and waiting for him at the front door where a few spectators, reporters and photographers had already gathered. On this journey to the US airbase he had an armed guard and a fleet of vehicles to ensure there was no repeat of the incident on his arrival.

Travis was in no mood for pleasantries at the airbase, a situation shared by General Thomas and Major Sutherland who kept in the background for fear of being confronted by the President, handing the job of the welcome party to junior officers. They need not have worried – on arrival Travis walked straight from his car and mounted the stairs to the aircraft which already had its engines running. Without even turning to wave goodbye or even survey the English countryside, he disappeared and the door was closed. Immediately the chocks were removed and the plane moved forward down the runway. Within a few minutes it had disappeared from sight.

Meanwhile reports of yesterday's activities were all over the newspapers. It was hailed as a victory for commonsense by reporters of the right-wing press, while the centre-ground papers were predictably neutral, but pleased the troops would be off the streets. Unsurprisingly, the left wing press saw it as a sell-out to the Americans.

Drakeford was on the phone almost continually, answering many calls. He phoned Joe Cole to thank him for his help in arranging meetings and making sure that at least some of the press reports were accurate. Later he had a telephone conversation with his sister, Jeanette. They spoke fairly often and he was well aware that in her role as a young doctor she had a passion for a modern health service. "I'm sure everyone's congratulating you on sorting out this mess, but you've sold the Health Service to achieve it," she complained.

"But once the Americans were in control it was never going to happen," countered Rufus. "At least now it's down to the British people. Either the Tory government changes its position or they'll get thrown out at the next election and the incoming Labour government will pick up the plan for the NHS."

She remained unconvinced.

For Travis it was a long fifteen-hour flight back to the USA, but the presidential plane was well appointed, with what was effectively a comfortable hotel room. Despite the drone of the engines he was able to grab a few hours' sleep and managed to catch up on yesterday's newspapers as he consumed a light meal. Nevertheless, it was late evening when the plane touched down in Washington and close to midnight as his car rolled into the White House driveway. He walked alone into the building, to be greeted by the uniformed guards, always on duty twenty-four hours per day. He made his way to the East Wing where all was quiet, the servants fast asleep and unaware that their boss was back in town. Based on earlier reports that his wife was not at home, he was hardly surprised to find there was no sign of her in the residence. He then noticed a large envelope on the table with the names David Travis and Tara Travis prominently displayed. Inside was clear documentation setting out claims for a divorce, something Travis was all too familiar with from previous occasions.

He decided to go to bed, but with the time adjustment and the shock of the legal proceedings served on him, he was unable to sleep. By four o'clock he decided there was no point in staying in bed, so he showered and dressed and made his way to the Oval Office to catch up on his paperwork and to grab the first editions of the morning newspapers which he took back to the residence. He stuck it out until seven o'clock when he decided it was time for breakfast, so wandered into the dining area where his head chef, Paul Robinson, was already on duty.

"Good morning, Mr President," he said enthusiastically. "Would you like your usual All-American?"

"Yes please, I need something to cheer me up."

"I take it you'll be eating alone?"

"Yes, you've probably gathered that the First Lady has decided to take a short holiday. Did she say where she might be going?"

"No, sir. She left three days ago. She was driven off by one of the chauffeurs, maybe to the airport. She just said she would be in touch later."

"Thanks, I'll make some phone calls."

Travis finished his breakfast and went back into the lounge and picked up the phone where he could dial without going through the White House switchboard. First, he decided to phone his son.

"Morning, Donald, sorry to wake you so early," said Travis. "Your stepmother's gone away somewhere, any idea where? I know she likes your place in upstate New York."

"No idea," he replied. "Are you ok? We've been reading all sorts of stories about you in the papers. She probably got fed up waiting as you were over in England and had no idea when you were coming back. Have you tried phoning Tamara?"

"No, that's my next call; I am fine by the way."

Travis then phoned his daughter, also in upstate New York. After some delay the phone was picked up as his daughter answered.

"Tamara, sorry to drag you out of bed. Is your stepmother with you?"

"Yes," she replied. "She's still in bed. Shall I get her to pick up the phone in her room?"

"Yes please. It's rather important."

There was some clicking on the line, then Mrs Travis answered: "Tara here, is that you, David?"

"Yes, just what's going on? I've come back to find you're filing for divorce."

"I should think it's rather obvious," Tara replied. "You're up to your old tricks again. You arranged all this just so you could go and see your English woman. What do you take me for? You don't expect anyone to believe that your presidential convoy was waylaid by a bunch of English cowboys who kept you prisoner for over a week. I bet they even had toy guns as well! Your bodyguards must be so embarrassed that such a story has been leaked out, only you would think you could get away with it."

"But that is what happened," protested Travis. "They were not cowboys, they were ex-military personnel. It was a well organised operation. Surely you saw the photo in the papers with me and Drakeford holding the New York Times, proving I couldn't be in two places at once?"

"Yes, I saw that. I'm sure you and Drakeford set that up. How much did you pay him?"

"It wasn't like that, he's a Lord over there, believe me he doesn't need the money."

"Everyone needs money," she countered. "I think you set it up with the three of you. I wouldn't be surprised if she wasn't the one holding the camera."

"You'll find it hard to prove adultery," responded Travis. "You need a name and you need witnesses. On this occasion there won't be any."

"I think you've got a track record going back a long way. You'll be hearing more from my lawyers." Tara replaced the receiver. She'd been waiting for this opportunity.

Travis just sat and stared out of the window for a few minutes. Eventually he stood up and decided there was nothing else he could do, events would take their course. Fortunately, he knew he could always spend his way out of trouble, his life would go on. Tara might have a change of mind, he thought, but somehow he felt this unlikely. It was now nine o'clock and he decided to walk over to the Oval Office as by now people were beginning to arrive for work.

First to arrive was the VP, followed quickly by Alan Dulles. "Good morning, am I glad to see you," he exclaimed. "We've had so many conflicting reports. It does seem that you've reached an agreement, the Brits are happy and the cost to us is not great. What's more you've got them onside; they appear to have seen sense over their allegiance with the Soviet Union."

"Yes, I think we sorted it eventually," replied Travis. "Unfortunately, my wife believes it was all a put-up job, the agreement was never an issue and she believes all this rubbish in the papers about my having an affair with an English woman. She's suing me for divorce."

The VP was clearly taken aback by this comment. "I'm sure she just lost patience with not knowing where you were and when you were coming back. I'm sure she'll know what's good for her; after all, she is the First Lady for this term and possibly four years beyond."

"I have my doubts," replied an unusually subdued Travis. "She's a very strong-willed woman. Anyway, let's get down to business, I can see a mountain in my in-tray."

* * *

The divorce process moved along apace with no holds barred. In the event Mrs Travis did not need to produce witnesses for the English excursion as plenty came forward from two previous affairs, including the actual women he had been involved with. They felt they had been misled, but at the time they had been given discreet payments to remain silent. The witnesses had always been available, despite the 'hush money' payments, and were merely waiting for Mrs Travis to decide enough was enough.

When accosted by a reporter Travis told him: "I'm not admitting anything, but I could do without the publicity right now. I need to get back to running my business, I can't afford to spend that sort of time in court. I've instructed my lawyers to deal with it, whether it's in court or out."

Travis offered a generous out-of-court settlement, including liberal expenses for everyone involved, while Tara settled back into her New York lifestyle. However, she was not to be cast aside this time and instructed her lawyers to proceed. Travis responded predictably, briefing his legal team to look into her private life for evidence that she had not led an exemplary lifestyle herself, particularly after she had moved away. This was not going to be resolved any time soon and likely to drag on for over a year.

Back in the UK a few weeks later a general election followed with just a 30% turnout as many voters saw the outcome as a cynical climb-down. Many people appreciated the efforts to bring about concessions from the American President and how close Britain had come to losing its independence, although this did not feed through to the ballot box. Standing in for Atlee, who did not stand for health reasons, Herbert Morrison's career was tainted in the eyes of his party's left wing. Churchill was installed as Prime Minister of a winning Conservative government who felt that at least they had the satisfaction of being democratically elected. US military personnel remained, but with a much lower profile. It was announced that a continued US presence was necessary to discourage any threat of USSR interference in UK affairs.

CHAPTER 21

BACK IN THE LIMELIGHT

After the President's return to the USA the British 'freedom fighters' made sure their friends in the US press and the Democratic Party were well informed as to recent events in the UK. Travis never admitted that he had been held captive, but boasted that he had taken charge of proceedings and reformed the political situation in Britain, allowing thousands of US military personnel to return home 'victorious'. In reality, the British concession to shelve plans for the NHS meant very little to the American public; consequently, Travis's claimed achievement was not likely to bring him much credit in the ensuing election.

It was now early 1948 and the Republican Party had to decide who they were going to back as their candidate. Clearly Travis was in pole position as it was highly unusual for anyone to challenge a sitting US President from within their own party. However, there were dissenting voices who felt that American voters thought Travis was weak and impetuous, having given in to British pressure. Some had expected Britain to become the newest state of the USA, possibly before Alaska or Hawaii, thus inflicting a serious blow to the ambitions of the USSR.

There was also a serious debate taking place regarding financial aid to war-torn Europe. Both major parties could see that this would provide post-war markets and trading partners for the USA, encourage stable, democratic governments and stem the tide of communism. There was popular support for this plan as a significant proportion of the population had emigrated from Europe in the 1930s and 40s and still had friends and families back there. However, people had long memories of Travis's controversial speech at his inauguration where he was advocating a strong line be taken, particularly with Germany.

A bitter campaign ensued within the Republican Party and it became clear in the Primaries that they were looking to dump Travis and select Thomas E Dewey as their candidate, their original choice to fight FDR in 1944. Travis decided to quit the selection process before the Republican Party conference in July and avoid further humiliation; after all, he was still the American President until next January and was determined to make the most of it.

At this point Travis may have expected an easy ride in the ensuing months prior to the election, but relations with the USSR had deteriorated significantly. The situation had reached a crisis point in Berlin where in June 1948 the Soviets blockaded West Berlin, which under the terms of the Potsdam Agreement was controlled by the USA, Britain and France. However, its location, deep inside Soviet-controlled eastern Germany made it heavily dependent on supplies travelling through a narrow corridor from the West. The move was a clear intention to persuade the West to withdraw from Berlin altogether and allow the whole of Berlin to come under Soviet control. The West collectively resisted this and quickly organised what was known as the Berlin Airlift in which aircraft carrying supplies operated a round-the-clock shuttle service between Allied airbases in West Germany to Tempelhof airport in West Berlin. Reports indicated that aircraft, mainly from the USA and Britain, were landing there at the rate of one every forty-five seconds. This continued into the next year.

While Travis remained President he was able to enjoy the trappings of power without the burden of having to conduct an election campaign within the USA. He travelled extensively and looked forward to being an honoured guest at the London Olympics. The opening ceremony of the London Olympic Games took place at Wembley Stadium, otherwise known as the Empire Stadium on the 29th July 1948, attended by eighty-five thousand people. Britain had originally been scheduled to host the 1944 games, but the four-year cycle had been suspended since the 1936 Olympic Games held in Berlin. It was a difficult time for Britain to be hosting the games, so soon after the war, and they became known as the 'austerity games' as all events used existing facilities and no Olympic village was built, with male competitors being housed in military camps at Uxbridge, West Drayton and Richmond Park, while female competitors stayed in London colleges. In all, fifty-nine nations took part, while Germany and Japan were not invited. In contrast to the 1936 Berlin games which had been fronted by Adolf Hitler, the London games were opened by King George

VI. He was accompanied by his wife Queen Elizabeth, his mother Queen Mary and his two daughters, Princesses Elizabeth and Margaret.

To their surprise, Lord Drakeford and his wife Christine had been invited to sit with the dignitaries at the opening ceremony. Clearly Drakeford had become a national figure in helping to bring about the confrontation with the USA and in some part helping to retain Britain's independence. They arrived, almost unrecognised, and took their places in seats which had been specifically allocated to them towards the back of a VIP area. As they looked around it was clearly a 'who's who' occasion, with heads of state, politicians, actors and dignitaries of several countries gathered in front of them. Then they noticed several rows in front of them President Travis, a late arrival and clearly enjoying the sense of occasion, taking in the smiles and the accolades before deciding to take his seat. As the two-hour ceremony ended, everyone filed away in a dignified manner to a reception held in a large marquee, erected on what was normally a car park. Everyone had a reserved place, indicated on a seating plan near the entrance, although heads of state were guided individually to their seats. A meal was served and once cleared away inevitably some speeches followed, after which people were allowed to mingle. Perhaps surprisingly Travis made a beeline for Lord and Lady Drakeford. "Well, hello again," he beamed.

"May I introduce my wife, Christine," replied Drakeford. "I don't think you met last time you were over here."

"I seem to remember I was rather tied up somewhere else," replied Travis. "What good causes have you been pursuing since I last saw you?"

"Oh, we've gone back to what we used to do, Christine as a political researcher, while I've gone back more or less fulltime to being a barrister. I still sit in the House of Lords on important debates, but obviously I'm no longer a spokesman for the government since the Conservatives are in charge. I serve on a couple of All Party Parliamentary Groups which I find interesting." At this point he could see Travis was glazing over, so decided to change the subject.

"Your guys certainly did all they could to track you down. The mechanic at my local garage was very surprised to find a radio transmitter strapped to the underside of my car when he came to service it! He had no idea where that came from," joked Drakeford, much to Travis's amusement. He went on: "I kept a diary all through my time with the BFG and I'm part-way through turning it into a book."

"That was very shrewd of you, I think I'd like to read it when it's finished. I suspect a few heads will roll when the truth is told," exclaimed Travis.

Drakeford continued: "Yes, I'm not short of material, that's for sure! I'll make sure you get a copy when it's published. The problem is knowing when to stop as the story is still unfolding. For instance, you may be surprised that Bill Johnson and Charlotte are now married,"

"I must say they were both very impressive," beamed Travis. "They're well suited, I'm sure. Please send them my congratulations."

"Yes, they'd been together for some time, although you would never have guessed. They met through the wartime secret service. Charlotte was parachuted into France a few times and managed to evade capture," explained Drakeford. "They were very professional while they were with us, no one had guessed until the very end."

"She certainly was not the waitress she pretended to be, no wonder I was impressed!" laughed Travis.

Christine changed the subject. "I hope you didn't take a dislike to our country as a result of your treatment during your previous short visit."

"No, I quite liked what little I saw of it, especially the time on the farm, it was like being on holiday on a Texas ranch. Unfortunately, that little holiday cost me my marriage," said Travis.

"I did read about that, but tried to scotch those rumours," countered Drakeford.

Travis responded: "It all came about because one slimy reporter staged a photo opportunity and made up a story, just to sell newspapers. I suppose we might call that 'fake news'. Unfortunately, my wife decided to believe the scandal and assumed you were in on the conspiracy."

"I guess we hadn't seen that coming, but it was the best we could do. We had contemplated a 'honey trap' that the spies use, just to get you to cooperate, but never carried it out. The contrived Bletchley incident was laid out in full public view and was as much an embarrassment to us as it was to you. We had no interest in putting your marriage at risk, we had nothing to gain. I had rather expected your wife would have second thoughts; in fact, I would have expected she would be with you today."

"Not a chance," replied Travis. "In fact, as divorce proceedings are grinding away I have to be seen to be on my best behaviour."

"I suppose now it's all about the November election. Sorry to hear you didn't get the Republican nomination, but at least it gives you more time to attend events like this?" remarked Drakeford.

"I was disappointed, but I think Dewey will win and I'll be campaigning for him; Harry Truman's just a lightweight," replied Travis. Then looking directly at Drakeford he added, "Actually I enjoyed our conversations back in the old manor, I don't get to speak to many people prepared to disagree, but you had nothing to lose."

Rufus was quick to respond. "Well most of your people are scared you're going to fire them, so they tell you what they think you want to hear. Even journalists have editors, so they will only push things so far."

"Yes, I admire your candour, let me know next time you're in the States, you'll be very welcome to pay us a visit."

With that he shook their hands, slapped Rufus on the back, kissed his wife, and moved on to meeting the next celebrity and another photo opportunity.

Drakeford turned to Christine. "Somehow I can't imagine us socialising with David Travis. I guess he was only being polite, I'm told that Americans often invite you to visit, but they're not serious, they're quite taken aback if you actually turn up! He seems to have mellowed somewhat, perhaps now the pressure's off, and he doesn't need to impress us. I must admit I was tempted to ask him what he thinks of 'losers' now, but I didn't want to spoil his day!"

"I would love to have seen him answer. He would probably have turned it round into some kind of victory. We're well rid of him now, let's look forward?"

"I agree, let's direct our energies to the UK situation. I'm particularly looking forward to the next general election, whenever that is."

* * *

Life moved on apace and it was now 3rd November 1948, the day after the USA Presidential elections. Against all the odds, the result was a surprise win for Democrat Harry S Truman. There were actually four candidates including two breakaway Democrats from the southern states, the so-called Dixiecrats, a distant third. Truman won 51% of the Electoral College votes and won 49.6% of the popular vote against Dewey's 45.1%. More significantly, the Democrats had gained control of both the House of Representatives and the Senate.

An article in the Washington Post explained that American voters felt the Republicans had not lived up to their promise to establish the USA as the superior world power, even though they had shaken the world by their use of the atomic bomb on Japan. There were rumours that the USSR was developing its own nuclear weapon, due to be tested anytime soon, and America's superiority as a world power was about to be challenged. The USSR was flexing its muscles and had significant areas of Europe under its control, and Communism was now a greater threat than it had been when Travis came to power four years earlier. As a Republican Thomas Dewey had inherited Travis's reputation for opportunism and showmanship. The British adventure had had little impact on American voters, except to underline Travis's impulsiveness and vulnerability to 'outside influences', particularly his dalliance with the ladies, something which offended staunch Republicans. The electorate decided it was the Democrats who were the more stable, a reputation gained over the years when FDR was in the White House. The Democratic Party's subtle message was 'be careful what you wish for' and it seemed to have got through.

A smaller article featured an interview with outgoing President Travis. He claimed: "I suspect there may have been some electoral fraud, I've heard reports of vote rigging and I'm sure in time these will all come out. I think the Republican Party made a big mistake in not re-selecting me, I'm confident that if I had stood I would have won, and won handsomely."

Elsewhere the New York press were running articles suggesting that Travis's business activities were in trouble and about to file for bankruptcy, implying that his family and trusted servants had lost control in his absence. When pressed for comment, Travis was dismissive, saying these were just rumours and total nonsense. "Just wait, now I'm back in my office all will be fine."

Travis was confident that his business interests were about to improve. In recent years his property companies had invested heavily in the development of several new ventures, and he had secured bank loans to make this possible. These projects comprised three new skyscraper blocks in New York City and a secure estate of luxury housing in the Queens suburb. Inevitably completion of these projects had slipped, adding to pressure being applied by the banks with rumours of bankruptcy. However, housing sales were now going well and income from rents of new offices and apartments were beginning to flow, with loans being repaid, giving rise to a new optimism in the Travis camp.

Despite his business apparently on the road to recovery, Travis was still resentful that he had been removed from the title race for a second term as US President. To consider his next move he called a meeting of his 'inner sanctum' to his palatial office on the top floor of his New York headquarters. Present were his son Donald, daughter Tamara, his faithful financial expert Joe Thompson and two long standing associates, Charles Kleinsmith and Arnie Hunter. Travis began:

"Thank you all for coming. Let's keep this between ourselves, but I wanted to talk to you about the possibility of another bid for the presidency in 1952. I see two main issues here: the first is finance, the second is policy. I'd like to hear what you have to say."

Joe Thompson was first to speak. "You're going to need a lot of money to launch a realistic election campaign. This was not an issue when you first became President as you were slotted in late as the running mate for Dewey in 1944. As you know, we felt that you should have fought the 1948 campaign more aggressively, having assumed that you were odds-on favourite as the sitting President, only to be ousted by your own Party. If you're going to fight it, you're going to need a lot of money upfront, not loans which have to be repaid, and I don't think even your business can find that sort of collateral. You'll have to set up a strong, forceful campaign in order to attract backing from big businesses."

No one disagreed with his analysis; in fact, the Travis family were quite relieved. They were concerned that a presidential campaign, whether successful or not, could bring down the Travis business empire. They had bitter memories of the 1948 campaign.

"I think we're all agreed on that, let's move on to see if I have a realistic chance," responded Travis with an uncharacteristic display of pragmatism.

Charles Kleinsmith stepped in at this point.

"It's becoming evident that momentum is gathering behind Dwight D Eisenhower. He's a former US Army General who had made his name as the Supreme Commander of 'Operation Overlord' and the D-Day landings, eventually leading to the defeat of Nazi Germany in 1945. That's one hell of a CV. So far, he's worked well with Truman, but he's recently declared his allegiance to the Republican Party and has quickly become a firm favourite. It's also clear with his current NATO involvement that Eisenhower will take a strong line with the USSR, a position previously taken by yourself when you were first elected. So, what will set you out against Eisenhower?"

"That's an interesting question. We could take an entirely different line on the threat of the USSR," countered Travis. "We're all aware that the USSR is becoming an ever-increasing threat to the world and is close to having its own atomic bomb. This could result in a stand-off and an escalation in arms build up which could last for years. Could we consider an alternative strategy, based on forming a partnership with the USSR in which both nations settle for what they have and allow citizens in the Western World to sleep more easily, knowing that the threat of nuclear war had been averted?"

The meeting stopped dead in its tracks – no one had seen that coming. Travis had previously made his attitude towards Stalin very public, so he was the last person to be named as an accomplice in his come-back campaign.

"How do we do that?" questioned Tamara. "Would Stalin even consider such an alliance?"

"Well, I met him at Yalta and again at Potsdam," replied Travis. "I think we developed a mutual respect and he might see sense in some kind of agreement. Perhaps I should make a business trip to Moscow and arrange a meeting with him, unofficially of course. He could sell such an arrangement to his people as an example of his statesmanship, a master stroke on his part, and I could do the same. The Russians probably fear the threat of a nuclear war even more than our own people. It would certainly be a different policy to any of our other candidates, that's for sure."

"But would the American people trust Stalin?" countered Arnie Hunter. "Before we go too far perhaps it might be worth floating the idea, maybe through a leaky journalist, just to test public reaction."

Donald Travis then entered the discussion. "If the Republican Party isn't interested, perhaps you should stand as an independent?"

"Now that's a thought!" responded Travis Senior. "I rather like that idea and it would mean I don't have to grovel to the Republican Party."

He concluded: "We have some interesting ideas on the table, let's leave it there and meet again in a few weeks' time. Thank you all for coming, we have much to consider."

The meeting dispersed and they all went away to resume their normal working day, even if concentration was rather difficult.

* * *

Just to add to Travis's busy schedule, his divorce case was now in the New York court. It was always going to be a high-profile case and the newspapers, radio and TV networks gave it maximum publicity. Travis appeared in person only when directed to do so, otherwise he let his lawyers do the talking. He reasoned he was paying them enough, they were the best in the land, so let them do what they do best. As predicted, Mrs Travis produced her own witnesses who claimed to have been charmed and then discarded by her husband. However, she produced no evidence of Travis's alleged affair while he was in the UK, even though it was those newspaper stories that had tipped her over the edge. He may have had his moments over the years, but the Bletchley 'affair that never was' meant she would have lost credibility, had she proceeded down that particular road without any actual witnesses.

After two weeks the court retired to allow the judge to consider the evidence over the weekend. On Monday morning everyone assembled in the court and waited for what everyone expected was just a formality. The judge, Clifford C Smith III, gave his verdict. "Not proven. I'm not convinced that the accounts I have heard prove that adultery has taken place. What actual proof is there, apart from verbal accounts? There is nothing in writing and no photographic evidence. I am more persuaded that the petitioners' motive is financial compensation."

Clearly this had come as a shock to all concerned, probably even to Travis himself. The media had not expected it; they assumed the verdict would be in Mrs Travis's favour, with the result that some rapid re-editing and change of headlines was necessary, even in the British press.

Mrs Travis left the court clearly distressed and refused to speak to anyone. Meanwhile, Mr Travis was persuaded to give a press conference in a nearby hotel, in a large hall that was normally used for banquets or occasional concerts. He sat at a large table at the far end of the hall, flanked by his lawyers on either side.

"Did you really expect this verdict?" asked a New York Post reporter.

"Of course, I had every confidence in the American legal system. It was the only verdict that the judge could have reached. What they offered was all lies and hearsay. You heard what the judge said."

"But you offered a generous out of court settlement to keep it out of the court. Wasn't that an admission that she had a strong case and would probably win?"

"No, that was to avoid any embarrassment on all sides and save a lengthy court process. To have so-called witnesses describe bedroom scenes in court is not my idea of entertainment. Unfortunately, my wife decided she wanted exactly the opposite, she wanted maximum publicity and a big payout."

The hall, full of reporters and photographers, all laughed at that remark. The questioner continued: "What will your wife do now? As the petition failed she is still legally your wife."

Travis smiled. "I hadn't thought it that far through. However, I can't see us getting together after such a public examination of our private lives. But I doubt if adultery will be the grounds for any future action."

Another reporter changed the whole mood of the conference. "Your wife's counsel objected to this particular judge, without success. They claim that you and the judge have known each other for many years. Is it true that he's about to purchase a large house in Queens that is part of a luxury development being constructed by one of your property companies?"

"I'm not aware of that," countered Travis. "Don't forget I've been out of the property business for the last four years. I think what you're suggesting is an insult to the judge, and that he would be influenced by that possibility. I suspect you may be hearing from his lawyers! With that, ladies and gentlemen, I think we should end this session before things are said that we might regret. I can see the lawyers licking their lips with cases of slander being contested!"

Travis stood up and, together with his lawyers and personal bodyguard, slowly made his way from the busy meeting room with reporters and cameramen still gathered round. They continued through the reception area, then down half a dozen stone steps which led onto the street where a large black Cadillac limousine awaited him. There was a small gathering waiting outside and yet more cameramen, Travis instinctively pausing while the shutters clicked. He looked around, enjoying the moment, then slipped into the back of the chauffer driven limousine. Travis's luck continued, on to his next challenge…

A few weeks later the American papers began running a story about Travis's possible election campaign for the 1952 election. It was clear they had been briefed by Travis's team as there were broad hints that he may run as an independent, with a declared policy of appeasement with the USSR on nuclear weapons. Within hours there was a reaction from the public on radio and television and next day letters to the press flowed in. Almost all reacted angrily to this idea, saying they couldn't trust Stalin, and even if he signed an agreement he would still continue making nuclear weapons in secret; his was a very big country where factories could be hidden. Within days there was a similar reaction from the USSR, with American correspondents stationed in Moscow reporting that Stalin had laughed at the idea, saying he couldn't trust the Americans, they would stockpile nuclear weapons anyway, using the excuse that a threat might come from elsewhere, possibly the Far East.

Predictably Travis was unsurprised by this reaction. "It's no more than I expected," he told reporters. "I think we have to make the case to the American people, explaining that we don't want another Hiroshima here in the USA, people need to sleep peacefully at night. I intend to go to Moscow and make the case to Stalin. I would have been surprised had he reacted any other way, but I'm sure he will listen."

However, Travis's campaign was slow to get underway. His team had approached potential sponsors, but none felt this approach was going to gain sufficient support from the American public. It was going to be a long uphill battle against the Eisenhower campaign which was now seen as the frontrunner.

* * *

Lord Drakeford sat at home in his customary place at the breakfast table with the *The Times* spread out in front of him. The news from America featured prominently and was well covered by the broadsheet newspapers. He looked up from his paper and couldn't suppress a smile. He turned to Christine and said, "I think we're well rid of Mr Travis. Leaving aside his indiscretions which we couldn't influence, on the political front it was worth the effort. I seem to remember four years ago we were sat here, very concerned about the future and who would be Roosevelt's successor. We decided to do something and shouldn't stand by and let Britain fall under the control of the Americans. With the aid of our friends, I hope we made a difference."

"I think we did," she replied. "Where would we be now if we'd sat back and done nothing?"

"Yes, I agree, it was worth the effort. However, if the rumours are true that he might run as an independent in fifty-two, then we could be hearing more from him," countered Drakeford.

Christine was quick to respond: "You really must get on and finish that book."

"Yes, it's coming along nicely. Just need to think of a title."

She replied smartly, "How about 'The Special Relationship'?"

END

APPENDIX: FACT OR FICTION?

Chapter 1:

The Drakeford family are fictional characters, as is their home. However, the SS-Jaguar was a popular high performance saloon (SS stood for 'Standard Swallow' after the coach-building company). The Morris 8 Series 'E' was a popular small four-seater family car.

The Beveridge Report was published in 1942 and became the foundation of Britain's welfare state.

The Travis family are fictional characters.

Thomas E Dewey was the Republican candidate in 1944, but lost the presidential election to Franklin D Roosevelt (FDR). FDR was wheelchair bound, having suffered from Polio since1921.

GOP is short for Grand Old Party, the American Republican Party.

J Edgar Hoover was head of the FBI and brothers John Foster Dulles and Allen Dulles, both lawyers and Republicans. Allen Dulles had recently returned from Switzerland where he had spent much of the war years as head of the OSS operation based in Berne.

The Germans had developed the V2 rocket and these were directed at London.

The atomic bomb was developed at Los Alamos in New Mexico, known as the Manhattan Project led by Robert Oppenheimer, an American scientist and world leader in Quantum Physics.

Chapter 2:

The Yalta conference began on 4th February, attended by Roosevelt, Stalin and Churchill. Yalta is situated in the Crimean peninsula and part of Ukraine. Provisional agreement was reached on the division of Europe when the war had ended.

The American Presidential Election took place on 7th November 1944 and Roosevelt was elected President for a fourth term.

On 12th April 1945, President Roosevelt died of a Cerebral Haemorrhage at his home in Warm Springs, Georgia, aged 63. He was succeeded by his Vice President Harry S Truman.

The war in Europe ended on the 8th May 1945 with an unconditional German surrender. Hitler was said to have committed suicide.

Churchill did make disparaging remarks about Atlee, but on 5th July 1945 Labour won the British general election by 146 seats.

After the German surrender the three leaders (Stalin, Truman and Churchill) agreed to meet at Potsdam, near Berlin, on 17th July.

Britain changed its team partway through the Potsdam conference, Atlee and Bevin replacing Churchill and Eden, much to the amazement of the other participants.

Chapter 3:

The Lend-Lease Agreement was intended to provide support for Britain in 1941. It was re-negotiated by the famous economist John Maynard Keynes in 1945.

The USA's first atom bomb, known as 'Operation Trinity', was successfully detonated on 16th July 1945 in New Mexico (as described in Chapter 3).

The actual decision regarding Japanese targets was controversial. Leslie R Groves was in overall control of the Manhattan Project and he wanted Hiroshima and Kyoto as targets, but Henry L Stimson, Secretary for War intervened as Kyoto had historic, cultural and religious significance. Thus Nagasaki was substituted for Kyoto.

The atom bomb was dropped on Hiroshima on 6th August 1945 and three days later another bomb was dropped on the island of Nagasaki.

A third bomb never existed. Japan surrendered on 12th August 1945.

Robert Oppenheimer was head of the Manhattan Project. He resigned shortly after the bomb was used on Japan. He was known to have communist sympathies and his security clearance was later rescinded.

It was actually President Harry Truman who said "Don't let that man near my office again".

Wernher von Braun led the German V2 project. He was recruited by the USA along with his team of scientists and engineers who willingly surrendered to the Americans.

Chapter 4:

Labour published its plans for public ownership to include coal, gas, electricity, steel production, the postal system, the telephone system, broadcasting, the banking system, water supply, railways, air travel and road transport. It went on to publish its ambitious plans for a National Health Service, to be introduced in 1948.

Sir Stafford Cripps was a left-wing lawyer who had become a Labour MP in 1931. He was expelled from the Labour Party in 1939 because of his connections with the Popular

Front which had communist connections. Following the formation of the coalition government in 1940 he was part of Churchill's war cabinet and became Minister of Aircraft Production. He rejoined the Labour Party in 1945 and later became Chancellor of the Exchequer in Atlee's government.

Britain had had a role in governing Palestine since 1918 known as the British Mandate, arising in part from the Balfour Declaration, calling for a national home for the Jewish people. The proposal to form a separate Jewish state was recommended by the United Nations Special Committee on Palestine (UNSCOP), resulting in the formation of Israel in May 1948.

Chapter 5:

The USA had 48 states until 1959 when Alaska became the 49th state, although America had purchased it from Russia in 1887 for $7.2m. Later in 1959 Hawaii became the 50th state.

The American Embassy was situated in Grosvenor Square in the Mayfair district of London.

Chapter 7:

Sir Walter Citrine had recently retired as TUC General Secretary and later became Lord Citrine. He was the author of the book 'The ABC of Chairmanship' published in 1939 and it remains a well-known guide for the conduct of meetings.

The statement '*If ivver tha dos owt for nowt allus do it for thissen*' is a famous old Yorkshire quotation.

Chapter 8:
Greenham Common, Upper Heyford and Brize Norton were US airbases in Southern England.

Chapter 10:
Bletchley Park was a wartime centre for code breakers. It still exists as a museum to demonstrate those activities.

The Auster was a single-engine three-seater light aircraft, a high-wing monoplane. Developed by an American company, Taylorcraft, they were made in the UK from 1938 and used by the Army and the RAF during the war for air observation. They later became popular with private owners and some foreign air forces.

The New York Post had a reputation for printing scandal and gossip.

Chapter 17:
During 1949-51 the USA paid the UK $4m for all subsequent usage of its jet engine patents, roughly equivalent to £70m in present day values. This was a risible sum in relation to the billions earned from worldwide sales in subsequent years.

Chapter 18:

At the end of World War II the army had vast amounts of equipment that was deemed surplus to requirements and these were sold off in large quantities to businesses who then in turn sold them to the public. This included motorcycles, many of which had never been used. The term ex-WD was used to describe all such equipment.

Chapter 21:

The 'Marshall Plan' was proposed by the US Secretary of State George C Marshall in 1947 and implemented in April 1948. It provided 13.3 billion dollars of aid for 16 countries, with the main beneficiaries being the UK, France, Italy and Western Germany. It relieved food shortages, helped rebuild industry and lessened the threat of communism in Western Europe.

The opening ceremony of the London Olympic Games took place at Wembley Stadium on the 29th July 1948. Because of the lack of resources it was known as 'The austerity games'. Germany and Japan were not invited.

The Berlin Airlift started in June 1948 when the Soviets blockaded the road, rail and canal access to West Berlin. This continued for 15 months when the USSR withdrew their blockade. It was a major factor behind the formation of NATO in 1949.

Harry S Truman was elected in November 1948 for a second term. The Dixiecrats had formed a breakaway party from the Democrats in the Southern States and they supported racial segregation. They were a distant third in the presidential election.

The USSR detonated its first nuclear bomb in August 1949. It was known in the USA as 'Joe 1'.

Dwight D Eisenhower was elected as a Republican in 1952 and remained US President until 1960, followed by John F Kennedy, a Democrat.

Printed in Great Britain
by Amazon